Gary Powell is a former London detective who served with the British Transport Police, retiring after thirty-three years' service. He is a frequent public speaker on his favourite subject: Britain's criminal history. He is also a guide at St Paul's Cathedral. He now lives in North Norfolk with his wife, Karen.

For those, past and present, who operate in the most unique of policing environments.

Gary Powell

MIND THE KILLER

Gary Powell

AUSTIN MACAULEY PUBLISHERS™

LONDON • CAMBRIDGE • NEW YORK • SHARJAH

A CIP catalogue record for this title is available from the British Library.

ISBN 9781398435759 (Paperback)
ISBN 9781398435766 (ePub e-book)

https://www.austinmacauley.co.uk

First Published 2024
Austin Macauley Publishers Ltd®
1 Canada Square
Canary Wharf
London
E14 5AA

I would like to take this opportunity to thank the small band of people who have shaped this book both in content and presentation.

Doctor Zoe Walkington of the Open University, who I have had the pleasure of working with during my service, for her guidance in relation to criminal psychology. Anne Armitage, former English teacher and RAF Education Officer, who moulded my grammar into something readable. My sister-in-law, Sharon Powell, who can read a book and deliver valuable feedback faster than anyone I know. Also Karen and Jay Moore, whose meticulous analysis of the narrative, fed back to me in a language I could understand, was invaluable; finally Kelly Warner, your wit and laid back attitude to all things forensic, and life in general, was—as always—wonderfully refreshing.

Thank you all, I'll be knocking on your doors again in the near future.

Prologue
1998

Two opposing commuter armies clashed as the tube train's doors opened at St Paul's London Underground station. Shoulders collided, tempers flared, as each refused to yield. For those passengers who alighted onto the platform, order quickly resumed.

Most relied on instinct to follow a familiar path, sipping coffee from fancy eco-friendly cups or guzzling the latest fashionable energy boosting drink. Any eye contact was an act of aggression. Few spoke; an eerie silence broken only by the sound of marching feet snaking in and out of tunnels as they sought the solace of daylight, cool fresh air, and another working day.

The train operator stifled a yawn, took a gulp of tea from a thermos flask and waited patiently for the guard's signal to proceed. So far the morning's shift had been dull and predictable. The two-hundred tonne train slowly eased forward into the blackness, quickly gaining speed, accelerating through a century-old tunnel, negotiating bends that seemed to defy the laws of gravity. The high-pitched screech of steel on steel was deafening. Powerful headlights cut through the darkness like lasers as amber signals turned green, encouraging the train to go faster and reach its maximum permitted speed.

Richard Talbot edged forward until his highly polished shoes traversed the bright yellow line inches from the platform edge at Bank station. He gazed into the black abyss of the tube tunnel feeling a faint draught on his face. The tunnel breeze grew increasingly stronger, swirling the aroma of the city streets metres above. Oblivious to the attention he was attracting, Talbot ignored a plea, via the platform PA system, to "Stand well back behind the yellow line"; he nudged ever closer to the edge.

Talbot placed his briefcase next to the headwall of the tunnel and removed his suit jacket in an orderly fashion, carefully folding it in half and laying it on the floor. The gust from the tunnel had increased to a roaring wind. Talbot jumped down onto the rails, snubbing desperate pleas from fellow passengers to return to the safety of the platform. He stood for a second looking into the abyss, as if he'd come to his senses and about to change his mind, before walking purposefully into the blackness.

The train thundered around the final bend before Bank Station. Talbot's ghostly white shirt reflected the powerful lights as he walked towards the speeding train, as if out on a Sunday stroll. The train's whistle blasted a meaningless warning—it was too late. Talbot had nowhere to go. Metre after metre of track disappeared as the emergency brakes were applied.

The operator could now see the man's facial features, eyes focused, filled with a pitiful sadness, a realisation that he was about to die. His last act was to stretch his arms out in cruciform and welcome death. The train operator, knowing the outcome could not be altered, prayed that somehow, metal and human flesh would avoid each other—there would be only one victor.

Chapter One
Present Day

'What is that stench?'

'Don't worry, sonny, it's only a dead rat.' Don Langley aimed the torch beam in the direction of his young companion, Tom Howley, trailing nervously behind him.

'How can you be so sure?' Howley replied as he peered further into the gloomy lift shaft. The stink was beginning to give him a headache.

'You come across all sorts in this job, sonny,' Don Langley grinned. He enjoyed showing apprentices the less attractive side of *his* world. It was a test to see if the college boys had the balls for a job like this. A little like a police officer attending his first post-mortem or a fireman climbing his first ladder. 'Cats, dogs, even deer sometimes. But it's been a while since deer roamed around Lambeth—normally rats.'

Langley was a chief mechanical engineer in the Lifts and Escalators Department on the London Underground. He lived and breathed his job, spending most of his leisure time travelling the length and breadth of the country observing and recording trains. He was stocky with black greasy hair combed over to hide an increasingly shiny pate.

Howley was amused by his boss' incongruous dress sense: smart shirt and tie with dirty jeans and black London Underground issue boots. In the short time, he'd been under Langley's tutorship he'd endured endless renditions of times past. Attempting to genuinely laugh every time his boss told him the job "was fucked".' But he'd developed a respectful affection for this short, stocky, railway dinosaur.

Howley had accompanied Langley to Lambeth North underground station to complete the final checks on two shiny new steel lifts fitted to replace the old wooden-panelled ones that had served the station for decades. The engineer suggested they take the opportunity to delve a little deeper into a disused passageway running from the base of the lift shaft heading in the direction of the Bakerloo line tunnels. Howley wasn't exactly frightened of the dark but tentatively agreed—as if he had a choice.

The powerful torchlight pierced the darkness, reflecting light off lumps of steel and cable littering the floor. The smell of dead rat had been replaced by damp and decay.

'Ah there it is,' Langley said. 'I knew it was here somewhere.' The beam highlighted a rusted steel door. Langley tried the handle—it didn't budge.

'Hold the light, sonny.'

'Where does it lead to? It doesn't look like it's been opened for ages.'

'I noticed it when I examined old maps of the area before coming down here. I never miss a chance to have a nose about. I doubt anybody has been through this door in decades.' Although the humid air seemed to be cooling, Howley could see sweat glistening across Langley's forehead. He was genuinely excited about what lay behind the door, and, if he was honest, so was he. Langley produced a heavy looking lump hammer from his leather kit bag and stepped back from the door.

'Hold that light still will you? You're shaking like a girl.' Although short, and somewhat out of shape, the chief engineer raised the hammer, with some energy, before the downward force struck the handle with an almighty bang. A cloud of dust descended, passing visibly through the strong light.

He has either loosened that handle or destroyed it, thought the young apprentice. Langley started to cough with such ferocity Howley wondered if his colleague would live. As the dust cleared and the coughing subsided Langley let out a satisfied grunt, and with one great heave, opened the door.

The musty dampness was much stronger in here. Both men stood in silence, in some weird homage, as a Bakerloo line train, so close Howley briefly looked over his shoulder in genuine fear of being mown down, rumbled past, dislodging a mist of black grime from the tunnel walls. Asbestos poisoning and a wretched death, before he reached forty, crossed the younger man's mind as he urgently covered his mouth and nose with a pristine white handkerchief his mother had handed him before he left for work.

'How near was that?' He coughed through, the now, blackened linen.

'I'm not sure, maybe four or five feet the other side of this wall. Can you feel a slight breeze?' Howley looked about quizzingly, as if one could physically *see* air.

'Yeah, I can, where's that coming from?'

'This used to be an old ventilation shaft which surfaces on Westminster Bridge Road somewhere.' Howley was unsure if he could see a speck of light above or he was hallucinating. Langley moved further on with a slow practiced step, as if he were avoiding landmines.

Howley jumped and dropped the torch as a rat, the size of a kitten, ran across his foot. The rodent screeched as a blind kick from Langley connected with some part of its anatomy.

'What your generation needs, sonny, is a bit of discipline—a spell in the armed forces. Go and fight those murdering bastards who plant roadside bombs and watch with glee as women and children are blown to bits. I was in the army— fought in the first Gulf War. You'd get a right kick-in from your mates if you gave your position away because of a bloody rat. Pick that light up will you.'

Howley could feel his face redden—glad his boss seemed unaware of his embarrassment. He kept the beam facing towards the tunnel floor until his heart rate slowed.

'Come on, I want to see how far this tunnel goes before you shit yourself and I have to change your nappy,' Langley chuckled.

'You'd better come here, Mr Langley.' The engineer felt a little guilty. Maybe he'd taken the banter too far, no sense of humour, these youngsters.

'What's up boy?' he enquired as he headed back to the light source. Howley gave no explanation but indicated, via the light beam, a skeletal hand pointing skywards from a grave of stone ballast, as if desperately pleading for help.

Chapter Two

'Another fourteen hundred quid wasted on this shower.' Ryan McNally crashed back down into his seat in unison with fifty-eight thousand other Gooners. Fourteen minutes into a new season and already one-nil down. McNally's blood began to boil as he watched the visiting supporters jumping up and down in celebration. He hated Mancunian supporters. He hated Scousers and Brummies. In fact, for ninety minutes on match day anybody who didn't support the boys in red.

'One of these days you're going to burst something. There's well over an hour to play yet.' McNally looked at the chilled out occupant of the seat to his left.

'Barry, I've known you for twenty-five years. We've been watching Arsenal for God knows how long, travelling all over the country. The one thing that winds me up most is your bloody laid back attitude. If we can't let off a bit of steam here, what's the point of coming?' McNally returned his attention back to the pitch and aimed his vitriol towards the manager's bench.

'It would help if we had a couple of Englishmen, with some backbone, in the team and an English manager.' His retort was met by a mixture of cheers and boos from those around him, depending on which side of the argument they stood in relation to the manager's competency to coach. He plonked his 6'1" frame back down. Resigned to another crap season, his only solace was they didn't support Spurs.

McNally momentarily lost interest with the action on the pitch. He turned, keeping one eye on the football.

'How's the world of security consultancy treating you anyway? How many boxes of paperclips you pushed around this week?'

'It's a living.' Barry Nash subdued a smile. He'd been a detective in the Metropolitan Police for fifteen years before taking a once in a lifetime opportunity to move into the private sector, initially with Barclays Bank.

'Yeah but working for some American pharmaceutical company isn't a patch on grabbing some scumbag's collar. I suppose the only worry you got now is somebody nicking the lab rats.' McNally smiled.

'Very funny you should've been a comedian. You're wasted in the old bill. Do you realise the billions tied up in these companies? I've got ten times the amount of responsibility that I had with Barclays. You ever heard of counter espionage?'

'What you on now, two hundred grand a year?'

Nash avoided eye contact, looking away at the crowd, preparing himself for the normal diatribe.

'I'm surprised you still sit with us poor people and not with those on *moon base alpha* upstairs—cheese and cress sandwiches and no bloody atmosphere.'

Suddenly everyone in the stadium rose as one, sixty thousand seats thumping against back rests as a strike of the ball, from thirty yards out, cut through the opposing team's defence. An interminable silence followed as the crowd followed the trajectory of the ball, willing it to dip below the crossbar, culminating in an agonising whine of disappointment as the ball crashed against woodwork.

'Is that your phone ringing Ryan?'

'What?'

'Your phone is ringing. You're the only twat I know who has the *Big Brother* ringtone. I can't believe anybody else within a mile of us would be that sad.'

'The kids put it on there and I can't figure out how to change it. You're an IT whiz, Barry. If you were a proper mate, you'd do it for me.'

'What and forego the pleasure of watching everybody looking at you and thinking "*what a knob*". That's your job phone—you on call?'

'Yeah, all weekend.' McNally shielded his eyes from the mid-August sun as he glanced at the giant south stand clock, the hands read 3.42pm. Placing the phone to one ear and plugging the other with a straight finger he answered. 'DI McNally.'

'Hi boss, sorry to disturb you. I see it's not going too well on the pitch.'

'Marcia, if you've just rung me on my job phone, knowing full well I'm on call just to take the piss, you'll be back in uniform cleaning up vomit in the custody suite before this game ends—what d'ya want?'

'A skeleton has been…' The crowd roared as if they'd all received the same news at the same time—as the Arsenal No.9 raced onto a delicious pass and was now one on one with the keeper. The roar fell away to a pathetic whimper as the ball dribbled passed the opposition's goalpost.

'No! I could have scored that.' McNally screamed, the veins in his neck bulging. 'Ian Wright, if you're in the commentary box put some boots on.' Returning to his call, 'Marcia, I couldn't hear the last part. You did say a skeleton?'

'Yes, been found in a lift shaft at Lambeth North station.'

'Well, if it's a bloody skeleton it's not exactly urgent is it? Can't you deal with it for now?'

'Plummer wants you on it.'

'Has the detective superintendent forgotten he's got a warrant card in his back pocket or can't he get out of his office with that chair stuck to his arse? That's the problem with retired senior Metropolitan Police officers coming over to the British Transport Police,' McNally ranted 'they think they're going to get another tasty pension for sitting on their backsides and doing fuck all, well it don't work like that.'

Marcia Frost gulped on the other end of the line and a difficult silence ensued.

McNally thought quickly, maybe he should keep such thoughts about his senior officer to himself. He was still unsure how trustworthy his new sergeant was. If she were to repeat his opinions to the wrong people, it wouldn't have been his greatest career move.

'Look it's nearly half time,' he said in a conciliatory tone. 'I'll leave before the rush for the bogs and bar start, meet you there. Give Sam and Stuart a ring, get them there too, this day *can't* get any worse.' As McNally took the stairs toward the exit, two at a time, he heard the muted celebrations of three thousand Mancunians. Two-nil down, the day just *did*.

Chapter Three

It had just started to rain as McNally got out of his job car. Pulling up his collar he walked head on into a wind that appeared from nowhere. Minutes before London's air had been stifling—even for an August day—but now it was lashing down. McNally, head turned to face the heavens, enjoyed a few seconds of the cleansing downfall before he entered Lambeth North station from Westminster Bridge Road. He was surprised that the station still appeared to be open until he saw the crime scene tape drawn tightly across the entrance to the stairs and the lift doors permanently open.

'Station supervisor is not happy having his station shut,' Marcia Frost said as she met her boss and walked him toward the lifts.

'When are they ever happy?' replied McNally, 'but I suppose he's got a point. I mean our victim's only been here for God knows how long. Are Hodge and Graves here yet?'

'Yes, both arrived half an hour ago. Sam is with the Area Manager for the Bakerloo Line and the two witnesses who found the remains; they are in the station supervisor's office. One of them is pretty shaken up. Stuart is down in the depths with our very skinny friend.'

'I take it you mean our victim? Have a bit of respect, sergeant.' McNally turned with a grin on his face—maybe she's going to be alright after all.

'The CSI is here, she's from New Zealand.'

'Wow, that's a long way to come. Didn't we have anyone nearer? And what the hell is a CSI?'

'A Crime…'

'Marcia, I know what it bloody well is, it was a rhetorical question,' McNally interrupted. 'You've been watching too much of that crap they send over from America. CSI is an "Americanism" adopted by senior officers over here, so they can appear to be trendy. In this country, we have Scenes of Crime Officers—you got that?'

'Yes, guv, actually, their official title now is Crime Scene Examiners…well for this month anyway. You're in a bad mood. D'ya want to know the final score in the football?' Marcia grinned; her dark brown eyes mischievously glinted. McNally turned around sharply.

'Don't…Let's go have a word with these witnesses before going down to the scene.' Frost headed for the lifts. McNally swerved in front steering her to the stairs.

'You on a keep fit regime? The lift is quicker.'

'No, I just hate lifts, got stuck in one when I was a kid,' replied McNally.

'Ok, the stairs it is then. I used to play on these stairs when I was a kid.'

'How come?' McNally allowed Frost to descend first. If he was honest, he wasn't great with stairs either but he wasn't going to reveal any further weaknesses to her.`

'I lived on an estate in Kennington, about half a mile from here. This, and Oval, were our nearest stations. Me, and my mates would ride around the tube all day; go all over the place: the airport, Oxford Street even went to Harrods once. We were as welcome there as a dose of the shits. You didn't see many black faces. Loads of Arabs and Japanese, but not people like us.'

'How many stairs to go? My back's killing me.'

'Not many, nearly there,' replied Frost.

'When did you decide to join our firm; couldn't have gone down well with your family?'

'I always wanted to be in the police. I never heard back from the Met. Mum and Dad were really proud when they saw me in uniform for the first time but they took a lot of stick over it and lost a lot of friends. My brother never really speaks to me anymore. But I was the first black woman from our estate to wear the blue uniform, and they loved it. The estate has changed a lot since then, people standing up against the thugs and drug dealers—it's a nicer place to live. We're nearly there, you keeping up, guv?'

McNally followed Frost down a small subway leading off the regular passageway.

'Where did you start in the job? You're not from London. You've got a bit of a northern twang on you.'

'Manchester. I originally joined the Transport Police up there, got to detective sergeant. That's where I met my wife Kate. She'd been out with her mates on Christmas Eve; she's a dental nurse, and was the worse for wear and fell asleep on a platform bench at Manchester Piccadilly station. Some pervert saw his opportunity and started to give her a grope—wrong decision. She woke up and punched him so hard the uniform officers who attended, had to arrest him and take him to hospital with a broken jaw. She's only 5'4 tall. I got the job on my desk, went and interviewed her, and within six months we were married.'

'You got any kids?'

'Yeah: a boy of eight, and a girl of fourteen. When Max was six and Ava twelve, I got the chance of promotion to Detective Inspector. I'd been overlooked for promotion in the north west a couple of times, so we made the move down here.'

'Looks like it worked out OK.'

'Well, for me it has, but Kate has never really settled and Ava is struggling at school.'

'So, if you're from Manchester, how the hell did you end up supporting Arsenal?'

'My dad was originally from Liverpool but was a blue and hated Liverpool.'

'A blue?'

'He supported Everton. It was my sixteenth birthday. We sat in front of the telly and he gave me a beer to celebrate. It was the Liverpool versus Arsenal championship decider. Arsenal had to win by two clear goals to steal the title off the Scousers. Dad spent the whole game shouting at the telly and was ecstatic when Arsenal scored in the last minute to win the game two-nil and take the title. Ever since that day I followed the Gunners.'

Frost opened a heavy door and entered the station supervisor's office. It was a small space not improved by their presence. The walls—painted in a sickly yellow colour—were covered with memos about health and safety and the obligatory dos and don'ts. One wall was home to a couple of CCTV screens, which flicked between the two Bakerloo lines platforms, the station entrance, the booking hall and the spiral staircase they'd just descended. McNally looked around at the occupants before introducing himself.

'I'm Detective Inspector Ryan McNally from the British Transport Police Major Investigations Team this is Detective Sergeant Marcia Frost.' McNally showed the occupants his warrant card. A man in a smart dark suit stood and offered his hand to McNally. Frost asked to use the staff toilet and was given directions back along the corridor.

'Inspector, I'm Lawrence Regan, the area manager for this group of stations. I'm obviously quite keen on reopening the station as soon as possible, especially as the incident is well away from public view. Even though it's the weekend, the station caters for many customers. At the moment, we're running the trains through non-stop on both the north and southbound platforms. Obviously, I realise that you have a job to do and I'm keen to assist whenever and wherever I can, but do you have a timescale?'

'Mr Regan, I've yet to see for myself what we face, but I assure you that we'll be as quick as possible. I'll have a better idea when I've spoken to the SOCO.'

McNally looked through a doorway leading to a further space which served as a small mess room with a kettle and a stainless steel sink. He could see the back of Sam Hodge's head. The detective constable was in conversation with a rotund balding man whose face was pale with shock, and a younger man who looked excited, as if this had been the most memorable experience of his life. Hodge could feel his boss's presence.

'Afternoon guv, these are two members of the London Underground lifts and escalators department. They were the unfortunates who found our friend downstairs. Mr Don Langley and his apprentice Tom Howley.' Frost re-joined the group.

Langley barely acknowledged the detective, but the eager young man jumped up and offered his hand which McNally accepted before introducing Frost.

'Are you okay, Mr Langley?' Frost enquired. 'Can I get you a drink of water?' Langley declined stating that he just wanted some fresh air, the room was very stuffy. Frost took the lead and asked Langley what they'd been doing in a disused tunnel.

'I was just being nosey, I suppose. I like to look around when I get the chance, bit of a passion of mine. Should've just done my job and pissed off home.'

'Our victim may never have been found Mr Langley, if that were the case,' McNally interjected. 'DC Hodge is not going to keep both of you here much longer. Please provide the officer with your full contact numbers and details of your working hours over the next few days and we'll arrange to take more detailed statements. Please don't discuss what you've seen with each other, as you'll each remember different aspects of the incident.' McNally laid a hand on Sam Hodge's shoulder. 'I'll see you downstairs when you've finished.' Hodge nodded and turned back towards his witnesses.

Chapter Four

Ruth Ward hadn't seen her school girlfriends for nearly ten years. To be honest, calling them friends was stretching it a bit far. Ruth had been an overweight teenager with a complexion often compared to a coalface. Any of the defining features of her approaching womanhood, enjoyed by her peers, were merged into her body mass. She had little self-confidence and withdrew into a fantasy world of catwalks and skinny, self-centred models, where eating *two* lettuce leaves was seen as pigging out.

She left school as early as the law allowed, with no qualifications, no ambitions, and started work at her father's south London export company.

She was good with figures and spread sheets, developing a knack for identifying wasteful practices, where operational costs could be cut, which pleased her father and made him richer.

Ruth soon became aware that she not only attracted praise from her proud father but admiring looks from several of the companies' single men, and a few of the married ones as well. By the time she reached her twenty-first birthday, she'd lost nearly five stone, trimmed her body fat with the aid of a fitness coach, both in and out of bed, and gained enough confidence to take her accountancy exams.

Ruth enrolled on a Saturday course in Canary Wharf. She studiously worked towards her final AAT exams. It'd only been in the past twelve months or so that her self-confidence had grown to a point where she joined several social media groups. Within weeks, she'd been contacted by several former school friends. Ruth had sworn to herself, the day she walked out of those school gates, for the final time, she would never return or ever make contact with any of her former tormentors again. Ruth's new-found confidence, and the fact that all of them seemed to have grown up and matured, softened her hard stance and she relented.

They met in a Docklands bar after she'd finished college. Her preconception of how some of the girls had turned out was way off. Jane had been Ruth's main detractor, a self-opinionated, nasty bitch. She hugged Ruth with what seemed a genuine show of emotion, possibly even guilt. Alice had been a boy magnet with beautiful black hair and big brown eyes. Now, having borne three children in as many years, she looked worn out; a few grey hairs were fighting for prominence and the bags under her eyes were large enough to carry her purse in. She'd gained a lot of weight and wore clothes that were probably at least a size too small; the skirt looked as if it had been levered into place with a crowbar. Everybody had been full of praise for Ruth's appearance, several of them failing to initially recognise her.

The evening had gone well. For the first time in her life, she felt comfortable with who she was and how she looked. She boarded a Jubilee line train from Canary Wharf station a little after 8 pm, having arranged another meet with Jane, Alice and the other girls in a month's time.

Ruth skimmed a crumpled copy of yesterday's *Metro*, taking in a little of the Brexit debate. Her thin lips broke into a smile as she remembered how shocked some of her former classmates had been at her appearance. The train rattled at speed towards London Bridge, where she would change for a southbound Northern line train to Clapham South.

Her fellow passengers, made up mostly of couples and groups, were generally in a good mood. Ruth often amused herself by watching people and how they interacted with one another. She was aware that she'd attracted the attention of a fellow passenger sitting half a carriage length away. The passenger stared at her intently, his cold piercing blue eyes visible, just below a tight-fitting beanie hat, were filled with hate. Ruth broke the spell and looked quickly at her wristwatch and the tube map above her head—anything to distract her. She wanted to look again but felt genuinely frightened to do so; it was an unwritten law of the London Underground: avoid eye contact.

The automatic train announcer robotically informed passengers that the next station was London Bridge. Ruth collected her belongings and discarded the newspaper in her vacated seat ready for the next bored passenger. She stood straight and purposefully in an attempt to make herself look bigger and more confident then she really felt, smiling at the irony. She glanced covertly at different carriage windows to try and catch a surreptitious look at "blue eyes". When failing to locate him, Ruth took a deep breath and looked directly at the seat he'd occupied, he'd disappeared.

The train came to a smooth halt and the doors and security gates slid open in unison. Ruth had travelled this route many times, alighting from the carriage directly opposite the passageway leading to the Northern Line. Comforted by the safety blanket of humanity surrounding her she moved with the crowd enjoying, for once, the jostling, the stale smell of perspiration and the closeness of her fellow human beings. By the time she reached the southbound Northern line platform, she'd almost forgotten the scary encounter—just another oddball, she thought.

The train indicator read "Morden 2 Mins".

'Yeah right,' she mumbled to herself. 'That's two London Transport minutes—five minutes in the real world.'

The platform was fairly busy with happy people talking about where they'd been and who with. Ruth realised that she too had, surprisingly, enjoyed the company of her former school mates. She drifted towards the platform edge as the smell of a takeaway curry wafted in her direction. She looked to her left as piercing lights broke the darkness of the tunnel, tonnes of metal roared into the platform like a ghost train at a fairground.

For a split second, she thought: how rude, as she felt the pressure of a flat hand on her back, we all want to get on this train. It was a funny sensation—floating through the air. Fear—the last emotion she would ever experience—had yet to arrive. She knew who was responsible, a pair of blue, hate-filled eyes, appeared from her subconscious. Hysterical screams from onlookers rang in her ears as her face smashed against the steel rails, rendering her unconscious, before she was cut to pieces.

Chapter Five

McNally and Frost returned to the main office and asked the station supervisor—a jolly Irishman called Heaney—to lead them to the crime scene. Heaney gulped down the contents from a filthy looking mug with a faded London Underground motif and a reminder to "Mind the Gap" on corresponding sides. Wiping a dribble of coffee from his chin with his jacket sleeve, he jumped to his feet and put on his orange high-vis vest, which at a stretch just covered his huge belly, collected a torch he checked was working, before guiding the detectives out of the office.

'I once found a severed foot between the tracks, it was never claimed. It's probably still rotting in the Lost Property office at Baker Street.' Heaney laughed raucously. McNally and Frost politely gasped and laughed in the right places, hoping they would get to their destination before he would tell them how he'd always wanted to be a policeman.

Heaney directed the detectives towards the lift shafts and then into a dark passageway. The supervisor shone the torch ahead warning the detectives to mind where they trod. McNally looked around at the damp brickwork covered in green slime, where water had seeped through over the years. He'd been in situations like this many times during his twenty-two years of police service; walked along miles of railway line and through dozens of tunnels. He always respected the railway environment, among the most dangerous environments to work in—he imagined—after coalmining and deep sea fishing.

The atmosphere became increasingly muggy and oppressive the further they progressed. As he peered into the distance McNally could see bright light emanating from a hefty steel doorway. The form of a uniformed police officer took shape, initially shielding his eyes from Heaney's bright light, but stiffly standing to attention when he recognised the DI. McNally thought the young constable was about to shout 'who goes there' and challenge them with his baton.

They identified themselves to the young officer who just looked glad to see another human being.

'How long have you been here, PC…?'

'Wakefield, sir, I started the cordon log at 4 pm, so about four hours.'

'You got a first name, PC Wakefield?'

'James sir…Jim to most people, that is.'

'How long you been in the job, Jim?'

'Coming up to three and a half years.' Wakefield puffed out his chest, as if lasting so long in the police was an achievement in itself.

'Who's logged in so far?' Wakefield turned the scene log towards the light.

'The crime scene examiner.' McNally winced, Frost just smiled. 'The coroner's officer and one of your detectives: DC Stuart Graves. My duty inspector wanted a peek but I pointed out that maybe that wouldn't be a good idea—the fewer people going into the scene the better, he went off in a bit of a huff, looks like I'll be getting all the shit jobs for the next few weeks.'

'Don't worry about that, Jim, he probably wanted to update his CV with the fact that he'd attended a possible murder scene to impress his next Chief Inspector's board—the job is full of 'em. Good, come and see me if you ever fancy CID, Jim, we could do with some forward thinking detectives.'

Wakefield entered the two detectives into the log whilst McNally and Frost stepped into forensic suits, gloves, and overshoes. They nodded at the young PC and ducked under the tape after thanking a disappointed looking Heaney for his assistance.

McNally and Frost headed towards the bright crime scene lights which replaced the need for a torch. An approach path had already been set out so those attending the scene didn't wander and disturb any evidence underfoot.

'I'm not sure how much we're going to recover from here' McNally mused.

Although both the SOCO and Stuart Graves were dressed in standard forensic suits and faces covered by masks, it was very evident, from a distance, who was who. Stuart Graves was a big man—6'2", with broad shoulders against the diminutive figure of SOCO Sally Cook. As they approached, Graves raised a hand to acknowledge McNally's arrival and issued a mumbled greeting.

'God, it's hot down here,' Frost complained as sweat started to form on her forehead and trickle into her eyes. The masks they wore were essential to protect the crime scene from being contaminated by their own DNA. But in these circumstances, they helped greatly to minimise the inhalation of decade's worth of dust thrown up by passing trains.

Cook was on all fours, carefully removing railway ballast from what was instantly identifiable as a human skeleton. She looked up, got to her feet and indicated back towards the entrance. She removed her mask.

'Hi, I'm Sally Cook, Force Headquarters Scientific Support, nice to meet you, dude.' She offered a gloved, dirt-covered, hand. Stuart Graves came over to join them.

'Evening, guv, fancy seeing you here.' He gave Frost a discourteous nod. McNally noticed, and made a mental note, of a tension between two of his detectives that he would need to address at a later stage.

'So what we got, Sally?'

'Basically, a pile of old bones. I've uncovered most of the remains; it seems to be a complete skeleton. I'm no pathologist, but as far as I can see, so far, we've got a head, torso, two arms and two legs. There is a massive hole at the back of the skull and no sign of any clothing on the body or nearby. I mean, the rats would've had a field day even though the body was covered in ballast, but I would expect to still see signs of clothing, so I would say it was stripped before being dumped here.'

'Any idea how long it's been here?' Frost asked expecting an estimate in years.

'Probably since 6 February 2000,' Cook replied with a devilish smile. McNally was intrigued and waited for more but Cook was playing with them and maintained the silence. McNally looked at Graves, who just raised his massive shoulders in a "don't ask me" gesture.

'Okay,' McNally smiled, 'tell me what you got.' Cook produced a small plastic evidence bag, which she held up against one of the lights. McNally, Frost and Graves peered at it.

'It's a Nat West bank cash deposit slip, dated 6th February 2000. It must've been dropped at some point, maybe when the clothes were stripped from the body.'

'There's a Nat West bank across the road.' Frost said. So our victim deposited cash sometime before he or she was killed.'

McNally broke the thoughtful silence.

'Or the killer did.' McNally examined the exhibit in torchlight before manoeuvring his DS a few feet away from the group. 'Marcia, I know its

Saturday, but let's start some enquiries with the bank. Sooner we find the identity of our victim the sooner we might be able to solve our mystery.' Frost nodded. 'And what's with the *dude*?'

'Don't worry, guv, she calls everybody she likes *dude*. If she refers to you as *sir,* you're basically an arsehole. Anyway the original use of the word dude describes a young man as 'dandy' a "stylish dresser".' McNally gave Frost a quizzical look.

'Anything you don't know, sergeant? What book did you read that in?'

'Bradley Walsh asked the question on *The Chase*.' McNally turned back towards Cook and Graves. 'Good luck, *sir*,' Frost added, suppressing a smile before quickly disappearing into the dark.

'Ok, Sally, what're our options?'

'Well, the bank receipt gives us a good head start but, as you mentioned, it could belong to our killer. Either way we need a more definitive identification of our victim.' McNally considered telling the new SOCO that he'd done this sort of thing before and to stop patronising him, but he held his tongue. Cook seemed to read the DI's mind.

'Of course, you'll already know this but bear with me. I've called a forensic anthropologist who'll help me recover the skeletal remains, and their examination during the post mortem will confirm the sex of the victim and assist with the method used to kill. As far as identification, I'll take dental impressions for comparison with any possible dental records you recover later, and as a backup samples from the femur, that's the bone in...' Cook saw the look on McNally's face and realised that maybe she was taking her condescending style a little too far, but she was enjoying the wind-up.

'Or pulp from one of the teeth to produce a DNA profile for later comparison. If you do identify our friend here, a hair or tooth brush would be helpful if they're still available. Got that?'

'Yes, even a thick bastard like me can understand that. I suppose this makes a change from examining kangaroos.' McNally gave a satisfying grin which was soon wiped off his face.

'You mean sheep,' McNally looked confused. 'We got loads of sheep in New Zealand but no kangaroos, they live in Australia. They can't jump that far.' McNally mumbled something uncomplimentary and asked, 'When will the post-mortem take place?'

'Monday, at the earliest.'

'I suppose you gotta have a day off?'

'Not me, but pathologists need to put their feet up.' Cook replaced her mask and muttered just loudly enough for McNally to hear, 'You have a nice weekend, *Sir*,' before melting back into the gloom.

Chapter Six

McNally breathed in the evening air, leaving the musty atmosphere of the underground behind him. His mobile vibrated, alerting him to a missed call and a voicemail. The screen displayed his home number. Momentarily deciding to ignore it, he attempted to process the information gleaned in the past half an hour, but Kate rarely called him at work unless it was urgent.

'Hi, love, it's me. You OK?' He knew from the first word his wife uttered that she was not.

'What's up?'

'Ryan, it's…' McNally could hear a slight tremor in her voice before she let it all out in a gush of almost incoherent torment. 'Ava's gone missing. I have contacted all her friends. We had a big argument. She stormed out about three hours ago. She's not answering her mobile; it's getting dark, I'm worried sick.'

'Ok, calm down, you know she's done this before. What'd you argue about?'

'The usual, her going back to school in a couple of weeks, how she hates it in London and how she wants to go back to Manchester. What shall I do, call the local police?'

'No, I'll be home in thirty minutes. You stay there just in case she comes home or calls you. You know what she's like, goes off in a huff, cools down and comes home, sulks for a few days and then she's ok.'

'It was different this time. She was so angry, blaming you and me for bringing her down here, away from all her friends.'

McNally switched his phone off and retraced his steps into Lambeth North station.

'Marcia, I gotta go home, family emergency. Wrap it up here. Tell Stuart and the others we'll have a full briefing on Monday morning. Nothing's going to happen until then. Anything else I need to know about before I go?'

'No, it's all quiet apart from somebody under a train at London Bridge, uniform are dealing with it.'

Chapter Seven

Marcia Frost looked troubled when she returned to the crime scene.

'You OK, dude?'

'Yeah good, thanks, Sal, the boss had to shoot off home. He looked worried, some family problem, didn't want to talk about it. Just told me to wrap things up down here, how long you gonna be?'

'The forensic archaeologist will be here soon so we'll retrieve the remains and take them to a local mortuary. Nothing is going to happen until Monday. It's hardly an urgent job is it? I got another call to London Bridge; an apparent suicide isn't looking as clean cut as they thought.' The joke flew way over Frost's head. 'Oh well, never mind, you Brits have got no sense of humour,' she sighed. 'Uniformed officers have got a witness, some dotty old lady, swears she saw the young girl being pushed. The CCTV is inconclusive so they're erring on the side of caution and want yours truly to have a look.'

'Ok, thanks for your help on this, Sal. Looks like we could both be in for a busy weekend.' Frost turned to Stuart Graves.

'Stuart, the boss said to leave this with forensics. He wants a briefing with the rest of the team at headquarters on Monday morning. I'm going to try and get something moving with Nat West.' Graves just grunted. Frost let his response go. She stripped off her over suit, mask and shoe covers and placed them in a property bag which she handed to Graves.

'What you got planned for the rest of the weekend, presuming we don't end up at London Bridge?' Graves just hunched his shoulders and walked towards the station stairs.

'What's your problem, Stuart? I've been on this team for a few weeks and everybody has been great except you—you've hardly said a word to me, why don't you get what's troubling you off your chest here and now, just me and you? I'm a big girl, I can take any shit you can throw at me.'

'Yeah right, 'course you can, love,' the detective looked at Frost with undisguised contempt.

'Well, out with it. Is it because my mother was a dinner lady and my dad a bus driver and I'm from south of the river rather than a leafy west London borough, where I presume you crawl in from every day? Or is it a bit more basic than that: my age or my sex maybe or the fact that I have been promoted over you, or does it just come down to the plain old colour of my skin?'

'Well, as this is *just* between you and me; with respect, sarge, piss off.' Graves turned and took the stairs two at a time. Frost took in a few deep breaths and tried not to blink as her eyes filled up.

Chapter Eight

McNally, with the assistance of a blue light and sirens, covered the distance between Lambeth and Finchley in twenty-two minutes. Turning right after Finchley Central station, the contents of his stomach headed north as he spied a yellow ambulance, blue lights flashing, parked in the middle of his road, adjacent to his house. McNally abandoned his car and rushed to the rear of the emergency vehicle. Dozens of scenarios raced through his mind. He didn't know whether to laugh or cry as his elderly next door neighbour waved at him from the ambulance's bed.

'Hi love. Just got home, have you? I'm off to hospital. Fell over—these lovely young men think I've broken my wrist. Can you ask Kate if she can pop in and feed my fish while I'm away?'

'Yes of course, Lizzy, don't you worry. Looks like you're in good hands.' One of the paramedics winked at McNally.

'I think it's just a sprain,' explained the paramedic, 'but you can't be too careful with a lady of such mature years.' Lizzy giggled.

McNally skirted around the ambulance and moved his car out of their way. Having parked, in the only space available, he jogged back to his house and was relieved to find his daughter fast asleep on the couch with an exhausted looking Kate gently stroking her hair. Kate indicated towards the kitchen as she gently laid Ava's head on a cushion.

'What…?' Kate placed a finger against her lips anxiously, looking back into the lounge.

'She was found at Euston station by a PCSO who'd seen her approaching random people asking for contributions for a ticket to Manchester Piccadilly. Ryan, she was trying to go back. God knows what would've happened to her if she'd gotten on a train on her own. Where would she have gone? She could have been picked up by some pervert and raped, or even worse.' Kate started to sob, muffling her cries with the crook of her elbow. McNally pulled her to him and let her cry.

'How'd she get back here?'

'The PCSO arranged for her safe return, a uniform car brought her home, they left just before you arrived. What're we going to do? Her school work's suffering. I think she's being bullied about her accent and it's having an effect on Max. He keeps on asking why his sister's always crying.'

'I'll talk to her. She just needs more time to make friends. We need to set up a meet with her teacher and headmaster, perhaps even move her to another school, maybe private. We can work it out, love.' Kate returned to the lounge as McNally's telephone vibrated in his trouser pocket.

Chapter Nine

Frost had just sat down with a glass of chilled Pinot in her favourite chair—her only chair—in her pokey, first-floor flat in Stockwell, when her mobile bellowed the theme tune of *Hawaii-Five-O*.

Ten minutes later, having carefully reintroduced the contents of the glass to the bottle, she was driving the short distance up South Lambeth Road before turning right into Bonnington Square, Vauxhall.

McNally had been apologetic about calling her out after the day she'd had but it was minutes from her place and she *was* on call. Frost had thought about asking him if everything was OK at home, but his tone of voice suggested that particular question should wait until Monday.

She'd done some checks on the ground floor flat occupied by 75-year-old Felicity Wright with, as expected, no flags or warnings. Frost had rung the telephone number, passed on by McNally, but received no reply so decided to take a reasonable chance that the elderly occupant would be at home this time of night.

She reached the address just after 10 pm and rang the bottom bell of four, the only one not to have the name of its occupant scrawled on it. Getting no reply, she pushed the outer door and, to her surprise, it yielded.

The entrance lobby was dark and smelt slightly of damp. Frost took out her mobile phone, the torch lit up some of the hallway ahead until she located a dirty plastic push-operated light on the far wall. On reaching a set of stairs, which led to the upper floors, she steered to the left. The ground floor flat was at the end of a corridor which had no further lighting but the dim hallway light provided enough illumination to plot a course to the front door of the ground floor flat.

It became obvious why Felicity Wright hadn't heard the outer doorbell or the earlier ringing of her telephone as the sound of her television pounded through the heavy wooden door. Frost rapped her knuckles against the door, as hard as she could, until the sound inside diminished slightly.

'Who is it?' a frail voice asked.

'Mrs Wright, its Detective Sergeant Frost from the British Transport Police Major Investigations Team. I'd like to talk to you about the incident at London Bridge station earlier this evening. Can I come in?' Frost was about to try and pass a further message when the door creaked open as far as the security chain would allow. 'Hi, Mrs Wright, I'm Marcia, let me show you my identification.' A spindly liver-spotted hand emerged through the gap and took the warrant card. Seconds later the chain was unfastened and the door opened revealing a fragile lady with thick-framed glasses and grey hair tied tightly back in a bun. She wore a grey, baggy, cardigan, which she'd pulled across her in a protective fashion.

'Come in, dear, that was quick, it only happened a couple of hours ago.'

Frost looked around the room and, for some reason, was surprised by how orderly everything was. The volume on the TV set was still deafeningly high until Felicity Wright turned it off completely.

'I was just about to put the kettle on, dear, would you like some tea?' Frost thought wistfully of the bottle of wine she'd returned to the fridge half hour earlier and a stomach that was now demonstrating its emptiness with discernible growls.

'A cup of black tea would be wonderful, can I help?'

'No, you sit down and relax. I know how busy you officers are.' Frost wandered around the comfortable room, looking at family pictures. She seemed to have a big family, several children of differing ages, in various school uniforms, smiled back at her. She sat down in a comfortable armchair as she heard the clatter of bone-china tea cups, carried on a brass-framed tray arrive from the kitchen.

'You have a lovely family, Mrs Wright, are those all your grandchildren?'

'No, no, dear, most of them are great grandchildren. I have three. Do you have any children? I suppose in your job you don't have time. Would you like a biscuit or a bit of Victoria sponge?'

'No thank you, tea will be great.' Frost's stomach objected with another growl. McNally had suggested to her, earlier on the telephone, that this was probably just a PR exercise. The uniform and duty late turn CID had viewed CCTV coverage of the incident in which a young woman, whom they'd now identified as Ruth Ward, appeared to throw herself in front of a southbound Northern line train. Other witnesses had come forward, but only observed the victim falling to her death, and the hysterical aftermath.

Felicity Wright had rung the Anti-Terrorist hotline, a number she often called with sightings of suspicious people, to report what she'd seen—the victim had been pushed. New Scotland Yard had passed the information to the Transport Police control room with a warning that Felicity Wright was a serial caller.

Frost glanced at her watch as the frail old lady poured the tea into a strainer and added milk into one cup and handed the second to her visitor.

'You're the first lady police officer I've had visit me here, dear. Are you on your own? It's a bit dangerous isn't it?' Frost was amused at how many questions Wright could ask without drawing a breath and giving her no opportunity to answer. She would make a good television interviewer on a breakfast news show. 'The nice chaps from Scotland Yard normally come in twos. That's why I've always got plenty of cake in.' Frost took a sip of her tea, which was lukewarm.

'Felicity, is it OK if I call you that?' Wright nodded her agreement. 'You reported to police officers earlier that you thought you saw the woman at London Bridge, who tragically died under the wheels of a train, pushed to her death. Is that right?'

'I maybe a dithering old busybody with glasses resembling the bottom of milk bottles constable, but please don't sit there, in my own living room, and patronise me—I know what I saw—not what I *thought* I saw.' Frost was taken slightly aback by the sternness in Wright's voice, but accepted the rebuke and started again.

'I'm sorry, Felicity, my choice of words were insensitive. I was never questioning your integrity. Please call me Marcia, and I'm a sergeant. Could you just explain to me a little of the background to you being at London Bridge and what you subsequently witnessed in as much detail as you can.'

'Well about once a month I meet up with some friends in Borough Market. We have a bite to eat and a chat about the old days. We were all in the RAF. I even got a medal. I don't drink anymore; it doesn't agree with me, dear. We went our separate ways. I'm the only one who lives south. The other girls catch the Jubilee Line up towards Baker Street. I made my way down to the southbound Northern Line platform and sat on a seat towards the north end, where the train arrives from. I'd just missed one so the platform was fairly empty. I love watching people and noticed the girl enter the platform; she reminded me a bit of the younger me. She had a great big smile on her face and looked really happy. She had a nice figure, a bit of meat on her, not like some of these young girls on the front of magazines who look like they need a bloody good meal.'

'Can you describe her any further?'

'Just a minute, I'm coming to that. She had blond hair—it looked natural enough. I'd say she was late twenties, quite heavy makeup, which she didn't really need. She had something alien stuck in the side of her nose, silver in colour—didn't like that. As she passed me she gave me the most beautiful, sweet, smile. I thought she was going to stop for a chat but seemed to change her mind at the last moment. I remember looking at the destination board which displayed the next train in six minutes. The girl moved about fifteen feet further up the platform.

'As the minutes ticked by the platform filled up considerably. I felt a warm draft coming from the direction of the tunnel. I got up and moved a few feet further along towards the front of the train—the first double door of the carriage I board, stops adjacent to the exit at the Oval Station.'

Felicity took a few sharp breaths and a mouthful of tea. Marcia saw that her hand had begun to shake ever so slightly.

'Take your time. This must be very distressing for you. Could you see the young woman from where you were?'

'I did glance in her direction and could see her blonde hair. I remember that she had a red hair band, but there were a number of passengers between us and I was more interested in jockeying for a position. Most people respect the elderly but you still have to use your elbows strategically on occasions. I managed to worm my way towards the edge of the platform with my toes touching the yellow safety line. I looked towards the tunnel entrance; the train does come in at quite a speed. Then…then I saw her.' Felicity removed a used paper tissue from the inside of her sleeve and blew her nose noisily.

'She almost flew from the edge of the platform in front of the train. I could see the utter shock on the face of the poor train driver, there was nothing he could do.' Marcia waited patiently for her to continue not wishing to interrupt her thoughts. 'The whole thing must have taken a second or two, but it seemed to play out in slow motion. I can hear the noise of brakes, the arcing of electricity, the crunching of bone and the smell of blood.' Frost remained silent as her witness retreated into her own thoughts. The timing was never going to be right, but the question had to be asked.

'Felicity, did you see anybody push her?' Wright looked up at the pictures of her grandchildren and gave each one of them a smile in turn. She looked at Frost for a few moments, realising the importance of the question.

'No dear, I didn't, but she fell from that platform to her death in a straight upright position with great force; not head first or at least in a crouched position as you would expect if she had jumped of her own accord. That confident young lady had been full of spirit just minutes before. She looked as if she were about to embark on a new exciting phase of her life, not ending it in such tragic circumstances. Believe me, sergeant, she was pushed—it was murder.'

Chapter Ten

McNally rang Frost first thing Sunday morning.

'How'd it go?'

'I believe her, boss. I think she was pushed. Yes, I know the CCTV doesn't show anything, and yes, there were no other witnesses who saw Ruth Ward actually being pushed but…'

'But *what*, Marcia?' McNally sounded grumpy; if she wasn't careful, she might be winging her way back to divisional CID.

'According to the witness, she looked happy; her exact words were "like she was about to embark on a new exciting phase of her life, not end it in such tragic circumstances". Uniform officers have searched her flat, there is no suicide note. There are dates on her calendar, for example: her dad's birthday party next week. Her bank statements reveal she was in good nick, financially. There is an ansaphone message from a local plumber thanking her for her call, confirming he would be around first thing Monday to fix a leaking toilet. Does that sound like a woman who, having had a nice evening out with friends, walks onto a tube platform and throws herself under a bloody train?' Frost knew she was getting close to the line with her boss but had thought of little else since she had left Felicity Wright's flat. Even half a bottle of Pinot hadn't induced sleep.

'Look Marcia, it's been a long weekend so far, I'm tired and you're tired. Let's talk about this after the briefing tomorrow. If you want to do something in the meantime, on a rare day off, have a word with Sally Cook and track down the coroner's officer. See what their take is on it. Obviously, there will have to be an inquest, but from what I've seen at the moment there is nothing for us, and unless you've forgotten, we've got an unidentified murder victim with a big hole in its skull. I want you fresh for Monday.' Frost could hear McNally's wife whisper something to him.

'Look, I gotta go, Marcia. I need to spend a bit of time with the kids while I can. I'll see you tomorrow and by the way, before I forget, welcome to major crimes.'

Chapter Eleven

McNally looked through, from his office, into the incident room at British Transport Police Headquarters on Camden Road. It was a bit different from the cramped conditions he'd experienced in Manchester. The Major Investigations Team was well equipped although, on a larger enquiry, there were never enough work stations, so a few of the detectives had to "hot desk" on occasions.

Frost, like him, had been in early contacting the Nat West Bank, having faxed over a Data Protection Act form that he'd signed. She had frustration written all over her face. Dealing with banks wasn't always that easy, especially when the police wanted information about their customers—which he could appreciate. Frost put the phone down and waved a piece of paper in McNally's direction, a triumphant smile signalled success.

Hodge and Graves walked passed McNally's office.

'Good morning, boss,' said Hodge. Graves gave just a curt nod of the head with a mumbled greeting. He could be a right miserable bastard when he wanted to be. McNally's phone rang.

'Morning boss, it's Ray. The team are here, what time do you want to start this briefing? Sally Cook is running twenty minutes late.'

'OK Ray, give it ten minutes and I'll be in. Did you manage to get an indexer for HOLMES?'

'Yes, I've borrowed Marie Relish; she just finished a fraud job during which, she told me, she frequently questioned the meaning of life. She jumped at the chance to work with us on this. So I'll tell the others ten minutes, might give that miserable twat, Graves, a chance to cheer up.' McNally liked Ray Blendell. He'd been with the Metropolitan Police for years but fancied a change and a better pension. He brought over bags of experience as an office manager.

'What's the new DS like? She seems keen; got in before me?'

'Marcia? She's going to be ok. I think she might need reining in a bit, every now and then, she's really keen to make an impression and is quite opinionated—

but in a good way. I think she'll be a good addition to the team. Keep an eye on her and Graves though, Ray. I think he might give her a bit of a hard time.'

'Yeah, I know he's a bit pissed off about her getting the DS' job over him but if he'd kept his nose clean…'

McNally replaced the receiver before lifting it again and dialling his home number. The telephone rang before a quiet voice answered, 'Hi darling, how're you?'

'Hi Dad, a bit tired I'm just going to chill at home. Is that OK with you?'

'Of course it is. Ava, we need to have a long talk when you're up to it about the future. I know you hate it at school but there are other options we can discuss.'

'I'm really sorry about the other day, and what I put you and Mum through. I don't know what I was thinking. But I hate it here. It's OK for you and Mum you're adults with jobs. Everybody is on my case at school. I'm an outsider Dad, I don't fit in.'

'It's OK, love, just calm down. We'll sort it out. I have to shoulder some of the blame. When I got offered this job, I jumped at the chance without really considering all your feelings. It's a bit easier for me, I know, I'm working in a similar role that I did before, just a different location. But London will offer you and your brother so many more opportunities. Look, I gotta go. Love you lots and we'll speak later.'

McNally put the receiver down and walked the short distance to the toilets. Splashing water over his face he examined his reflection in the mirror, 'you selfish bastard,' he mumbled.

Chapter Twelve

McNally walked into the briefing room, his thoughts split between his daughter and murder. The room settled down as he looked around at his team.

Two were untried entities in relation to a murder enquiry. Marcia Frost: young keen and proving to be capable, and Sam Hodge: the youngest detective on the team, who had a lot to learn but was showing real promise. He was more concerned over that lazy bastard Stuart Graves. He needed to get rid of him; he was going to be disruptive, already having some influence over Sam Hodge. Up till now he'd been able to deal with Graves by acknowledging, to himself, that every team has a 'Stuart Graves.' But his patience was wearing a little thin. McNally looked at Ray Blendell and nodded curtly.

Ray opened the briefing with a summary of Saturday's discovery at Lambeth North station. Sally Cook had sent an email from the mortuary, describing briefly the cause of death—a blow to the back of the head which would have caused major brain trauma, no surprises there. If any of the detectives had any doubt, they were dealing with murder, it was now crystal clear.

Blendell outlined the make-up of the team introducing himself as office manager to those who didn't know him, and indexer, Marie Relish. McNally watched Graves whisper some—no doubt—lewd comment about the indexer into Sam Hodge's ear. Hodge reacted with an awkward, embarrassed smile.

Frost was to head up the outside enquiry team with Hodge and Graves, the latter doubling up as exhibits officer. Everybody nodded their understanding. McNally got to his feet.

'We know we're dealing with a violent death several years old; our first priority is to identify our victim. Sally Cook was pretty optimistic that a confirmed identification can be made via dental records, we just need a name and to identify a dental surgery our victim used. As Ray outlined, a bank deposit receipt was found at the scene which gives us a number of possibilities. Firstly it's our victim's, secondly it belongs to the killer or thirdly it may have been dropped by a passenger and found its way down through an air vent, train tunnel or a hundred different other ways and is irrelevant to our enquiry.' McNally and the rest of the team looked in Frost's direction causing her slight consternation before she recovered and cleared her throat.

'I served a data protection form on the bank at 7am this morning and spoke to the bank's fraud investigation branch. They were, eventually, really helpful and have come back, literally, in the last fifteen minutes with a result. The account—which has lain dormant since the date on the receipt—6 February 2000—is still active, with a balance of £121.30p, and belongs to a male called Liam Brennan, who had an address in Brixton Road about halfway between Stockwell and Brixton. His date of birth—13th July 1957—meant he would have been, forty-two. I've done a voters' check on the address but nobody by that names lives there anymore, couple that fact with the redundant bank account, I think we have our victim.'

'Let's not assume anything at the moment. Ray, make a visit to this address a number one priority. Give the action to Marcia, as she's already started the enquiry.' Blendell nodded and scribbled a note.

'Marcia take Sam with you—door to door enquiries with any neighbours and try a few local dental surgeries. Hopefully he was a good boy and visited his dentist every six months, we might get lucky. Dental records are going to be the fastest and most conclusive identification we can get at this moment.'

'Stuart, can you do all the checks on this guy Brennan, you know: Police National Computer, Department of Works and Pensions, DVLA, etc. We could do with a picture of him ASAP,' Graves nodded. 'Include HMRC to see if he was working, and the Home Office for any passport. When you've done that, get hold of somebody from London Underground, maybe that area manager who was at Lambeth North station on Saturday—can't remember his name...'

'Lawrence Regan,' Hodge added, 'not the most helpful of characters. Just wants an easy life—I got the feeling that trains *are* his life.'

'Well, you speak to him, Sam, and point out that this is now a murder enquiry. We need details of members of staff who worked at the station in February 2000, all of them, not just the ones who were on duty that day, including any contractors carrying out maintenance, and cleaners. Also, were any incidents or out of the ordinary occurrences logged in the station log book for say the previous week?' Hodge nodded.

'Bearing in mind the location of the body,' McNally continued, 'there must be a London Underground connection to this enquiry, be it either our killer or our victim—if not both. All understand what you've got to do?' The team nodded in unison. 'Any questions?' The room fell momentarily silent before McNally shuffled his papers and moved towards the incident room door.

'Marcia, a word in my office.' Frost grabbed her cup of coffee and followed McNally, shutting the door as she entered. She sat down looking a little apprehensive.

'What's the problem, sir?'

'Nothing relax, I just wanted to have a talk. This is the first time we've had a chance to have a proper chat since you joined the team. I know you're chomping at the bit to get out and progress this inquiry, but I need to clear up a few points, OK?' Frost nodded.

'I noticed the other day, when we were at Lambeth North, that there was a bit of tension between you and Graves.' McNally let the observation float in the air and was impressed when Frost didn't bite back at him with an ill-thought reply. He continued, 'Between me and you and these four walls, Graves can be a divisive pain in the arse. I know that he resents being passed over for promotion and that you may bear the brunt of that. In his eyes, you've got his job. But he only has himself to blame for that.'

'I know that he was up on a misconduct hearing recently.' Frost took a sip of coffee, giving herself time to consider if she was following the right path and testing the water with her boss before continuing. 'A complaint of sexual harassment from a witness on a previous investigation I understand.' McNally nodded and said.

'He was lucky to get off with a warning at a misconduct hearing, but sadly is not the kind of person to see it that way and keep his head down. I don't want to make a big thing of this, Marcia, but just be aware of him. He's actually a good detective, but I'm concerned what sort of impression he's going to make on Sam Hodge.'

Frost decided not to mention the conversation she'd had with Graves. She'd met bigoted bastards like him, throughout her career, and dealt with them, he would be no different.

'Okay boss, no problem. I'll keep an eye on the situation and keep you updated.'

'Good. I have asked for an extra pair of hands from the Detective Chief Superintendent on "B" Division, which includes the London Underground. We go back a long way. He said he'd see what he could do. I know they are pretty busy at the moment with a couple of rape enquiries but hopefully they can spare someone. Let me know when they arrive.' McNally looked at his watch.

'Ok, I've got to brief Superintendent Plummer, anything else?' Frost shook her head in a way that meant the contrary.

'What's on your mind?'

'I can't get that London Bridge suicide out of my head. I know we have to follow the evidence, and in this case, nobody saw Ruth Ward being pushed and the only witness we have is a lonely old lady who likes inviting detectives to her house to ply with cake and tea, and believes she was pushed but didn't witness the act itself.' McNally looked at his watch again and gave a frustrated sigh.

'I interviewed her, guv, call it gut feeling or a copper's nose, whatever you want. This girl had everything to live for; she didn't even leave a suicide note.'

'Okay, have a dig around but, if you haven't already done so, speak to the coroner's officer. This Lambeth North murder takes priority, is that understood? Don't use anybody else, you've all got enough to do,' McNally pushed himself up from his chair 'now clear off before Plummer starts yelling down the phone asking where the hell I am.' Frost stood up and left the office. Stuart Graves watched her as she walked across the incident room, a contemptuous look spread across his face.

*

Frost printed off statements from two of Ruth Ward's friends, whom she'd been with literally minutes before her life ended under a train at London Bridge station.

'I've got a car, sarge. All ready to go when you are.' Frost looked at Sam Hodge and signalled that she would be two minutes. She waited patiently and was about to put the phone down when a confident female voice answered:

'Whitestone's Banking Corporation, Canada Square, Alice speaking, can I help you?'

'Yes, good morning. I'm Detective Sergeant Marcia Frost of the British Transport Police Major Investigations Team in Camden. Is that Alice Harrison?' The voice wasn't quite as confident now.

'Yes, that's me, is this about Ruth? I've already given a statement, I didn't know her that well, and in fact when we met on Saturday, it was the first time since we left school. I explained that in the statement to the uniformed officer—you are a detective; why are you calling? Is there anything wrong?' Frost let Alice Harrison release the pent up tension, she was obviously still feeling, with an avalanche of questions before taking back control.

'Nothing is wrong, Alice. Your statement was very helpful in establishing Ruth's state of mind before she allegedly took her own life.'

'Allegedly—what do you mean?'

'Although the platform was fairly crowded before the arrival of the train we have some conflicting witness accounts that I would just like to try and get to the bottom of before the file goes to the coroner. I read that you believed her to be in a "good place" and seemed to be relaxed and talking positively about her future. It just worries me why somebody with such a positive outlook on her future, would throw herself under a train minutes later.'

'I can't figure that one out myself, detective. She even texted me just before she entered the underground. Sorry, that's not in my statement, with all that was going on I didn't read the message until the following day—yesterday. It scared the hell out of me. I was going to ring the officer who took my statement during my lunch hour today, but I guess you've beaten me to it.'

'What did the message say, Alice?'

'She sounded really happy. Hang on. Let me get the message up on my phone. I'll put you on loudspeaker so I can read it out. Here it is: *thanks for today, really enjoyed seeing you all again, looking forward to meeting up again in the near future.* Doesn't sound like somebody about to kill herself?'

Chapter Thirteen

Hodge guided the Ford Focus down Southampton Row towards Aldwych. It had started to drizzle, and the intermittent wipers cleared the windscreen every three seconds. Hodge was a north London boy—south of the river was an enigma to him. He headed towards Waterloo Bridge and then into the unknown.

'You OK, sarge? You've hardly said a word since we left Camden,' Frost answered whilst continuing to look out of the rain streaked window. London always looked so grey and miserable in inclement weather.

'I'm fine, Sam, just a few things on my mind. What d'ya think of Stuart Graves?'

'He seems okay. I don't really know him. First time I worked with him was on Saturday at Lambeth, and he seems to know what he's doing. He thinks quite a bit of himself and likes the ladies. I saw him chatting up the analyst, Marie Relish, before we left. She didn't seem too impressed and told him to piss off.' Frost smiled for the first time since getting in the car; she'd have to make an effort to get to know Marie better, she seemed like a real laugh.

'Okay, let's get our minds focused on the job in hand,' said Frost, 'I'm pretty sure that Liam Brennan is our victim, but McNally's right, we need to find evidence. The address we're going to is the last address the bank has for him, whether it was owned or rented by him or he lodged there is something we need to find out. Bearing in mind, he's probably been dead for at least twenty years, we might have a problem.'

'Do we have any idea what he looked like?'

'Not at the moment, hopefully Graves will come up with something during the database searches.'

'Do we need to advise the locals we're coming? I mean we don't want to start any riots do we?'

'Sam, Brixton isn't like it used to be. I mean you look at places like Brixton, Hackney and Shoreditch. They're full of people with money nowadays, people who want to connect with the working classes, be at the centre of the diversity revolution.'

'That sounds like a right load of bull. You're from south London. You don't believe that, do you?'

Frost directed Hodge over Waterloo Bridge and eventually onto Kennington Road.

'Of course I don't believe that, but the area has become more fashionable. People like me, like us, can't afford to buy there nowadays. That's why I rent. My parents' house, which they bought under the "right to buy scheme", is probably worth over half a million now. But local people are being forced out. It's like stepping back in time to the 50s and 60s and Peter Rackman.'

'Who's he?'

'Google him and educate yourself with a bit of social history. Landlords are charging exorbitant rents, changing the whole dynamic of the area. Now it's full of bankers, or should I say wankers, from the City. Turn left here this is Stockwell Road. It's the fifth turning on the right.'

'That pub looks a bit of a dump.'

'Ah, that's the Swan, Irish-themed, got a good reputation for giving Irish bands their first chance of stardom. It was police friendly, Brixton nick used to have their Christmas do's there every year as did the BTP at Stockwell. Before I joined the police, me and some mates tried to get in on an Irish night…big mistake, even though, in my drunken state, I tried to convince the doorman I was born in Dublin. Turn right here, Salisbury Road No. 24 on the left. That's it with the red door.'

Hodge found a parking space on the opposite side of the road and both detectives took a few moments to observe the substantial building in front of them.

'Blimey. This doesn't equate to somebody with so little in his bank account. It's got five floors and an attic, probably a cellar as well. It's bloody huge. Do your parents live in a place this size?'

'Most of the houses around here were constructed in Victorian times, when London started to spread out, built for those who had a few quid to their name but not enough to live in Belgravia, Mayfair or Bloomsbury, so they moved south of the river. But most of these places are spilt into flats and bedsits now. According to the voter's register and land registry the property owner is a lady called Paula Lentini who lives in flat 1.'

'Come on. Let's get this done' Hodge opened his door. 'I'm starting to get hungry.'

Flat 1 was the basement flat and Hodge pressed a brass bell button that sounded deep inside the premises. Below the bell, in scratchy black pen, was the name 'P. Lentini.' The sound of a barking dog got louder and louder before it hit the door with such force the detectives thought it was going to put it through, and took a step back. The barking lowered to a menacing growl as the canine sniffed their scent through the slightly warped door, sizing them up. Confident the dog wasn't coming through the door, Frost took a step forward.

'What is that awful smell?' she commented to herself.

Frost tentatively looked through the letterbox, the aroma coming from inside turned her stomach.

'Something has died in there and definitely not gone to heaven. I can hear some movement.'

A voice issued a command to the growling dog. 'Get back, go on.'

A soiled net curtain moved revealing a heavily mascaraed eye peering through a gap in the dirty window. It moved from one detective to the other and then back to Frost.

'If you fucking bible bashers don't fuck off, I'll set the dogs on you. I don't give a shit about you or your fucking religion. Have a bit of respect and leave an old lady alone.'

'Mrs Lentini, it's the police. Can you open the door please? We need a quick word. I promise it won't take long.' Frost raised her warrant card to the level of the eye which multiplied as the net curtain was drawn back a little further. They blinked at the brightness of the sunlight. It must be pretty dark in there, Frost thought.

'What d'ya want? My husband ain't here.'

'Mrs Lentini' Hodge spoke with a soft, compassionate, voice that impressed Frost. 'There is nothing to worry about. We are just making a few enquiries about somebody who, we believe, used to live here.'

'What's their name?'

'We can't really discuss it through a door. It's a little sensitive. May we come in? We won't take up too much of your time.'

The curtain shut and for a couple of seconds the detectives thought she'd walked back into the bowels of the flat and ignored them. They heard a door slam and presumed, well at least hoped, the dog had been secured. Seconds later the bolts slid from their housing at the top and bottom of the door. The door creaked open, as if it hadn't moved for years, the smell got stronger. Frost thought, dog shit or cat piss, took a deep breath and moved into the hallway.

*

Detective Superintendent Nigel Plummer sat behind his desk as if it were a safety barrier between him and Ryan McNally. Plummer was a short man, who wouldn't have made it into the force twenty-five years ago, when a 5'8" minimum height requirement was in place for anybody wishing to be a police officer. McNally guessed that Plummer was a good inch below that. He'd heard rumours that he wore built up shoes to give himself a more authoritative presence; he fought the urge to peer under the desk and check the rumour out for himself.

McNally had taken a dislike to his boss the first time they'd met. As far as he was concerned, he suffered from small man syndrome, and all the people he'd ever come across called Nigel, which to be fair weren't many, were absolute wankers.

Plummer had a face that reminded McNally of a piece of cheese, sort of soft and shiny, with no real distinguishing features. His mouth was small; beady, dull eyes peered through designer glasses that had a blue tint frame; a mass of unruly, wavy brown hair dominated the other features.

Plummer clasped his hands on a desktop devoid of anything official; a photograph of an attractive women grinned from a photo-frame. McNally wondered if that really was his wife or a cut out from a magazine. If it were Plummer's wife, he was boxing well above his weight, a tinge of respect entered McNally's sub-conscious.

McNally was aware that Plummer wasn't a career detective, a bit of a square peg in a round hole and well out of his depth as far as murder investigations go. This happened a lot in the world of modern policing. Instead of picking the right people for the right job and sticking with them, those officers would be moved on for 'career development' to a totally unsuitable position that didn't reflect their talents, pissed the individual off and destroyed any motivation they had to get the job done. Whoever thought of that policy probably got a knighthood, a big fat pension and developed a Do-I-Give-A-Fuck-Attitude when asked what they thought about the state of the modern police force.

'How're you settling in, Ryan?'

'OK, sir. It's been nearly twelve months now, the first six months were hard until the family joined me. Our son Max has adapted well but Ava's struggling a bit. She really misses Manchester and her friends. It will take time.'

'I know what you mean. I started off in Bristol before joining the Met in London. It's good to move around a bit, come out of your comfort zone, and challenge yourself.' Here comes the management talk. McNally suppressed a smile. Senior officers must be issued with a compendium of bullshit phrases as you climbed the greasy promotional ladder. He hadn't received his yet. One reason he was sure he'd reached his level.

So how's the investigation going? Do you need any more resources?'

'It's early days yet. We hope to positively identify our victim by the end of the day. DS Frost is in south London at a possible last known address. It was a bit of luck, finding the bank receipt near the body, but of course I'm still hoping it's the killer's. I've requested another detective from B Division, so we should be OK. The very dynamic of the investigation means nothing is going to happen at break-neck speed.'

'Good, but let's still try and wrap this one up ASAP. We don't know what's around the corner. How're the team? You have a couple of new faces on board haven't you?'

'Yes, all good, boss.'

'What about Stuart Graves?'

'I'm keeping an eye on him. I think there might be a bit of friction between Frost and him. He's a good detective with plenty of experience. But if he steps out of line, I'll come down on him hard.'

Chapter Fourteen

Frost and Hodge followed Paula Lentini into the front room of the basement flat; the curtains were partially open, letting in a modicum of light.

'Sorry about the state of the place. I don't use this room much since my husband died last year. We had him in here for a few days, in his coffin. To be honest, the room gives me the creeps, the dogs sleep in here most of the time now.' Hodge wondered if Mr Lentini had ever left; the smell was awful.

'I need to get my fags and feed the dogs. Sit down if you want. I can't offer you anything. I haven't been to the shops for a while.'

It was the first time either Frost or Hodge had had a chance to assess the occupant. She was a slight woman, with dark black, greasy, hair tied back into a ponytail, dressed in a wraparound silk dressing gown which she hugged to her body, revealing skinny forearms and arthritic hands. Frost guessed she looked, maybe, twenty years older than she actually was. Lentini left the detectives with their thoughts, half-closing the door.

Hodge pushed aside several newspapers to make room to sit.

'What's that?' Frost pointed to the cushion Hodge was just about to sit on.

'I think it's a lump of dog shit.' Hodge retched violently but managed to keep his rising bile somewhere between his stomach and throat. The detectives began to take a closer look at their surroundings, opening the curtains fully. Frost gave a shriek as something black and furry ran from behind an armchair.'

'What the fuck was that?' she said after composing herself.

'I think it was a cat,' Hodge offered unhelpfully, 'what a shithole! How can somebody live like this? Imagine what the rest of the place is like.'

Frost noticed the smell was even stronger near the windows. She peered over a second sofa and spied two large cat litter trays. The bottoms of the heavy draped curtains rested in each of the filthy trays; cat urine had soaked into the curtains, rising up the fabric several inches, leaving a damp yellow stain. As the detectives' eyes became accustomed to the dim light, it became evident this room was just one big pet toilet. Large piles of dog mess littered the room. Frost looked at her partner, who had suddenly gone very quiet. Hodge looked a little green and was breathing through his mouth.

'You okay, Sam?'

Hodge shook his head, beads of sweat appearing on his brow.

'I gotta get out of here soon, sarge.' Both heard footsteps approaching from the hallway.

'I'll be as quick as I can. Just keep breathing through your mouth and take a seat.' Hodge nodded. Before taking Frost's advice, he lifted a cushion. Tiny insects scurried to find the sanctuary of darkness again under a piece of clothing that had been stuffed down the side of the furniture. Hodge picked the item up; it was a pair of female knickers, soiled with faeces. He dropped them abruptly as Lentini came back into the room with a cigarette hanging from the corner of her mouth and a large register under one arm and sat in an armchair. Hodge tried to waft the smell of cigarette smoke into his nostrils.

'So you gonna tell me what this is all about?'

Frost perched herself on the very edge of the sofa near the window. Hodge remained standing, all colour now drained from his face.

'You're the owner of this house, Mrs Lentini, and you rent out the upper floors. Is that correct?'

'Yeah, that's right, it's all above board. I pay my taxes every year to those thieving bastards at the Treasury.' Lentini gave the detectives an accusatory glance. 'I got the register of people that 'ave stayed here over the years; my late husband—he was a restaurateur—kept the records. I've let them slip a little since his death, I must admit.'

'That's not the only thing you've let slip,' mumbled Hodge. Lentini either didn't hear or chose to ignore the detective's comments. Frost gave him a stern look before continuing.

'We are interested in somebody, we believe, rented one of your bedsits some years ago. His name was Liam Brennan. Can you recall him?'

'Bloody right I can. You lot came and searched his room, turned the place upside down. Luigi—my husband—had a right argument with them. You lot don't exactly tidy up after you.' Frost decided not to interrupt Lentini's flow and glanced out the corner of her eye at Hodge, who looked too ill even to say his name, let alone interrupt with a question.

'He just disappeared from the face of the earth and he owed us two month's rent.' She opened her register and turned several pages. 'Here he is—Liam Brennan. He was a long-term tenant, came here in January of 1995 and disappeared in early February 2000. Your lot came bursting in here on the 9th February. I remember it was that day, because we were 'aving a bit of a party for Luigi—it was his sixty-fifth birthday. They insisted on searching Liam's room. One of your lot, in plain clothes, waved a bit of paper at us stating it was a search warrant. They took a bundle of stuff away with them and we never heard a thing after that or saw Liam again.'

'When you say, our lot, Mrs Lentini, can you remember what police force they were from?'

'Your lot—Transport Police.'

'Did they say what they suspected Brennan had done?'

'Stole a load of money from a booking office at the station he worked at.' Frost couldn't disguise her surprise. 'He was a London Underground station supervisor at Lambeth North.'

*

Taking a statement from Paula Lentini had been exhausting. Sam Hodge just wanted to write anything down to get out of this hell hole. His head was thumping and he was finding it increasingly difficult to talk and breathe through his mouth at the same time.

'If he disappeared so suddenly, what did you do with his possessions?'

'I kept them in one of the bedsits upstairs. It's a bit damp, so we never rented the room out. I was going to sell some of the stuff off to recover some of the rent he owed when he disappeared, but I never got around to it. I suppose you wanna have a nose around, do you?' Frost jumped to her feet and grabbed the key from the landlady. She gave Hodge a half smile. Sometimes rank had its privileges. Hodge returned to the job in hand. Frost stopped in her tracks at Lentini's next comment.

'He was a bit of a weirdo, you know.'

'What do you mean?'

'I caught him a couple of times lurking outside the room of a young student who was staying in the floor below him. He always had an excuse—he had the gift of the gab. We have a communal washing line in the back garden and the young lady complained to me, on a number of occasions, that some of her underwear had gone missing. I always suspected it was Liam. I even caught him coming out of this flat once. Luigi was at work and I'd gone out shopping. I left a key under a flowerpot outside as I'm always losing my keys.'

'I got home late afternoon. Liam was coming up the steps from the basement and was really surprised to see me. He said he'd knocked on my door as he had a problem with a leaking tap. I told him I'd get Luigi to come and have a look later but he said not to bother. He would fix it himself. Out of curiosity, I looked under the flowerpot for the key—it was missing; in fact it was under an adjacent one. If I'm honest, I was glad when he disappeared.'

'Did you ever confront him over this?'

'No but I was right. When I cleared his room, I found several pairs of knickers under his bed; not only the girl's but also mine. They weren't even clean. He took them from the laundry basket!' Hodge glanced at the pair of filthy knickers he had launched across the room minutes earlier. He became even more nauseous at the thought of anybody taking the slightest, sordid, sexual pleasure out of this woman's dirty pants.

*

Marcia Frost ascended two sets of stairs and found the storeroom, which she unlocked with the key. The air was musty, but a relief from the aroma of cat and dog mess. A single light bulb, under a dusty pink light shade, illuminated the surprisingly big room.

The detective hadn't expected to find anything of great value to their investigation. She assumed her colleagues, who'd visited two decades ago, would've removed anything of importance.

Among the possessions, packed away in a couple of damp cardboard boxes, she found some old London Underground uniform, several documents about pension plans and RMT Union paraphernalia. Other personal items included: family photographs and a diary come address book. Frost dusted down an old chair, sat and read.

Most of the diary entries were around shift patterns and days off, together with a few birthday reminders and several weeks blocked out with the words A/L—annual leave and a couple of entries for other appointments—one being a dental check-up but no details of a dental practice. Appointments and holidays booked but never to be experienced. Entries that made Frost reflect on how fragile life could be.

She studied the remaining pages. On reaching the penultimate page, she found a small plain brown envelope with no writing on the outside. She took a pair of gloves from her handbag before carefully opening the envelope and removing several black and white stills, printed from a video. The quality was poor. She rotated the images a number of times before realising what she was looking at. Each image showed a woman partially naked in the process of relieving themselves. Although the images were shocking, showing the women in the most vulnerable of positions, knowing what she now knew about Brennan from his landlady, she wasn't completely surprised.

Something began to nag at the back of the detective's mind about the images. She'd learnt from experience not to zone in on such thoughts; her subconscious would retain it, work it out and return it to the present, in its own in time— normally the middle of the night.

She placed the images and envelope into a property bag, with several other items, including a toothbrush, hairbrush and the family photographs, and sealed them. She was unsure if the tooth or hair brushes could still yield a DNA profile after such a long time but it was something she could let Sally Cook and the forensic labs have a go at.

Frost returned to the basement flat as Lentini was signing her statement. She showed her a number of photographs she'd taken from Brennan's possessions through the transparent bag. The landlady identified the former station supervisor standing at the back of a family gathering. Frost thanked the landlady and turned to find Hodge; the young detective was already out the door.

Both detectives breathed in Brixton's air as they left the basement flat. Frost called Ray Blendell in the incident room with an update.

'That's good work, Marcia. You've confirmed what Graves has come up with via HMRC. We've just had a photo of Brennan emailed over to us from London Underground personnel.' Frost was a little miffed that Graves had gotten in before her, but she didn't dwell on the fact. She was delighted her next piece of information was more significant.

'Crikey, can the landlady remember when our lot called on her—was it long after he disappeared?'

'Yeah, she can. It was on the 9th February—her late husband's sixty-fifth birthday. They were having a family gathering to celebrate. The officers asked a lot of questions and searched his room—pulled it apart; she was pissed off that not only had Brennan done a runner, owing her a couple of months' rent, but brought the police into her house. We'll try and find this dentist mentioned in the diary. Obviously, we can't prove at the moment that Liam Brennan and the bag of bones at the mortuary are one in the same but it's looking that way. Can you do a PNC check, it seems Brennan was a bit of a pervert as well as a suspected thief; I'll explain when we get back.'

'Ok, I'll get that done. His London Underground personnel file is on its way over from 55 Broadway. I'll see if he had any disciplinary hearings or complaints from members of the public during his service. He must have pissed somebody off. I'll draw the archive file on any investigation carried out into the booking office burglary.'

Frost ended the call and returned to the car. The fresh air hadn't done the trick for Sam Hodge.

'You still hungry, Sam? There's a decent greasy spoon around the corner. I could do with a decent fry up. I only had muesli for breakfast.'

Hodge lifted his head up towards her, about to say something, when the contents of his stomach finally won the war with his throat muscles and erupted from his mouth and nostrils, splashing across the bonnet of their vehicle.

'Okay, Sam,' Frost smiled, 'maybe via a car wash. Get in, I'll drive.'

Chapter Fifteen

McNally stood next to his desk looking down onto Camden Road. He still couldn't get used to the volume of traffic, twenty-four-seven. It'd been difficult to get his head around the sheer size of the capital. He estimated you could fit Greater Manchester into the footprint of Greater London several times over.

It was a hot morning; the sun already high in the sky but dulled by a haze of pollution. McNally reflected on his meeting with Detective Superintendent Nigel Plummer. It had gone okay. If he was honest, he thought Plummer was going to stick his nose in where it wasn't wanted. That would come if he didn't get a result fast. With the revelation that their victim—subject to confirmation—was a London Underground worker Plummer would be getting extra pressure from above, both from the Chief Constable and senior railway officials. People like Plummer were always looking to take the next step up the ladder and a flawed murder investigation wasn't going to assist with that aspiration.

McNally opened his decision log and started to enter his strategic decisions; including the specific lines of enquiry he'd actioned at this morning's briefing. He also pondered over the fact that their possible victim had originally been suspected of screwing the booking office. He was disturbed mid-thought by a hesitant knock on his door.

'Come in,' a vaguely familiar face peered sheepishly around the door.

'Morning sir, I've been sent over from B Division to help on the Lambeth North investigation—PC Jim Wakefield. We met on Saturday at the scene. I was keeping the cordon log. If you remember, sir, you said if I ever fancied a go at CID, I should come and see you. Well looks like I'm here a little earlier then I planned and by the look on your face a little earlier than you would expect. The Chief Super on B Division apologises; I'm all he's got. I was due to start an attachment to CID today. All the CID teams are on active investigations—a series of knife-point rapes.'

McNally remembered the young officer, and the fact that he'd shown good common sense and some degree of initiative. He needed an extra pair of hands at the moment and wasn't particularly bothered if said pair of hands came with the rank of detective or not. He closed his decision log and told Jim Wakefield to report to Ray Blendell and bring himself up to date with the investigation so far.

McNally rang Frost's mobile number and got her to repeat what she'd discovered.

'Good work, Marcia. Give the SOCO's office a ring and get Sally Cook down to the address. I want all of Brennan's possessions forensically recovered and examined for fingerprints and DNA. I'm not sure if he's a victim or an offender or both yet, so let's play it safe.' McNally cut Frost off to answer an incoming call.

'Hi, Kate, look, this isn't a good—'

'Ryan, Ava's gone missing again. I left her for thirty minutes to get some shopping. When I got back, she'd disappeared.'

*

Fresh air and a decent brunch at some greasy spoon hadn't improved Sam Hodge's outlook on the day. Frost constantly glanced towards her passenger, worried that he was about to regurgitate the meal she'd insisted he consumed to *settle* his stomach. But Hodge was sure he could *still* smell dog mess and constantly checked the seat of his trousers and the soles of his shoes.

The rush hour traffic had settled down to a normal stream of heavy goods vehicles, buses and taxis as Frost steered the car north along Kennington Road. They'd struck lucky. The second dentist they'd visited proved to be the one they were looking for. Dental records bagged up in a property bag, they headed for Camden.

The thought that'd earlier been nagging at the back of her mind, since she saw the sordid images in Brennan's property, was quickly moving to the fore and she swerved the car from one lane to another just outside Kennington police station, instigating a torrent of abuse from a black cab driver. She pulled over and parked in a bus lane opposite Lambeth North station.

'I need the toilet, Sam. I won't be a minute.'

'You not feel too well either, sarge?' Hodge gave a satisfied grin.

'Don't be a wanker, Sam. I'm made of sterner stuff. Keep an eye out for traffic wardens.'

*

The whole investigation team had made it back to the late afternoon briefing at the Camden Road incident room. Ray Blendell and Marie Relish had been hard at work with detailed drawings of Lambeth North station, pinned up on the wall, together with crime scene pictures of the remains of their, as yet, unidentified victim.

The banter was in full flow. Stuart Graves pretended to throw up into an office rubbish bin. Frost had to smile along with the laughter but felt slightly guilty—well for a couple of seconds anyway—about telling the team of Sam Hodge's projectile vomiting over the squad car's bonnet. Hodge—whose normal colour had returned to his face—joined in, pointing out that he could still smell dog shit and asking if roundworm could be caught by humans.

'If you suddenly drop your trousers and shuffle your bottom on the carpet, best you go to see your doctor.' Marie Relish added.

'Or even your vet.' Graves was now in full flow. The banter calmed down only when McNally entered the room. Normally he would be pleased to hear the piss-taking, and in fact he would be more worried if there wasn't any. This was how cops dealt with the pressure and stress of what they saw and dealt with day to day. It used to be called "canteen culture" or "canteen humour" until some do-gooder on a police management board decided such references "professionally unacceptable". Probably the same twat who decided to get rid of all social clubs in police stations and any other unnecessary social activities—not part of the modern image of today's police service. The thoughts only contributed to the darkening of his mood.

The team sensed something was up and duly quietened down.

'I'm sure we all have things to be getting on with so let's get this over with.' McNally had toyed with the idea of jumping in his car and going home. Ray Blendell was more than capable of filling his shoes until he'd got the crisis at home sorted out. He opened his notebook and decision log and, without looking up, started the briefing with an introduction.

'PC Jim Wakefield has joined us on attachment from B Division. He will join up with the outside enquiry team led by DS Frost. Whilst he is here, he will be treated as one of the team without exception. Is that clear DC Graves?'

'A bloody wooden-top! They run out of detectives on division?' McNally looked at Graves with such intensity further words were unnecessary. Graves knew he was close to the line and started nervously shuffling some papers in front of him. Frost looked over at Jim Wakefield, who'd gone a slight shade of pink, and gave him a reassuring smile. Hodge was pleased he was no longer the new boy, and have the chance to deflect Graves' venomous tongue to another.

'Right, let's go around the room. Stuart, seeing as you have so much to say, you can start us off.'

'Yes, boss. I spent most of the morning carrying out checks on Liam Brennan and struck lucky with both the HMRC and then London Underground. Liam Brennan had been an employee of London Underground since the mid-eighties. He was recruited as a station platform assistant, working mostly on the Central Line, starting at Oxford Circus and going onto various other stations in that group: Bond Street, Tottenham Court Road etc. He got knocked back when he applied to be a train driver. He didn't have the mental application or temperament, according to his file. Apparently he was a bit pissed off with the decision, which meant missing out on a big pay increase, loads of holidays and a shortened working week. He appealed the decision via the RMT, claiming he'd been subject of prejudice.'

'What?' Frost interjected. 'He was white, male and heterosexual.'

'Exactly, and he paid his taxes, and for his prescriptions, didn't claim any benefits and sang *God Save the Queen* every night. In other words, he was part of the only group of people in this country that doesn't have any human rights.' Graves smiled, believing he'd scored some good points in front of his peers. He continued.

'He kept his head down for a couple of years and was promoted to a station supervisor at Pimlico station, before moving onto Lambeth North.' The atmosphere in the room had changed, concentration taking over from humour.

'On 6th February…'

'The day recorded on the bank slip found in the vicinity of our yet unidentified human remains,' Blendell reminded everybody.

'…there was a burglary at the booking office—remember them? For the younger members of the team they were glassed holes in the wall, where helpfully you could go and buy a ticket from an occasional friendly face, instead of trying to figure out how to manipulate a computerised ticket machine.'

'Dinosaur,' somebody commented from the back.

McNally didn't smile with the rest. Graves' was starting to grind on him. His phone buzzed in his pocket—a message from Kate. He tensed as he opened it. "She's OK, with Mum and Dad in Sheringham X". McNally visibly sunk back into his chair as the tension drained from him. Kate's Mum and Dad lived in the North Norfolk seaside town. Ava had travelled up there on her own during the school summer holidays on several previous occasions. He wanted to talk to her, to make sure she was okay, but knew she was safe with his in-laws. Anyway it would only end in an argument. Better to let Kate deal with it for now. He turned his frustration to Graves.

'For fuck's sake, Stuart, just get on with it, and keep your opinions, unless they're about this investigation, to yourself.'

'Sure, boss. The booking office was closed up just before 10pm that night. The booking clerk had knocked off ten minutes early. When it was opened again the following morning, the place had been cleared out—the safe door wide open and about twelve grand missing, give or take a pound either way. Police were called and headed straight around to the late turn booking clerk's home, a guy called Steve Wallis. According to the officer's notebook—a copy is attached to the case file—the booking clerk was still in bed. He was shocked but co-operated and allowed a search of his house and car without the need for a warrant. He was still arrested on suspicion of burglary and interviewed by the early turn divisional CID and bailed. I've had a quick read of his interview and his explanation. He stated that he left the booking office fully secured and his movements, after he left work, seemed pretty convincing.'

'Where did he go?'

'Well, Ray, he went to Lewisham Hospital maternity unit. His wife gave birth at 10.42pm. The only thing he admitted was that he left the station about ten minutes early when he got the call that she was about to drop a bundle imminently. Seems unlikely that he would decide to nick twelve grand of the company's money at the precise time his wife is about to give birth. The investigation concluded that he wouldn't, logistically, have had the time to get home and then to the hospital, he made it with two minutes to spare. The midwife remembered Mrs Wallis shouting "Where the fuck have you been?" The investigating officers took his office and safe keys from him. He was bailed for further enquiries but no further action was taken in regards to him.'

'So suspicion fell on our possible victim—Liam Brennan?'

'Yes, boss. Brennan was the late turn supervisor, finishing after the last train about 1am. Wallis told the officers that he'd called Brennan on the station's internal phone system after he got the call from the hospital and informed him that he was off and everything in the booking office was in order.'

'What about CCTV? Wasn't any seized at the time? Everybody turned and looked at Jim Wakefield, who went the colour of a tomato and hunched his shoulders as if to point out that it *was* a relevant question.'

'There was CCTV in operation along that piece of the Bakerloo Line but it was locally operated on a time lapse system which only showed the booking office entrance and front of the station for about five out of every fifteen seconds. It was recorded on VHS tapes in the supervisor's office. I remember the system well. It was more for the benefit of the railway, in relation to crowd control, rather than a policing or security purpose. They used to have a VHS tape or tapes for each day of the week, depending on the size of the station. It was the early turn supervisor's duty to change the tape each day so any recording only had a life of seven days until it was recorded over again. Sometimes the tapes were not changed, some days they went missing. Most were of bad quality, some due to the constant over-recording and in black and white. It never really changed until the 7/7 bombings.'

'The terrorist attacks on the tube in 2005, when fifty-one people were murdered by fanatics.' McNally explained to one or two blank faces in the room—God, did he feel old.

'I was on that enquiry,' continued Graves. 'We had hundreds of coppers all over London from BTP, the Met and City of London trawling around collecting thousands of VHS tapes just in case our dead terrorists appeared on any. As it happened they arrived at Kings Cross Thameslink station. The quality was terrible. The digital videoing age was well underway but the attacks hastened the investment needed to update CCTV recording on the transport network. When the officer who attended the station early Sunday morning, when the burglary was discovered, went to seize the video tape surprise, surprise, it was missing.'

A couple of heads turned as SOCO, Sally Cook slipped through the door to the rear of the room. McNally nodded his head as she took a seat. She looked exhausted. Her jet black hair a little dishevelled and the dark rings under her eyes suggesting she'd had a longer weekend than any of them in the room. The team mentally digested what Graves had outlined. Ray Blendell was the next to speak.

'What was the outcome of the investigation?'

'Brennan's rented flat in Brixton was searched.'

'In a manner of speaking,' interrupted Frost, 'I found a lot of documents and photos that give a clearer picture of Liam Brennan's character, which were overlooked or deemed irrelevant by the searching officers at the time. To be fair to them they were investigating a £12,000 burglary and not murder, as we are.' Frost let her words hang in the air before Graves continued, a little miffed at the interruption.

'They did at least seize his passport so knew he couldn't flee the country— well legitimately anyway. There are several printouts in the file in relation to the use of Brennan's staff barrier pass, days after the burglary. These passes were issued to all members of London Underground staff in those days. We used to be issued with them as well until several Met officers abused them by travelling on their warrant cards and letting their other halves or children use the rail pass. There can't be another occupation in this country who fucked things up for themselves more than the "Old Bill". A few murmurs of agreement circulated the room.' Graves continued.

'But these records weren't obtained for a couple of weeks—post incident— so again the CCTV covering the locations, where the pass is used, they presumed at the time by Brennan, was non-existent. It's noted here that the last recorded use of the staff pass was on the 11th of February 2000. He then disappears from the face of the earth.'

'Is the investigating officer still with the force?'

'Yes, guv—John Danes, he's a DI in Birmingham, due to retire next month,' said Blendell.

'OK, raise an action for somebody to have a word with him. See if he can remember anything about Brennan that's not in the file.'

'Brennan is still circulated on PNC as wanted and his photograph has appeared in the *Police Gazette* and Danes made an appeal on the tenth anniversary of the burglary on *Crimewatch* for information regarding Brennan's whereabouts. There were a few phone calls about possible sightings around London and in Spain but they came to nothing.'

'Ok, Stuart thanks, but let's move on. Sally any update on our pile of bones?'

'Yes, dude, just got a phone call, on my way here, from the forensic odontologist.' Marie Relish sank her face into the crook of her arm to stifle a snigger. 'She can confirm a match between the dental records recovered and our man, end of mystery.'

'Good, progress at last,' McNally allowed himself a smile. 'So we now know that Brennan is our victim. We know he was alive and breathing mid-afternoon from the time on the bank receipt. We know he was alive at just before 10pm that night because the booking office clerk—Willis—spoke to him on the internal phone before leaving the secured booking office. Stuart have a look at the names in the file of any other staff who were on duty early and late turn on the 6th of February and the early turn who opened up the following morning. Presumably he or she can confirm the station was locked from the previous night.' Graves nodded as he made notes.

'Marie, I want you to dig as deep as you can into Brennan's private life. See if you can uncover a possible motive for our man's murder. Liaise with Marcia regarding the search of his flat. Jim, get a photocopy of Brennan's diary. Use gloves. I want it fingerprinted—go through it and construct a timeline of his movements for January 2000 and the first few days of February before he died and a list of appointments for the rest of the year that he sadly wouldn't make.'

McNally glanced at his watch. He needed to speak to Kate and his in-laws; one of them was going to have to travel to Norfolk tonight, they couldn't both go. He didn't want Max taken out of school.

'Marcia and Sam, you went to our man Brennan's address. What you got?'

'A lot of the documents, I recovered from the flat, back up what Stuart reported. The landlady—Mrs Lentini thought he was a bit of a loner. He didn't seem to have any friends. She put it down to his long hours at work and the difficult shift pattern. She did find him lurking around her flat once and suspected he might have been poking around as the spare key she'd hidden had been moved when she checked. I also found a couple of pairs of women's underwear among his clothes. One of the items—which were rather soiled—belonged to the landlady herself.' Frost broke off to look under her desk and retrieved an evidence bag which she raised above her head and passed around. Most were relieved to see it wasn't a pair of soiled knickers.'

'I discovered these stills, inside the back lining of the diary, lifted from a video. They feature several women in compromising positions basically about to...'

'Have a piss,' Graves shouted out.

'Stuart, one last chance…'

'Yeah, sorry, boss. Just trying to help out our young detective sergeant who seemed to be struggling to explain what was in front of her.'

'I saw a programme, on this sort of thing, on the telly the other night,' explained Hodge. 'It's a serious problem in South Korea, they call it *Molka*.'

'What you on about Sam. This sort of thing's been going on for years. It's an extension of voyeurism, that's all, just using technology instead of standing in a bush with your todger in your hand.'

'You should know, Stuart.' Graves turned on Marie Relish and gave her a lecherous smile. Relish wished she'd kept her mouth shut.

'No honestly. It's a huge problem over there; they are calling it a 'voyeurism epidemic,' Hodge continued. 'They had a case recently, where female workers in some tech company were well chuffed that their boss had a new toilet seat fitted in the ladies' loo until one of them found a tiny camera fitted on it. You can get five years over there if you're caught; makes our recent "upskirting" law look a bit lightweight.'

'Let's get back on track.' McNally weighed in.

'They are pretty amateurish,' Frost continued, 'and look to be recorded from a fixed, presumably covert camera. The green and white wall tiling rang a bell with me but I couldn't place it until we were driving back to Camden along Kennington Road towards Lambeth North station. Then it dawned on me. I went and checked, and my hunch was right, these were covertly taken in the ladies' staff toilet at the station and I think we can all figure out by whom. If we needed a motive for murder, I think we have one.'

Chapter Sixteen

An air of anticipation swirled around Craven Cottage, replacing one of utter misery just four months earlier. Last season's campaign had been disastrous for Fulham Football Club. But the team had performed brilliantly in their first two games of this new season, and there is nothing more atmospheric than an evening game.

The floodlights gently coaxed away the evening sunshine, accentuating the greenness of the playing surface. A slight breeze from the Thames crept through gaps in the stands, disturbing the corner flags and warning of autumn's approach. The sounds and smells of football were everywhere. An aroma of onions and pies wafted up through the Johnny Haynes stand. As kick off approached a buzz of excitement pulsed through the crowd like an electric current.

Laura Marston had been a Fulham fan since the age of eight. Uncle Alby—her mother's brother—had taken Laura to Craven Cottage as a special birthday treat. She remembered it vividly, the walk from Putney Bridge station, grasping her uncle's hand as if her life depended on it. The brightness of the floodlights, the roar of the crowd as the players appeared on the pitch; naively asking which colours Fulham were playing in. From that moment on, she'd been obsessed by the game.

Laura had met her husband Mark at the ground when he spilt a red-hot cup of Bovril over her beige raincoat. She'd been mad at him, but not for long. He replenished her drink, and promised to pay the dry-cleaning bill, as long as he could see her again. A seven year marriage, and a three-year-old daughter, later, they both enjoyed a once-in-a-while break from everyday life to watch their favourite team and dream of premiership domination.

The mood wasn't so optimistic on the way back to Putney Bridge station. A 2-1 home defeat had dampened the enthusiasm as much as the light rain that seeped through summer clothes. Laura was a "glass half filled" person. Husband, Mark, was the opposite and often sulked for days when their team lost. She chatted about her day and how their daughter seemed to be accepting nursery school life, even hinting that it might be time for another baby.

The throng slowed to crawling pace as the young couple joined the orderly, subdued, snaking queue into the wholly inadequate station entrance. They split in order to pass through separate automatic gates, manned by uncompromising revenue protection officers who slowed the flow, as they checked the validity of every passenger's ticket. Laura breezed through the gate-line and headed to the stairs leading to the eastbound platform. She looked back and saw Mark stuck behind a passenger whose ticket was being examined. Mark waved her on; she knew this wouldn't improve his mood. He was looking a little red-faced; normally a pre-cursor to him losing his patience and on occasions his temper.

She had little choice but to move on as the crowd pressure behind her grew and a metallic voice instructed her not to block the stairs. She didn't worry as they always boarded the District Line train at the same position on the platform, allowing them easy, fast access to the Piccadilly line on arrival at Earls Court. So Mark would know where to find her.

On reaching the top of the stairs, it was obvious a train hadn't departed for some time. The information board informed the crowded platform that the next two trains were delayed. Everybody was requested to move along the platform to make more room for even more people to squeeze on. Laura crooked her neck back towards the stairs but couldn't see Mark. When she reached their boarding point, Laura stuck her heels in and pushed towards the platform edge; the indicator board sprang into life with an estimated time of one minute until the next arrival. If push came to shove—literally in this crowd—she would board the train and wait for her husband's arrival at Earls Court.

She could see the train's lights cutting through the darkness as it approached the crowded platform at a precautionary, reduced speed, blowing its warning horn to the accompaniment of station staff, advising passengers to stand clear of the platform edge.

Her blood turned to ice as a loud roar of away fans filled the air close behind her. Further down the platform several fans, from opposing sides, fought each other. A bottle was thrown smashing into the side of the train. Laura felt the surge of the crowd, most of who were trying to escape the mayhem. She inched dangerously nearer the edge. The train was now only feet from her position and had gathered speed. An iron grip held her right arm. She turned to remonstrate.

A set of hate-filled blue eyes met hers. Her lips formed a silent scream as she was violently pushed to her death.

Chapter Seventeen

McNally drove at speed north up the M11 and onto the A11 arriving in the small north Norfolk seaside town of Sheringham just after 10pm.

He'd left the briefing at Camden in the capable hands of Ray Blendell. He was pleased with the progress of the investigation. They knew the identity of their victim and the kind of person he was. The discovery of the video stills and the theft of women's underwear opened up one line of enquiry in relation to establishing a motive for his murder.

McNally had discussed, with Kate, who should go to Sheringham and pick Ava up. Kate wanted to go with him, but they had nobody to look after Max, so they decided he would travel up to Norfolk as soon as he could get away from work.

He drove down Station Road, Sheringham. Nothing seemed to have changed a great deal since the last time he and the family had visited at Christmas, apart from a couple of new charity shops. He passed the *Robin Hood* pub, which seemed very quiet for the time of year.

Christmas in Norfolk was always a special time for his family: the New Year's Day dip in the sea, he and Max running in at full pelt, Ava and Kate cautiously dipping in a toe each before they all retired to *The Kitchen* cafe for a welcome hot chocolate.

The properties on Nelson Road offered one of the best views of the town and the North Sea. His in-laws' bungalow sat, almost precariously, at its highest point. McNally steered the car onto the gravel driveway. A curtain twitched, allowing a slither of light to escape. The front door opened a few inches as McNally approached. Ava's faced peered out, she looked scared. McNally felt sick to the stomach that his arrival could cause his daughter such stress.

'Hi, Dad,' her voice was so soft he could hardly hear her. He'd decided on the journey up that she needed some harsh words and home truths regarding her selfish behaviour but his heart melted when his daughter's beautiful blue eyes released a cascade of tears that streamed down her face. McNally choked back his own emotions, temporarily incapable of forming a sentence. He simply held out his arms and embraced his daughter in the knowledge that she was safe.

'Hi, darling, let's get you inside. It's a bit chilly out here. Where's Nan and Grandad?'

'Grandad has gone to bed. He's going fishing at three in the morning. Nan is making you something to eat in the kitchen. Dad, I can't face going back to school in a couple of weeks. I needed to get away from London. I called Mum as soon as I got here.' McNally guided his daughter into the kitchen and was met with a warm sympathetic smile from his mother-in-law.

June Cartwright was in her early seventies but had kept her youthful looks with unblemished skin and soft blue eyes. The only hint of her mature years was some restrictive movement, due to the onset of arthritis in her hands and lower joints. She beckoned her son-in-law to sit at the kitchen table and placed a plate brimming with chilli and rice in front of him—it smelled delicious and reminded him that he hadn't eaten since lunchtime.

'I just spoke to Kate. She is relieved that you arrived safely.' McNally nodded, suddenly feeling very weary. June Cartwright placed an arm around Ava and pulled her close to her.

'She suggested Ava stay here for the rest of the week. She's going to bring Max up on Thursday, once he's finished his football practice.' McNally had forgotten that Max was attending a three-day coaching course at the Arsenal Youth Academy.

'Is that OK with you, sweetheart?' Ava nodded her approval; she felt safe here, and she loved her grandparents. 'We need to have a long chat about school and the future maybe when Mum comes up at the weekend. We're all too tired to talk about it now. Is that ok?'

'Yes, Dad, I'm sorry for being so selfish and putting you and Mum through all this worry.' Her voice cracked. 'I hate that school,' she raised her voice in anger, 'I've got no friends and everybody takes the mick out of my accent and it's your entire bloody fault. Can't we please go back to Manchester, I hate it in London.' McNally didn't know what to say. He'd never heard his daughter swear and be so aggressive towards him. Her grandmother held her tightly and subtlety shook her head from side to side at McNally to warn him not to react. She calmed Ava down with some soothing words.

'Your Dad is very tired, Ava. Let's all sleep on it. We don't want to wake Grandad up. You know how grumpy he'll be.' June gave her granddaughter a kiss on her forehead before guiding her towards the stairs. 'I've made the back spare room up, Ryan; you can't drive back to London tonight.' McNally stood and nodded his thanks.

'I'll sort this out. I promise.' Ava didn't look back.

McNally sat down to his meal, all of the sudden he'd lost his appetite. June returned and placed a reassuring arm around her son-in-law's shoulders.

'Ryan, I'm sure you'll all get through this. She's at a time of life when she's probably at her most insecure and vulnerable—Kate was the same.'

McNally sunk into a luxurious armchair. Fatigue started to overwhelm him.

'When Ava sat down to dinner tonight, I noticed that she had marks, thin cuts on her left forearm; I think she's self-harming. She told me she'd got them climbing through a bush in your garden, but it wasn't a convincing story. She got really angry and defensive when I pushed it a bit more so I backed off. I'll discuss it with Kate when she gets here, you need sleep you look exhausted.'

'Thanks, June, I'll get a few hours. I've got to be back in London by 9am.' McNally retired to the spare room next to where his daughter was now fast asleep. He lay looking at the ceiling, listening to the North Sea crashing onto the beach below, knowing he wasn't going to sleep for a while.

*

Frost topped and tailed a couple of actions and submitted them to Marie Relish.

'Long day?' Relish enquired.

'You bet. I can still smell cat's piss.'

'That's what it is? That's a relief,' the indexer smiled. 'Thought it was your perfume, you need something a bit sexier if you want to pull Stuart Graves.'

'I'd prefer to stick a red hot poker up my arse, Marie.' They both laughed.

'He's a bit creepy,' said Relish, 'every now and then I look up and catch him eyeing me. Most people would look away at that point, but he just carries on staring.'

'Yeah, I know what you mean; we've already had a couple of run-ins. I think he believes us women are in the police force for one thing only and it's not catching villains. What time you finishing? I fancy a large glass of wine. You interested?' Marie Relish nodded enthusiastically as she closed her computer down.

'Great! I'll get my coat, see you downstairs in five.'

*

Frost plonked two large glasses of Pinot Grigio on the table, pushing one across to Marie.

'Cheers!' they said simultaneously, raising their glasses.

'Never been in here before, Marie, is it your local?'

'No, not really, I don't normally socialise much after work but some of the officers and staff on the fraud investigation, I've just finished on, used to come here now again. After some of the tedious days I experienced on that job, I needed a bloody drink. You ever worked on fraud?'

'No, not really, apart from the usual run-of-the-mill credit card scam when on divisional CID. You never thought about joining our side?' asked Frost.

'I did, after I finished university, but Mum and Dad weren't too impressed. Thought I could do better for myself. I studied law. All they could see was me standing, adorned in wig and gown, in court one of the Old Bailey. But getting into a law firm nowadays isn't easy and they've got their choice of the very best, which didn't include average me. So I applied for a few jobs with both the Met and BTP. Started as a custody officer at Victoria—I looked like a sack of spuds in uniform—so applied for an indexer/analyst job when it became available. Anyhow, you've done pretty well for yourself, detective sergeant on the Major Investigations Team at the age of 30'ish.'

'You cheeky cow, I'm only twenty-eight,' Frost smiled, she really liked this girl. 'To be honest, Marie, I like to keep myself to myself. The police service is the sort of job that you get on well with certain people you work with. You have to really. It's all about looking after each other, when the world seems against you, and you can have a real laugh. But rarely is it a job in which you make lifelong friends; you move on in different directions in your career and frequently lose touch.'

'You ever dated a copper?' Frost took a substantial gulp of wine before she answered.

'Yeah, a couple of times, when I was in uniform; never worked out with shifts and extended working hours, just a bit of fun, nothing serious. What about you?'

'Only the once, it did get quite serious—a DI on B Division, wanted to know where I was, who I was with, turned into a bit of a nightmare, even started to stalk me. Thankfully some other loser came on the scene, probably making her life hell now.'

'Really, what was his name?'

'Mind your own business you're not interrogating a suspect now; anyhow who says it was a man. Let's change the subject. What do you think about the boss?'

'Who? Plummer?'

'No, not him—McNally.'

'He seems OK—bit of a family man by all accounts. I picked up he's having a few problems with one of his kids, the daughter, I think. But he seems fair. I know he's losing patience with Graves. Who isn't?'

'I worked with him a couple of times when he first came down here on promotion from Manchester; he led a rape enquiry. Really looked after his staff, but rarely went for a drink with the troops, even though it was ages before he was joined by his wife and kids. By the way, your handbag is vibrating.'

'Bloody hell! Hang on a minute, Marie. I'll have to pop outside. It's getting a bit noisy in here—got to get it, we're still on call.' Frost pushed her way to the exit, surprised at how busy the bar had got in the time they'd been there.

'DS Frost—can I help?'

'Hello, Marcia, it's Alice…'

'Hang on a minute. I can't hear you.' Frost placed her hand over the mobile to block out the noise of a group of office workers who followed her out of the bar. They'd been tanked up when she and Marie arrived half an hour ago. One of the males made a lewd comment towards her and was just about to get a swift kick, when he was pulled away.

'Come on, Ozzie, you couldn't afford her.' They headed in the direction of Camden Town station.

'Sorry about that. DS Frost this end. I didn't catch your name.'

'Alice Harrison. You rang me the other day about—you know…'

'Hi. Yes of course, you're the friend of Ruth Ward. You sound a bit shaken, Alice, what's up, love?'

'I…I was approached by a man, when I left work this evening. He said he was a freelance reporter and he wanted to discuss Ruth's death with me. I told him to go away and that I didn't want to talk about it but he followed me to the station. He said that he didn't think Ruth committed suicide and that there were other victims. I saw a police officer nearby and warned him that if he didn't leave me alone, I was going to make a complaint about him. I started to walk over to the officer when this guy shoved a card into my hand and said ring me. The last thing he said was, "Ruth didn't kill herself—she was murdered!"'

Chapter Eighteen

Frost was up early. She'd decided to see Alice Harrison at her workplace in Canary Wharf. She'd left the job car at Camden the previous evening, after a couple more glasses of wine with Marie Relish.

As she walked to Stockwell station she texted McNally a message about her plans, not mentioning what Harrison had told her. To be frank she wasn't quite sure she'd heard her correctly, what with the noise of Camden Town at 10pm in the background, and drinking on an empty stomach. She was a little nervous that McNally, who hadn't been in the best of moods when he shot off yesterday afternoon, would blow his top when he found out what she was doing. But the words "press reporter" and "murder" had stuck in her mind and she needed to act.

She made an appointment to see Harrison at No.1 Canada Square, an iconic building which seemed to reach the edge of earth's atmosphere. She stood at its base, looking upwards, the occasional cloud, in an otherwise beautiful morning sky, made the building look as if it was moving. She approached the massive reception desk, behind which sat several efficient business-like receptionists. She checked the floor plan for Alice Harrison's company and produced her warrant card for the next available receptionist to examine. She hardly glanced at her picture, which worried her slightly, as this building must be one of London's main terrorist targets.

Frost was directed to several comfortable leather sofas. She selected one that offered a view of the whole reception area and the lift lobby. Frost had always been good at picking people out of a crowd, whether it was a thief or a sexual pervert. She'd been one of the first officers in the BTP to receive behavioural awareness training. Her instructor had been a short, bald, detective called Mick, with bags of experience, and a really good sense of humour. The course was all about the basics of observation—looking at people. Skills that had been lost to the service as police officers spent more time sitting on their arses in cars and vans.

It wouldn't be difficult to pick Alice Harrison out of the crowd. She would probably be feeling apprehensive about speaking to the police, which would be evident in her body language. She would be looking around her—something she wouldn't normally do in such familiar surroundings if she were going to lunch or going home. Frost was sitting close to several other visitors to the building, three of whom were white women. She was confident that Harrison wouldn't identify the only black woman amongst them as the police officer. She was right.

From the two telephone conversations with Alice, she'd formed a mental picture and was taken slightly aback at how wrong *she* had been. For starters Alice was black, rather plump, and although she had pretty facial features, with immaculate make-up, she looked worn out. She was dressed in an ill-fitting suit, which had, at one time, probably fitted her, but was in denial about the pounds she'd gained. Before she embarrassed herself anymore by asking the one remaining white woman, if she was a police officer, Marcia extricated herself, with some difficulty, from the sumptuous leather sofa and introduced herself.

'Hi. Alice?' Harrison looked a little surprised but seemed to relax quickly as she looked at the smiling detective's face and maybe realised that this wouldn't be such an ordeal after all.

'Hello…'

'Marcia Frost. I'm a detective sergeant, with the BTP Major Investigations Team. We've spoken a couple of times on the telephone. Sorry about last night but I could hardly hear you, and to be honest, I'd had a couple of glasses of wine on an empty stomach after a very long day. Can we go somewhere and talk?' Harrison nodded and made her way to the lifts. Frost watched the movement of people in and out of at least a dozen lifts that came and went with the utmost efficiency. They entered a plush lift with several other people; a couple nodded their recognition to Harrison, who pushed the button for the thirty-seventh floor. Frost could see that she was a little uncomfortable in the presence of her colleagues and decided that any small talk wouldn't be appreciated at this particular time.

The lift took a few seconds to reach its destination, where most of its occupants spilt out into a plush lobby area. Frost was glad McNally wasn't present—sod walking up all those stairs.

Harrison held back a little and turned in the opposite direction to the others and guided Frost into a small featureless room, with two chairs, a table and a flask of coffee. She indicated a seat to Marcia, who removed her lightweight suit jacket and placed a notebook from her bag onto the desk.

'Would you like a coffee, sergeant?'

'Yes, thank you, that would be nice—first of the day, black no sugar and please call me Marcia.' Frost noticed a slight tremor as Harrison poured the coffee. She was putting on a brave face but seemed to have been badly shaken, firstly by Ruth Ward's death, and probably even more so by the revelation from a reporter, who believed her friend had been murdered. Frost cast her mind back a couple of days to the interview with Felicity Wright, before turning her attention to Harrison, who began picking at highly polished fingernails and shifted in her seat before she settled down.

'I know this is going to be hard for you, Alice. I've read your statement you gave to the uniformed officer, outlining the events of the night of Ruth's death, but I just want you to tell me in your own words what happened yesterday—in as much detail as possible.' Harrison took out her mobile telephone, opened the protective case and withdrew a business card, which she handed to Frost.

'I left here about 5.30 last night and was walking towards the Docklands Light Railway—I live in Greenwich and catch the DLR to Island Gardens. The guy whose name is on the business card…'

'Ben Scrivenor,' Frost said. Harrison nodded and continued.

'He was walking towards me and asked if I was Alice Harrison. That really scared me. The look of shock on my face must have given him the answer he was looking for. I have no idea how he knew who I was.'

'Maybe he picked your name and photograph up from a *Facebook* page, either yours or Ruth's. So what did he say?'

'He told me he was a freelance investigative journalist, looking into a number of unexplained deaths on the London Underground. He asked me if I knew Ruth well and I told him that we'd been at school together and on the night of her death, Ruth, I and a few other school pals had met up for a bit of a reunion. To be honest I said more than I should've but he was quite nice about it all and didn't pressure me into saying anything. He asked if he could record the conversation but I wasn't happy with that so he said he wouldn't and I believed him.' Frost raised a dubious eyebrow and scribbled down a few notes. Harrison paused and waited until Frost looked up again.

'He asked me if I found it a little bit strange why Ruth would take her own life after a great night out with friends and had everything to look forward to. I hadn't slept since Sunday, when I was contacted by the police, thinking exactly the same thing—why?'

'He then begun telling me about other similar incidents that he'd uncovered over the last few months, where seemingly successful, happy, secure, self-confident women had come to the same fate. No evident signs of mental anguish or illness noticed by close family or friends and the lack of explanation via a suicide note in any of the cases. All these women were of a similar age and all blond. It was, at this stage, that he started to frighten me. I had no proof that this guy was who he said he was—he could have been some psychopath, and me his next victim. I was surrounded by thousands of people but felt so alone and scared. That's when I asked him to leave me alone and threatened to approach a nearby police officer.'

'Did he go into detail about any of these other incidents?'

'No. I didn't give him the chance. I told him to leave me alone otherwise I was going to scream. This seemed to do the trick and he backed off telling me to get in touch if I wanted to know more. I got home still pretty shaken and then I rang you.'

'You did the right thing, Alice. Leave it with me. I'll speak to this guy.' Harrison nodded and both women got to their feet. Frost was escorted back to the reception area and shook Harrison's hand.

'Give me a ring if he attempts to contact you again before I get the chance to speak to him, and ring me if you have any questions.'

'I've got one now. What if he's right—and all those women *were* murdered?' Harrison turned sharply, not wanting to hear the answer, and headed back towards the lifts, leaving Frost alone with her thoughts. The enormity of what she'd just been asked fell on her like a shroud. She reached for her telephone.

Chapter Nineteen

It had taken McNally nearly three hours to drive from north Norfolk. He'd left his in-laws' house just after 6am, looking in on Ava before he did so. She was fast asleep and he didn't disturb her. If he was honest, he didn't want another argument. The M11, from the Stansted Airport turn off, south towards the capital, was busy all the way down to the North Circular.

He'd been accompanied for the last leg of his journey by country/rock singer, Jimmy Nail, whose profoundly meaningful lyrics, about love and the challenges that life throws at you, always got inside his head. Although Nail is a Geordie, the theme of many of his songs—a working class boy brought up in an industrial northern city, its identity eroded over time—often resonated with McNally reminding him of his working class upbringing in Manchester. As he drove through the gates on Camden Road he tapped his fingers to the chorus of *Crocodile Shoes*.

The drive had been quite therapeutic, allowing him time to think some of his problems through. Just before he'd moved down to London the family lost a great friend, a Boxer dog called Bruno. The kids and Kate missed him, but McNally was hit hardest. When he'd needed a bit of time on his own, away from the kids and work problems, he would walk the dog for miles. The pressures of balancing a demanding family life and a challenging professional career melted away. He could talk through anything with his loyal canine companion, who never, ever, judged him or answered back. He was thinking that maybe they should adopt another dog. It might settle Ava down and give her some responsibility. She could choose the dog. The only conditions being: it couldn't be a breed he could ever be seen dead walking, the breed's name wouldn't end with "ooo"; and it wouldn't cost a fortune to groom—he would speak to Kate later. Ava was safe. He felt a lot more relaxed than he'd done for a couple of days. His mobile signalled an incoming message; his good mood was about to disappear.

*

McNally had called his office manager, Ray Blendell, and Frost into his office. He sat behind his desk fingers arched under his chin, and looked from Blendell to Frost without moving his head. He had read the earlier text message from Frost and decided to leave the subject until the end of the meeting. He wanted to concentrate his attention on any progress on the Liam Brennan murder. Blendell started.

'We have five members of London Underground staff to trace and interview: three men and two women, who were on duty at Lambeth North either on late turn on the night of the burglary and Brennan's disappearance or the following morning when the burglary was discovered. Graves is liaising with LU to locate them—they may well be retired or dead.

'I sent Sam Hodge up to Birmingham to talk to the original investigating officer, John Danes, whom I also spoke to on the telephone late last night. He remembers the case and always thought that Brennan was probably dead—he just seemed to disappear from the face of the Earth and now we know why. As far as he was concerned it was a simple case of burglary. They'd discovered a number of betting slips in his bedsit: football, horses, cricket and darts, he would bet on anything that moved. They interviewed a local bookie. This was well before all the online betting sites we have now, and he was up to his neck in debt.

'Danes believed Brennan had waited for the late booking clerk to book off, taken the spare keys in his possession, stolen the money, and cleared off. A large number of season tickets had also been stolen and a theory they considered was Brennan could've been murdered when attempting to sell these tickets on. The serial numbers of the stolen tickets were circulated to revenue inspectors on both the underground and main line stations, but no tickets were ever recovered from passengers using them.

'Didn't he interview any of these staff members?' McNally asked.

'He did, but no statements were taken for some reason. I think, reading between the lines, he expected a quick result and lost interest when he didn't get one.'

'OK. Obviously the burglary line of enquiry in relation to his death is out, the fact he was found, still on London Underground premises, rules out Brennan's involvement in the burglary and Danes' suspicion regarding motive. So at the moment we are left with the sexual pervert angle in relation to the images found in his room. I doubt if any of his victims, filmed in the staff toilet, ever realised what he was up to, but such pictures always opened them up to blackmail.' Frost nodded and added.

'From the impression I've got of this creep so far, from Mrs Lentini, he was a watcher rather than a doer. I think he got his kicks from sneaking around in ladies' underwear drawers and wanking over a few pictures.'

'You're probably right, Marcia, but somebody smashed him over the head, stripped him and concealed his body and without a nosey lift engineer, he would still be there. Let's interview the staff members again, if we can, particularly the women. I doubt he restricted his perversions to staff members. Let's chase up London Underground for any recorded complaints against him—especially from women, you know the sort of thing: suggestive behaviour, flirting or worse.

'Get Sam Hodge to ask DI Danes about those movements on Brennan's staff pass during the few days after he'd been murdered. I know we won't get CCTV but did he investigate further? We know it couldn't possibly have been Brennan as he would've been decomposing under a pile of ballast—so who was using the pass? Our killer, most probably, in order to suggest to investigators that Brennan was still alive and on the run,' Frost nodded.

'Ok, let's move on.' Blendell was half out of his seat when McNally raised a hand in the air. 'Ray, I want you to stay for a bit, but what we're about to discuss stays in this office for the time being, Marcia...'

Chapter Twenty

McNally and Blendell listened intently to Marcia Frost's account of her meeting with Alice Harrison. The room fell silent for several seconds. Frost was tempted to speak but saw a slight annoyance on McNally's face and thought it better to keep her mouth shut. She looked at Ray Blendell to try and gauge his reaction but he just looked slightly shocked at her revelations. Both waited for the boss to break the silence.

McNally rubbed a hand over a shadow appearing on his face, remembering he hadn't shaved that morning, fearing he might wake Ava. He stood and walked to the partially blinded window and ran a hand through his thick black hair. He peered through the slats and watched the ever present traffic on Camden Road, wishing he was back in his car with Jimmy Nail, before returning to his desk. He often found that engaging his brain before opening his mouth had served him well in the past.

'Ok, Marcia. Set up a meeting with this reporter...'

'Ben Scrivenor.'

'I want any evidence he has on his claims, and emphasise to him this is strictly on the QT at this stage—I don't want to create a panic, with the travelling public, that a serial killer is stalking the underground, murdering blond women at will. Can you imagine the tabloids getting hold of it? It worries me that he didn't come to us first, probably means it's all in his head at the moment. Ray, see what you can find out about this guy. Who he's worked for in the past and any articles attributed to him. Have a look on social media. Has he leaked any of his suspicions? This has got to stay between us three at the moment, at least until we have spoken to Scrivenor. He must've been fishing for facts, when he stopped Alice Harrison, to substantiate his theory.' Frost took a deep breath; she had been holding back one very important fact. McNally picked up on her anxiety.

'Marcia, get it off your chest. It looks like there may be something more to Ruth Ward's death, as you originally suspected. What else you got?'

'There was another death last night at Putney Bridge station in south west London. A woman fell under a train. The new on call team, led by DI Atwood, is dealing with it.'

'Why are *they* looking at a suicide?'

'The platform was crowded with football fans from the Fulham home game. A fight started between rival fans near to where the victim was standing. It's not clear yet whether her fall under the train was suicide or as a result of the fracas or something more sinister. Uniform officers, who were on the platform, have arrested a number of fans from both sides for affray and suspicion of manslaughter. I know one of the Detective Sergeants on Atwood's team and I've left a message to call me but they're going to be pretty busy. It sounds like it may well have been an accident as a result of people trying to distance themselves from the fight. The only thing that worries me is that the victim—Laura Marston—was blond.'

*

Hodge arrived at Birmingham's New Street station just after 10am. He'd been to the station once before, maybe a decade ago—for an NEC exhibition with his father—and was astonished at the change. The concourse and exterior façade had been completely rebuilt. Hodge stood and observed some of the thousands of passengers, who passed through this Midlands hub every day, as they made their way to or from the newly refurbished platforms, utilising brand new escalators or crowding into shiny new retail outlets.

Hodge had decided to catch the train from Euston that morning; it was quicker and a lot less hassle than the M40.

He liked being part of a team, and working closely with his colleagues on the Major Investigations Team. Every day had been a steep learning curve for the young detective. But he also liked his own company and being able to carry out enquiries at his own pace. He was methodical and that didn't always suit everybody else—certainly not Stuart Graves. After initially liking him, Hodge had become ever more cautious about what he did and said around Graves. It was just a feeling that he had, and he was rarely wrong about people.

Hodge followed a sign for the British Transport Police station and introduced himself to the reception officer, explaining that he had an appointment to see DI John Danes. He was shown in and directed to a mess room and invited to make himself a cup of tea or coffee as DI Danes was in a meeting, which was over-running. He had a quick chat with a uniformed officer he recognised from a training course, but it was obvious neither could remember the others' name as the main form of address was simply "mate". Following a few pleasantries, the officer rushed off in response to a radio call which sounded pretty urgent.

Hodge sat at a table and sipped his black coffee, opening his notebook and re-reading the computer generated action that had brought him to Birmingham. He was aware of a figure entering the room and looked up.

'D.C Hodge?'

'Yes, sir, that's me.'

'I'm DI John Danes.' Hodge accepted the outstretched hand and followed the DI through a door just off the main CID office and sat in a chair the DI indicated. Danes was stocky with collar length, jet black hair and a moustache that any 1980s porn star would have been proud of. His Brummie accent was soft and monotone; he sounded a little like a member of the Shelby family in *Peaky Blinders*, but lacked the menace.

'So, young man, I've spoken to one of your colleagues in London about a burglary that I investigated when I was a detective sergeant in 2000.' Hodge nodded. He didn't like the patronising address normally, but Danes was "old school" and didn't mean it in a derogatory way.

'Yes, sir, I'm not sure how much info you were given over the telephone but your main suspect—Liam Brennan—was found under a pile of ballast in a disused storage area near to the lift shafts at Lambeth North underground station. The post-mortem revealed he'd been struck on the back of his head, stripped of his clothing and buried. It was by luck not judgement that he was ever found. You've had a little time to think back to the case, sir. I was hoping that you might remember some details that aren't in the file that may give us a different line of enquiry to follow, other than the sexual pervert angle we are concentrating on at the moment.'

Danes looked a little puzzled and ask for clarification. Hodge brought him up to speed on the discovery of the covert pictures, found by Frost in Brennan's bedsit, lifted from a video concealed in the staff toilets at the station.

'OK. I didn't see that coming.'

'Did you or your team interview the staff on duty before, at the time and following the burglary?' Danes used one hand to smooth over his impressive moustache, pausing to pick out some morsel left over from breakfast, which he examined and flicked away.

'Yes, of course. Is there some question over the competency of my investigation?'

'No sir, of course not,' Hodge quickly backtracked. 'You were dealing with a burglary not a murder.'

'I think there was half a dozen staff members interviewed as witnesses, but nothing formal. I thought it was a pretty simple case: find Brennan and I'd find the money. I had no other suspects at the time or since. I think I told the detective I spoke to on the phone that after a year or so I suspected he was probably dead—maybe a feud with another criminal—was one theory.'

'We looked deep into his past, spoke to family members and the Garda Siochana in the Republic of Ireland. He'd come to their notice in the past for some strong Republican views and frequently passed over the border into the North, but there was no suggestion that he was involved in Republican terrorist activity. This was a short time after the signing of the *Good Friday* agreement and the laying down of arms by the Provisionals. But also the emergence of splinter Republican groups, such as the Real IRA, who carried out several targeted strikes in London, the highest profile attacks were a rocket fired at the MI6 building and a bomb in a black cab in the vicinity of the BBC Television Centre in 2000 and 2001.

'We made a few enquiries around the Irish Republican community mainly in the north London area and via Special Branch at New Scotland Yard, but there was no trace of our man.'

'Did all the staff get on with their supervisor?'

'Well, that's what's intriguing. I got a call from a woman around Christmas time that year, so ten months or so after the burglary and Brennan's disappearance. She wouldn't talk to anybody else but me. It was a couple of days after the first *Crimewatch* I did. She was a member of London Underground staff. She said she'd worked with Brennan before but wouldn't say where, and in what capacity. They'd fallen out when she caught him hanging around her locker and suspected that he had rifled through it—a few things were out of place. She didn't say anything to anybody, but was wary of him from then on. She told me that one of Brennan's staff at Lambeth was a staunch protestant and he and Brennan would often have serious arguments about Irish politics and religion. She heard from another member of staff, who'd moved from Lambeth, that, on one occasion, they had to be separated in a local pub. She was loath to tell me his name, but eventually blurted it out before she put the phone down on me.'

'Can you remember his name sir?'

'Patrick…' Hodge waited patiently knowing to interrupt Danes' thought process would be counter-productive. His patience was rewarded.

'Mullen…Patrick Mullen.'

*

Sam Hodge sat on the train back to London, feeling pretty pleased with himself. This was why he loved this job, unearthing little nuggets, like a name, that might well be a significant step in the investigation. Danes had gone on to tell him that Mullen was interviewed about his relationship with Brennan and admitted they didn't get on but of course at the time they were looking for a burglar not a killer.

Hodge was frustrated by the lack of a signal on his mobile. 'For God's sake,' he muttered under his breath aware that several other passengers were in close vicinity. 'How can the hub of the British railway infrastructure not be served by 4G?'

The train pulled out on time and as he looked over the former industrial sites of Birmingham his mobile pinged into life. It was a message from Graves to give him a call in the office.

'I suppose you've been sitting on your arse, doing fuck all, and now you're going to have a Balti somewhere, while I do all the work.'

'No, actually mate, I've got some good stuff from the DI up here and the name of a possible suspect—Patrick Mullen. He apparently worked with Brennan and they often fell out, especially when they'd had a drink. I think he's going to be worthwhile interviewing again.'

'Best you make your way to see spiritualist then, clever clogs…he died of a heart attack in May 2004.'

Chapter Twenty-One

McNally and Frost sat one side of a table in the corner of the saloon bar, facing the door, and waited. McNally would have preferred the interview to have taken place in a police station and be recorded visually and audibly—he just didn't trust the media. At times, they could be extremely useful to an investigation. He usually found a balance between what he wanted, and what they demanded, but Ben Scrivenor had insisted the meeting take place in a public location of his choosing.

The *Skinners Arms* was a pub McNally had visited a few times in the past—a popular venue for police officers to celebrate reaching the magical thirty years' service. It was a welcoming pub, with a real log fire, roaring away during the winter months. The food was basic pub grub, but of a good standard.

McNally looked at his watch. It was just gone midday and the pub was starting to fill up. He hated people who had no sense of punctuality, and was starting to get annoyed, when he got a dig in the ribs from Frost.

'That's got to be him guv.'

She nodded her head towards the entrance. A male in his mid-thirties scanned the bar and spied the two detectives, who were seated exactly where he thought they would be. Scrivenor had long wavy brown hair with darting eyes which—having identified the detectives—scanned the area for anybody paying him or them particular attention, before moving towards McNally and Frost who noticed that he walked with a slight limp.

'You're a bit nervous.' Frost commented.

'Served in the British Army in Iraq and Afghanistan—old habits die hard. Good to see coppers are as easy to spot as always.' He gave them a friendly smile before extending his hand. 'Ben Scrivenor. You must be…'

'DS Marcia Frost and this is my boss DI McNally.' All three exchanged handshakes and Frost offered Scrivenor a drink. As she stood at the bar she looked at her boss and the reporter with great interest. McNally didn't—in her opinion—look like a copper. He had an ease about him, a calmness, that she found quite attractive, but he did seem to carry a bit of stress around with him, more from outside the job than within, she guessed. In the few short weeks she'd worked with him, she knew he was a very capable detective; she should know, she'd worked with her fair share of losers.

Scrivenor was a bit more of a conundrum. Yes, they'd only met, literally, two minutes ago but she could normally tell who and what was in front of her and quickly come to a decision that, more often than not, proved correct. He looked quite smooth and sounded educated, probably an ex-Sandhurst man. He wore the "uniform" of an ex-military man: a check patterned cotton shirt, dark corduroy trousers, brown suede boots and a canvas bag, that only a man with extreme self-confidence could carry, hanging from one shoulder.

She picked up the half of lager he'd requested and strode back to the table, interrupting a casual conversation about politics, a subject she'd never heard her boss refer to in the past. Scrivenor nodded his appreciation and took a large gulp before settling back in his chair. Frost took the lead.

'I understand that you approached a police witness, at her work address in Canary Wharf yesterday, and asked her several questions about an active police investigation. Is that right?'

'Look, let's cut the bullshit here. Firstly, you know I did, and secondly there is no criminal investigation into the death of Ruth Ward or any of the others.' McNally jumped in, slightly agitated with the reporter's know-it-all attitude.

'Mr Scrivenor although this meeting—to a degree—is off the record, there is a limit to my patience. Firstly let me point out that any death, unexplained or suspicious, will be investigated so that a file can be submitted to a coroner in order to establish the facts surrounding that death. At the moment the officers, dealing with Miss Ward's death, are satisfied that she took her own life and are conducting that investigation on that basis. But if you have any *evidence* that may change the course of that investigation, now would be a good time to hand it over.'

Both detectives waited for Scrivenor to make the next move, they didn't have to wait long. Unfastening the flap of his fashionably worn bag, the reporter removed a buff coloured file with contents two inches thick made up of: photographs, newspaper articles and some official looking documentation.

He looked suspiciously over his shoulder at a small group of suited men and women who'd taken up a position at the bar. McNally couldn't figure out if

Scrivenor was being over-dramatic for effect or was genuinely concerned about what he was about to reveal to them. He laid out three photographs of women, all young and blond. He pushed the middle image towards the detectives. McNally picked it up and examined it before passing it on to Frost.

'Her name is Cheryl Meade. She was…' both detectives picked up on the hesitation as a little emotion crossed the reporter's face before he quickly regained his composure. '…thirty-one years old and worked for the NHS as a sexual health specialist nurse in a major London hospital. She was married with two children. Her husband is a financial advisor in the City of London. On the 29th May, this year, having the day before booked a holiday of a lifetime to Florida, she allegedly threw herself under a train as it entered East Finchley station on the northern end of the Northern Line. The platform was packed and witnesses saw Cheryl disappearing under the train, everybody screaming—utter chaos, but nobody saw anything else.'

McNally picked up the photograph again and looked deep into the eyes of Cheryl Meade, seeking answers. Why would a successful woman, who'd just booked a holiday with her husband and children, throw herself under a train? During his service he'd known a couple of fellow officers that had committed suicide. It was a tough job with stresses and strains that can affect the hardest of individuals. Sometimes it could be the most innocuous event that proved to be the final straw. McNally himself had seen death, both violent and self-inflicted, but he'd always been able to compartmentalise it—keep it in a box safely chained and locked away somewhere at the back of his mind. He'd often wondered— even recently with the events with Ava—what if something happened in his life that would force that box to the forefront of his mind, unlock it, and release all those images he didn't want to think about again. He looked at the photograph again and wondered if that had happened to Cheryl Meade. Had something, so catastrophic, so sudden, occurred in her life that changed the course of it and ended in her death? Or was she murdered and they had missed it? He looked at Frost and saw that she was probably thinking the same.

Scrivenor pushed the two remaining images towards the detectives.

'The one to your right is Ruth Ward. She died in similar circumstances a week or so ago at London Bridge station. The one to the left is Laura Marston, who died under a train at Fulham Broadway station a couple of nights ago. You lot are treating her death as manslaughter or just an accident, after a large fracas on the platform, following a football match.' McNally was impressed, but

91

slightly concerned, with the depth of Scrivenor's knowledge. 'These deaths are being treated as tragic isolated incidents. All these women were murdered, Inspector. They are all roughly the same age, all have blond hair, and all had their lives mapped out in front of them. They had no financial worries, and two of them had children. You have got a lunatic running amok on the London Underground system—one thing is for sure, he has probably killed before these women, and will definitely kill again, if you don't take this seriously.' McNally drained the rest of his drink and got to his feet. He needed time to consider the allegations.

'Mr Scrivenor. We're grateful for bringing your suspicions to our attention. You have my word that we'll look into your claims but, on the face of it, they do look like tragic accidents. However, we're always open to receive new information, should it come your way, as long as it is not based on pure speculation. We need hard evidence.'

Chapter Twenty-Two

McNally and Frost sat at a red light on Euston Road. It had taken them nearly twenty minutes to reach the junction with Hampstead Road. Neither had spoken a word to the other during the journey. McNally still couldn't get his head around where all this traffic came from in London and where it was going to. He looked at his sergeant, who watched the set of lights intently, waiting to accelerate forward. To be fair to her she'd had doubts about the circumstances surrounding Ruth Ward's death from the off. Maybe he'd been too dismissive of her initial suspicions, but even listening to what Scrivenor had told them, and keeping an open mind, he still couldn't accept they had a serial killer running around the system murdering blond women. It sounded too far-fetched.

'What *if* he's right guv?' Frost broke the silence.

'*If* my aunty had bollocks she'd be my uncle.' McNally watched an impatient cyclist edge his way up the inside of their vehicle, he thought about opening the door and telling him to wait like everybody else, he wished he had when the cyclist nudged the wing mirror as he passed. 'We need evidence, not some theory from a freelance journalist trying to make a name for himself.' He sounded harsher than he'd meant to. 'I don't think he will go to a newspaper—yet. All he has at the moment is hearsay and suspicion, which gives us a little time. Let's get the Liam Brennan briefing over with first and then come into my office with Ray Blendell and we'll decide where to go from there. I don't want anybody else on this at the moment and I don't want Plummer getting a sniff of it. He'd shit himself for starters and, God forbid, may want to run the job.'

'OK.' Frost nodded, as the traffic lights changed to amber. 'Let's hope we don't get another one in the meantime.' Frost accelerated forward. She was in no mood to wait for the light to change to green.

*

Wakefield looked at his reflection in a passing shop window. The suit he was wearing—his only suit—looked sharp, complemented by a plain purple tie and brilliant white shirt. His first full day on the Major Investigations Team had been a good one. Tasked by Graves, basically because he couldn't be bothered with something so mundane, to identify the whereabouts of members of London Underground staff that'd been on duty before, at the time and after Liam Brennan's disappearance, he'd set off from Camden full of enthusiasm.

He'd enjoyed his time in uniform, but had always wanted to be a detective— just like his father, who'd served thirty years in the Metropolitan Police. He'd taken a bit of stick from his old man, when he proudly announced that he had been accepted by the BTP. As far as his father was concerned, there is only one police force to join.

He had hoped to get an attachment to a plain clothes unit such as the Pickpocket Squad or dealing with sexual offences. He would never have predicted the opportunity that had befallen him, and he intended to make full use of it.

Living in the East End of London meant a lot more travelling to get to Camden, having to change trains a couple of times. The hours seemed to be basically nine to five rather than the shifts he was used to. If he was honest, he was feeling a little out of place at the moment. He knew people like Graves were not impressed with a mere 'uniformed officer' being attached to the force's premier investigations team. But, sod him, he'd have to get used to it because, as far as Jim Wakefield was concerned, he was here for the foreseeable future. He just hoped DI McNally saw it that way.

He'd been a little lucky with his task for the day; he already had a contact at London Underground headquarters, which made his investigations much simpler. He looked down at his notes. Five names were listed with each individual's current status in relation to their employment with the company. The list read:

Patrick Mullen—Died in Service—Heart Attack May 2004.

Comfort Ikande—Female retired to Nigeria 2013—pension still paid.

Elizabeth Wood—Still employed station assistant—St John's Wood.

Henry Hayhurst—Retired 2007—Retired ill health. Pension still being drawn.

Devon Lorne—still employed—a train driver on Victoria Line.

Wakefield had fed the information back to the incident room for trace and interview actions for each on the list to be generated, apart from the late Patrick Mullen, of course. He was keen to get on and start with Wood or Lorne, who, he believed, could be located quickly. Graves put him right on that one and reined in his enthusiasm.

'You can't just piss off and do what you like, *PC* Wakefield. If we don't keep a handle on what people are doing, we're likely to end up with two of us sticking our heads up the same arse and being covered with the same shit. We don't have the resources for that. Get back here. The boss has called this evening's briefing forward to 5pm.' Of course Graves was right but he would never win any prizes for motivational speeches and the emphasis on his rank—and inference that he was just a uniform bod—did sting.

Chapter Twenty-Three

The briefing room was buzzing. It had been a long day, but most present felt they'd made progress. Stuart Graves—who never missed an opportunity to be the centre of attention—was regaling a story to Sam Hodge and Jim Wakefield, who both sat mesmerised.

Frost stared at her computer screen, pre-occupied by her own thoughts and what she had unearthed around the earlier meeting with Scrivenor.

'…the traction current had been turned off between Notting Hill Gate and Holland Park. We all had large plastic evidence bags and set off.'

'Who reported it?' asked Wakefield.

'A member of the public had seen this guy go through the emergency door at the end of the carriage to gain access to the smoking carriage. In those days you had two cancer carriages, one towards the front, and the other to the rear. He lost his footing and fell down between the carriages and disappeared. Anyway, the first thing I saw was a leg with a nice shiny shoe attached to one end. I don't know if you've ever picked up a leg. I tell you it don't half weigh a lot. I got it in the bag—the leg that is—having searched the pocket for any clue as to who this guy was, and we carried on further. We found the other leg and an arm hanging from the cables on the side of the tunnel. He looked like he was waving at us.' All three laughed loudly. Marcia Frost looked over at Graves with contempt.

'Eventually we found the torso but couldn't find the guy's head. The train was checked at the depot; sometimes body parts can be found mangled in the undercarriage, but it was nowhere to be found. We got a phone-call from the mortuary. Mystery solved. His head was in his stomach.'

McNally came out of his office with Ray Blendell in tow and looking like a man in a rush.

'Boring the arse off everybody as usual, Stuart?' McNally did allow a smile to appear on his face.

'Just entertaining the troops, boss, you know, keeping morale up.'

'OK. Let's go around the room quick. Sam, how did you get on in Birmingham?' Each member of the team briefed the rest on their day's work. McNally looked up from his decision log.

'Marie, we need to find out more about this Mullen character. Dig into his background has he any family left in London, if not, where are they. There is obviously a history of confrontation between him and Brennan; he could be the strongest suspect we have at the moment. He had the motive and certainly the opportunity. I see he was late turn with Brennan and Elizabeth...'

'Wood, sir,' Wakefield reminded his boss.

'Well obviously we can't speak to Mullen but we can trace and interview Wood. Ray, allocate that action to Stuart and Jim as a priority.' McNally looked over at Graves. 'Stuart get hold of her tonight.' Graves nodded.

'So the burglary could just have been a cover for murder. Lead us to believe it was down to Brennan, who'd disappeared, when in fact he was lying under a pile of ballast one hundred feet below.' Blendell said.

'It's as good a theory as we've had so far,' the team seemed to agree with several nods of heads. 'Sam, see if you can trace the Nigerian woman—Comfort Ikande. According to London Underground, she is still in receipt of her pension at the full rate. They must have an address for her. You'll need to serve a data protection form. Knock one out tonight. I'll sign it. In all probability, it was Ikande who contacted DI Danes. But don't get any ideas about travelling to Nigeria, if that's where she is now—not with our budget. Ray, allocate the trace and interview actions for the other two: Henry Hayhurst, who is retired and Devon Lorne, who is still employed, to Stuart as well. I want these people found and interviewed as quickly as we can. I still think our murderer will be one of these five or a mixture of them anyway.' McNally was up from his chair and back in his office before any questions could be asked.

Chapter Twenty-Four

McNally undid his tie, flopped down in his chair, and indicated to Frost and Blendell, who'd closed the office door behind him, to take a seat. McNally was about to speak when he spied Graves walk past and peer through the window. He waited until he was sure he'd gone before opening his notebook and read the details of Scrivenor's allegations. The other two remained silent.

'I can't go to Nigel Plummer with this.' McNally waved a hand over his notes and shook his head. 'He would laugh me out of his office. Marcia, have you come up with anything else to substantiate what Scrivenor is claiming?'

'I have spoken to the coroner's officer, who dealt with Cheryl Meade. On the face of it, she committed suicide at East Finchley station three months ago. The inquest has taken place and recorded suicide. The CCTV was inconclusive, but witnesses said she seemed to dive onto the track a second before the train went over her. The driver had no chance of stopping the train, even though it was slowing down to stop. Her husband, who attended the inquest, gave evidence to the coroner that she would never have contemplated taking her own life; she had everything to live for. As with the other two—Ruth Ward at London Bridge and Laura Marston at Putney Bridge—there was never any suicide note found.

'Cheryl Meade's NHS line manager gave evidence that they'd chatted at lunchtime the previous day about how much she was looking forward to her holiday with her husband and two children, and how anxious she'd been to tie all her paperwork up so she could have a clean break?'

'The fact that none of these women left a suicide note is worrying.' McNally offered whilst stifling a yawn.

'I spoke to our Suicide Prevention and Mental Health Team here at headquarters. I asked them that question. I was surprised to learn that, actually, most people who take their own lives don't leave a note so it's not that unusual. But what bothers me is there are too many similarities. They are all blond, of a similar age. All three seemed to have their lives sorted, if you like, you know—

established relationships. Two of them had children, all had good jobs, and we've evidence that all were planning ahead, be it a holiday or exams to further careers.' They all sat in silence for a few seconds as if paying their respects to the dead and those they'd left behind. It was Frost who broke the silence first.

'What if these women were not random victims?'

'You mean is it a possibility that they knew each other or were at least connected to the killer?' Blendell offered.

'Hang on a moment. We're getting way ahead of ourselves now.' McNally raised his voice a little louder than he'd intended. 'We've no evidence at the moment to suggest that any of these women were murdered, apart from the claims of a freelance journalist, who makes his living out of sensationalising and spinning everyday events. I agree there are concerning similarities between these deaths. I would even go along with the fact that Scrivenor may have something here. But we need more before I can go and speak to Plummer. What I need now is a result on the Liam Brennan murder to keep Plummer off my back. So I want all our efforts on that, understood?' Frost and Blendell nodded their understanding and stood to leave.

'Marcia, have a quiet word with Marie Relish. I've worked with her before. She can be trusted. Tell her this is confidential at the moment. Get her to have a look at the three women and see if she can come up with any connections between any of them; you know the sort of thing: previous occupations, schools they attended, and get her to have a look at social media and any links they may have had there.'

Chapter Twenty-Five

Graves turned right off of Watford Way onto Page Street in Mill Hill. The annoying voice—that resembled his former headmistress—mechanically relayed directions. The display informed them they were less than three quarters of a mile from their destination.

'That's where Saracens play now.' Jim Wakefield indicated a stadium just visible in the distance to his right. Graves looked at him dumbly.

'Who the fuck are they?'

'You obviously don't follow rugby union. They're one of the most successful teams in Europe—well until they got relegated for bending the rules financially, allegedly paying their players well over the permitted amount. That's what the papers say anyway.'

'That's a game for you posh boys. When I was at school, it was football or netball for the girls.' Graves paused as he negotiated a mini-roundabout. 'What d'ya think the boss was talking to the dynamic duo about when we left?'

'No idea, as you keep telling me, I'm only a visitor, a *mere* P.C, how would I know?' Wakefield replied with a little more venom than he'd intended.

'Good point. I was just thinking aloud, something else is boiling and it's not about our friend Liam Brennan, otherwise it would've come out during the briefing.'

'You don't like DS Frost much do you?'

'She's too young, with too little experience. She should be cutting her teeth on divisional CID, not on a team like ours. You need to keep an eye on her and that ex-Met tosser Blendell. He's just here for the money, already got his Met pension. Now he's after another one and has got the ear of McNally. Most of these ex-Home Office coppers come over to us thinking they're going to get any easy ride, play with a few trains, take themselves back to their childhood, until they realise how much shit we deal with, and they might have to get their fingers out of there arses and chip in.'

Graves followed directions by turning right into Pursley Road. A large housing estate appeared on their left. Wakefield wondered if there was any subject he could raise that wouldn't get the sharp end of his colleagues tongue. Graves's hadn't finished yet.

'We must be near now. Obviously this was one huge council estate at one time. You can tell which houses are still owned by the local authority. They've got the same-coloured doors and new roofs. The privately owned ones, purchased for a song in the days of Maggie Thatcher's government and the 'right to buy' scheme, are the smarter ones. People tend to take greater care of their properties when they own them. But I dare say you know that coming from Surrey or Sussex, I would guess.'

'Actually, I was born in Homerton Hospital in Hackney, where were you born?'

Graves turned left into Brookfields Avenue, ignoring the question and turned the satnav off.

'Peace at last. It's like being at home. What number was it?'

'Eleven. It's on the right, the one flying the Union Jack.' Graves followed the local's example and parked the car on the kerb.

'What's this guy's name?' Wakefield looked at the paperwork.

'Henry Hayhurst.' He was on duty at Lambeth North station on the Sunday morning from 9am. By the time he turned up, the burglary had been discovered so he probably won't add much to what we know already.'

'I bet you he's ex-military. The flag's a bit of a giveaway. Let me do the talking. You just listen and learn.' Graves noticed a few net curtains twitching. He wanted in and out quickly. He'd arranged to see Elizabeth Wood at 8.30pm at St John's Wood Station.

The house was mid-terraced and a little shabby looking, with a front garden that could have done with tidying up. Wakefield rang the bell but heard no sound from inside so knocked on the door. They'd taken a chance on a cold call. Hayhurst's landline number was ex-directory; they both hoped they hadn't wasted their time.

'Who is it?' The voice didn't sound friendly.

'It's the police,' Graves answered 'Mr Hayhurst, can we have a quick word? It's nothing to be worried about.' The officers heard a chain being removed and the door swung open. The smell of curry wafted from the direction of the kitchen.

Hayhurst, according to the records the detectives had, had retired from London Underground through ill health at the age of forty-seven. He was now sixty but looked in his early seventies. He was vastly overweight and wore dirty knee length shorts and a tee shirt that stretched so tightly across his enormous stomach it looked as if it were about to rip and release an avalanche of visceral fat, in several directions, at any moment.

Hayhurst examined the warrant cards produced by the officers.

'Transport police, what d'ya want? I left London Underground years ago.' He showed them into the living room, which was surprisingly tidy and indicated a black leather two-seater sofa, which both officers sank into and accepted his offer of a cold soft drink.

As they waited for him to return from the kitchen, both officers looked around the room, which badly needed decorating, taking in as much information as possible. The furniture was quite dated. A few family photographs were dotted around the room. Graves smiled and nudged Wakefield, indicating a maroon beret sat on a side cabinet with a gleaming metal Parachute Regiment cap badge affixed to the front. Hayhurst returned with the drinks and sat down in an armchair on the other side of the room.'

'What's this all about then?'

'Do you live here on your own, Mr Hayhurst?' The occupant looked at them a little curiously, mentally questioning why they needed to know that, but decided to go with the flow.

'My wife died two years after I retired. I was her carer. It was a tough time for both of us.'

'I see you were in the Parachute Regiment, sir' Wakefield was surprised with the sudden change in attitude and the respect Graves showed to the former soldier.

'Very observant, I served with the Paras in the early 1980s. I did two tours of Northern Ireland. It's not about that is it? I see in the news how ex-soldiers are being hunted down and persecuted for serving Queen and country, whilst terrorists, pardoned by the Government, wander around as free men.'

'No nothing of the kind, sir' Graves saw he was hitting a raw nerve and swerved away from the military and turned the conversation to Hayhurst's employment with London Underground.

'Can you tell me when you started with London Underground?'

'Well I can, but you probably already know, as I presume you traced me through my pension or personal file. I came out of the Regiment in the early 1990s. Was at a loss for a while, done a few jobs: delivery driver, postman and some work for the local council. But I missed the routine of military life. I was told by a friend of mine that London Transport—as it was in those days—were recruiting station staff. I had another mate who I was in the Para's with. He'd applied and got in the year before. He loved it. You were told what days you were working, when and where you had to be, and you got a uniform to wear. Like being back in the mob, plus you got free travel and the money was OK.'

'Where did you start?' Wakefield nervously asked his first question, keeping Graves in his peripheral vision; he was damned if he was just going to sit there. Yes, he was inexperienced, but how was he going to gain that experience if he sat there like a nodding dog?

'I wanted somewhere around here, especially when you're talking about starting at 5am. I got posted to Camden Town, which wasn't too bad. I stayed there for a couple of years and then moved onto the Bakerloo line. I tried to get a driver's job but my eyesight wasn't as good as they required so I settled down as a station assistant. I was never interested in promotion, to be honest, even in the army I wasn't one for telling people what to do. It was hard enough looking after your own back, let alone other people's.' Graves took control again.

'Can you remember an incident that happened at Lambeth North station back in February 2000, when the booking office was broken into? From our records of the investigation at the time, you were on early turn the following morning when the burglary was discovered.'

'Yeah, I remember that. The station supervisor—a bloke called Brennan— disappeared with the lot. I don't think your lot ever found him.'

'Did you know Brennan well?'

'Not well. I was at Lambeth North that morning covering for somebody who was on annual leave. He was a bit of a self-opinionated tosser, big supporter of the Irish cause—you know—independence. We never saw eye to eye for obvious reasons. He was always making snide remarks about my regiment. I had to keep my hands in my pockets on a few occasions and think of my pension; it would've been very easy to put my fist through his face. He was always winding my mate up. I think they came to blows on a few occasions.'

'Can you tell us your mate's name?'

'Yeah, he was the same guy who gave me the heads up on the job. He passed away a few years back. I went to the funeral, Patrick Mullen.'

Chapter Twenty-Six

Graves showed Henry Hayhurst into an interview room, and asked him if he wanted a drink.

'A large brandy would go down well.' Graves smiled and told Wakefield to sit with him while he made a couple of phone-calls. Hayhurst had become very defensive when he'd learned of the discovery of Liam Brennan's body after twenty years and even more so when asked about the relationship between Brennan and his pal—Patrick Mullen. Graves decided to stop the informal interview on Hayhurst's own ground and up the pressure a little by asking him to attend the police station voluntarily and be interviewed. Graves was sure that Hayhurst knew more than he was willing to discuss with them, at his home.

The first phone-call was to cancel the appointment with Elizabeth Wood, the station assistant at St John's Wood, and the second to inform his boss of the actions he'd taken. McNally was initially sceptical, but after hearing of Hayhurst's reticence to answer some pertinent questions in relation to the investigation, he gave Graves his support and told him he'd be there within thirty minutes.

The interview room was standard: a desk with three chairs with built-in digital recording equipment, both audible and visual. McNally turned up within twenty minutes and was briefed by Graves and Wakefield. Graves was eager that he and Wakefield conduct the interview. McNally agreed, and would listen in from a different room. This was a chance for Graves to impress rather than piss off his boss; he cleared his throat and started.

'First of all, Mr Hayhurst, I must remind you that you are not under arrest and are free to leave at any time you wish. Do you understand?' Hayhurst bit his bottom lip. The confidence he'd shown at home had disappeared. He looked around the bleak characterless room and nodded his head.

'You'll have to answer the questions with words rather than gestures.'

'Yeah, I understand that I can leave, but I don't understand why I'm here in the first place. One minute I'm sitting in my armchair, not a care in the world, next thing I'm in this shithole.' Hayhurst looked sheepishly at the recording equipment. 'Sorry. Let's just get on with it.'

'We asked you earlier about your friendship with a man called Patrick Mullen. Can you tell us a little more about that relationship? Where did you meet?'

'In the mob—the Paras, we did our training together. I was posted to 2 Para he to 3 Para, we never served in action together though, just remained good friends. He came out a few years before me and got a job with London Transport. When I came out, he gave me a call and I told you the rest.'

'When was the last time you saw him?'

'A couple of weeks before he died; it was pretty sudden. He had a heart attack. He liked his food and his booze. He never did anything in moderation.' Graves looked through a few papers that he had in front of him. He wanted to give Hayhurst a little thinking time. He then went straight to the point.

'Did you have anything to do with the murder of Liam Brennan, Henry?'

'What the fuck! I thought I was here to help you lot out. Now I'm being accused of murder. This is a complete new ball game.'

'I'm not accusing you of anything, Henry. I'm just asking you a straight question to which, I would like a straight answer to.'

'No I did not—clear enough?'

'You've already told us, in an earlier conversation, that Mullen and Brennan often clashed about the Northern Ireland issue, and, in fact, had come to blows over the subject on a few occasions. Now I want you to think very carefully before you answer my next question, Henry. To your knowledge, did Patrick Mullen have anything to do with the killing of Liam Brennan?'

'You know what, officer. You can kiss my arse. Patrick Mullen was a good soldier and a fucking good friend of mine. If you think I'm going to sit here and talk ill of the dead, you're mistaken.' Hayhurst got to his feet, throwing his chair back violently. 'If you think I had anything to do with Brennan's death, then charge me. If not, I'm off home.' Wakefield rose to his feet, as Hayhurst opened the interview room door but Graves grabbed his colleague's arm.

'Just escort him out of the nick, Jim.' Graves put together his papers and ended the interview formally for the tapes and waited for McNally, who entered the room shortly afterwards.

'That's an interesting interview technique, Stuart.'

'I didn't think it was worth pussy-footing around with him. He doesn't possess too many brain cells. What d'ya think boss?' McNally waited for Wakefield to return and take a seat.

'He ain't happy, especially when he realised he had to get the tube back home,' remarked Wakefield.

McNally said 'From listening in I think he knows more than he's letting on. If Mullen *is* our man and he did kill Brennan then he took that with him to the grave. But I can't believe that in the four or so years between the murder and Mullen's death, these two old soldiers never discussed what happened. I'm not convinced Hayhurst was involved in the killing, but I do believe that he knows who was, and proving that may just be beyond us.'

Chapter Twenty-Seven

The mood was positive in the incident room at Camden. The aroma of bacon, sausage and strong coffee swirled around the room. Everybody had had a good night's sleep and keen to get on and tie this enquiry up. They could sense some sort of result, although most now accepted it improbable the investigation would conclude with the snapping of handcuffs around a suspect's wrists. McNally got the meeting underway.

'Ok. Quieten down everybody. Last night Stuart and Jim Wakefield pulled in an associate of Patrick Mullen, a man called Henry Hayhurst, whom he met when they signed up together and trained in the Parachute Regiment in the early 1980s. It was Mullen who was instrumental in getting his mate a job on London Transport.

'Mullen, in my opinion, is looking more likely to be our main suspect for the murder of Liam Brennan. Mullen had both the opportunity, as he was on duty with Brennan on the night of his murder, and a degree of motive. We have witnesses to the often volatile nature of their relationship, rooted in their hatred of each other's views on the situation in Northern Ireland. We have evidence that Brennan had been a supporter of the Provisional IRA's campaign, although we have no evidence to suggest that he'd been actively involved in facilitating that cause through fundraising or being part of any terrorist network.'

McNally loosened his tie before continuing.

'In contrast, Patrick Mullen had been a very vocal opponent of Irish nationalism and with his history in the Paras, having been on several tours of the province, this relationship was always going to explode—but did it explode into a violent assault on the night of 6th February 2000?' McNally asked Graves to give the rest of the team an update.

Graves drained the rest of his coffee.

'To be honest, we didn't get a great deal more out of Hayhurst at the police station than we did at his home address but we…' Graves shot Wakefield a quick glance. '…well *I* thought it worth a shot dragging him in to try and hammer home the seriousness of the situation, but he remained pretty cool throughout. He got a little agitated when I suggested that he might be complicit in some way in the death of Liam Brennan, but other than that he remained calm and stuck to his story about when and where he'd met Mullen and the extent of their relationship up until Mullen's heart attack in 2004.'

'Can I add something, sir?' Marie Relish raised her hand as if she were still at school McNally nodded his assent.

'I've done some more background checks into Hayhurst's military past via military intel. It's no surprise he was cool under pressure. He's been interviewed several times in relation to an incident of attempted murder in 1992 whilst in Northern Ireland. He was cleared of any wrong doing at the time, but as we've seen with many of our veterans, they are currently the subject of a witch-hunt. A number of them have been charged and awaiting trial for alleged offences thirty or forty years ago, which were thoroughly investigated at the time, and of which they were exonerated, whilst the terrorists were given a "get out of jail" card.' Relish suddenly realised she'd got carried away and been a bit too political; she was pleased when McNally pushed on.

'What's your gut feeling on Hayhurst?' McNally directed the question at Graves and Wakefield, who was the first to speak.

'He did seem genuinely surprised to see us on his doorstep, and equally so when we told him that Brennan was dead.' Graves nodded his agreement before adding.

'He couldn't remember where he'd been on the 6th February 2000, but if asked, neither would I. I still believe that he knows more than he's letting on. They both knew and hated Brennan, and he was best mates with Mullen. The subject of Brennan's disappearance must have cropped up in conversations with each other over the last four years of Mullen's life. But we can't prove that. He got a bit upset last night, but, on the whole, he's been co-operative with us, but that would change if we formally arrested him for conspiracy to murder. He would shut up shop and we'd have nothing but supposition to put to him.' Marcia Frost interrupted the gloomy silence as the earlier positivity seemed to slip out of the room's ill-fitting window frames.

'What about a search warrant for his house? We still have outstanding property belonging to Brennan. His uniform that he was wearing on the day of his disappearance and his staff gate pass, used several times during the days after the murder, have never been recovered. Or maybe he got sloppy with some correspondence between him and Mullen. It might be worth shaking his tree one last time.'

'Let's move on from Hayhurst for now. Listening to the interview, I'm not sure he's worth the effort at the moment. We still have a couple of Underground staff that were on duty that day to trace, they may be able to give us more.' McNally looked in the direction of Sam Hodge and nodded. Hodge cleared his throat.

'Yes, guv, I managed to trace Comfort Ikande. She's now retired and returned to Lagos in Nigeria. I spoke to her last night and this morning. She admitted, when I put it to her, that she was the person who made the phone call to DI Danes.' Hodge turned a couple of pages in his notebook. A couple of telephones rang in distant offices leading from the incident room but remained unanswered.

'On Saturday 6th February 2000, she'd been working early turn at Lambeth North station and finished about 2pm. She saw Patrick Mullen briefly as she walked up Westminster Bridge Road, on the completion of her shift, towards Waterloo, where she catches a train home to Clapham Junction. He almost knocked her over as he bowled out of the Horse and Stables pub. She remembered that he was in a pretty bad mood, and looked as if he'd been out all night. He was quite dishevelled and stank of alcohol which surprised her as he was about to start his duty. They exchanged a few words before he made his way towards Lambeth North station. She had a few days' holiday booked and didn't return to work until the end of that week, by which time everything had got back to normal.

'She was interviewed by DI Danes' team regarding the burglary and asked for her opinion of the missing Brennan. She painted a picture of a man who paid little respect to women and would often mimic her Nigerian accent but she didn't tell them anything about the friction between Brennan and Mullen. She told me that she felt no need to, at the time, as there was no suggestion Brennan had come to any harm. She saw Mullen on very few occasions after that day as their shift patterns rarely aligned.'

'Did she know Henry Hayhurst, Sam?' Frost asked.

'I telephoned her again this morning and asked her that very question. She struggled to remember Hayhurst physically, but the name seemed familiar. She believes their paths crossed at various different stations over the years, but she couldn't describe him.' McNally's mobile vibrated on the desk in front of him; the display revealed a London number. He re-routed the call to his voicemail.

'OK. You've all got work to be getting on with. I want the other two members of staff traced and interviewed ASAP. Stuart, Jim split them between you and let's get it done today.' Chairs scraped the floor as the hum of conversation returned. Computers were switched back on, mobile phones returned to audible.

McNally beckoned Frost, Blendell and Relish into his office. His telephone bleeped alerting him to a voicemail message. He sat down behind his desk as the others followed him in. They were all frustrated that they didn't have anything concrete, just supposition. They stood looking at their boss, his face flushed with anger; the message wasn't what he wanted to hear.

*

Graves didn't like the feeling that something was about to come off that he didn't know about. Was a new job about to break? It certainly looked that way in relation to who the boss had invited into his office. Whatever it was, at this stage, it looked like he wasn't part of it, which pissed him off no end. A new job meant a new budget and more overtime. He didn't want to be stuck on this dead end enquiry into a twenty-year old murder, where the most likely suspect had been dead for sixteen of them. He needed to know what was going on and he wasn't going to fuck about finding out. He made two cups of tea and wandered along the corridor and luckily enough, the Detective Superintendent's door was half-open.

Plummer sat behind his desk with a file open on it. The Superintendent seemed deep in thought, but Graves' wasn't letting this opportunity go by. He knew Plummer despised him, and he would have only a few seconds to get his attention. In one quick motion he knocked on the door, pushed it fully open and walked in.

'Made an extra cup of tea, boss. Jim Wakefield has disappeared out, thought you might like one, you know—waste not want not and all that bollocks. One of my mother-in-law's sayings—well not the bollocks bit of course; she don't swear.'

'What do you want, Stuart?'

111

'Nothing, boss, just wanted to put myself forward for the new job that's about to break—you know, sir, show willing.' Plummer closed the file, turned it face down and put it to one side, and let out a long sigh.

'What new job? No investigation comes into this department—new or otherwise—without first crossing my desk. I'll then decide which team is allocated it, understood constable?' Graves nodded, as he extended the tea towards Plummer, whose expression left no doubt that it was not required.

Graves returned to his desk, where he had a diagonal view of Plummer's office door and looked at his watch.

'I'll give you five minutes, you pompous wanker,' the detective mumbled. He smiled as Plummer crossed the threshold of his office in 3mins 45 seconds.

*

'Do you want us to give you a few minutes, boss?' McNally shook his head at his office manager and indicated for Blendell, Frost and Relish to sit down.

'Shut the door please, Marie.' McNally passed his fingers through his dark, thick hair and rubbed his skull as if trying to release the pressure building up inside. He looked at his mobile again and waved it in the air.

'From our friendly reporter, Mr Scrivenor,' McNally pushed the play button.

Tried to ring you earlier—no answer. I can't sit on this story much longer. It's going into a Sunday paper this weekend. Ring me back to discuss.

'Marie, have you come up with any connection between the three women that Scrivenor believes were murdered?' Relish flicked through a number of computer printouts and hand-written notes.

'I've looked at each woman: Cheryl Meade, Ruth Ward and the latest Laura Marston. They were all successful, independent women, living in very different parts of London. From enquiries made by the coroner's officer and statements given by next of kin, they were all very dissimilar. None seemed to have a connection through interests or educational back grounds. Only one went to university, another left school at sixteen and worked for the family business. I have checked social media accounts, but can't find any association between any of the three there either. The only connection being all were young women with blond hair and died under the wheels of a train in circumstances deemed to be non-suspicious by our uniform colleagues and none of the three left a suicide note.'

'OK. I'll need to speak to Plummer about where we go from here. Ray make sure we tie any loose ends up on the Lambeth North murder. I want the remainder of the statements from London Underground staff on my desk by morning, together with the pathologist's report and identification evidence. Marcia, get hold of anything recorded regarding Mullen's death. I'm assuming if it was a heart attack there would have been no inquest. Try and track down his next of kin. See if they can shed any light on Mullen's relationship with Brennan. I need to be in a position to answer the coroner's questions in a day or two.' A knock on the door interrupted McNally's thought process before bringing the meeting to an abrupt finish.

'OK. That's all for now, from the look on Mr Plummer's face, the shit is just about to hit the fan.'

Chapter Twenty-Eight

Wakefield walked through the ticket barriers at Burnt Oak station on the Edgware branch of the Northern Line, with twenty minutes to spare before his appointment with Elizabeth Wood. It had taken him less time than he had anticipated, catching a direct train from Camden Town. A glance at a local map on the booking hall wall located Silkstream Road which, he estimated, was a three or four minute walk.

Wood had seemed a little hesitant to speak to him at her home address, when he made the appointment, until he emphasised the urgency of the situation, and that it couldn't be delayed until her next duty in two days' time, she reluctantly agreed. What he thought a little strange was she never asked him what it was about.

No.17 Silkstream Road was an end of terrace, brick-fronted, former council house not dissimilar to Henry Hayhurst's in nearby Mill Hill, a few miles from where he stood. The small front drive was empty. As he approached the navy blue glossed front door, the front room net curtain of the next door neighbour's moved ever so slightly. He pushed the brass door bell and took a few steps backwards. The door opened within a couple of seconds.

Elizabeth Wood looked a little older than her fifty-one years. Her blond hair was greasy and a little unkempt; her pale complexion was accentuated by a black blouse. She wore a pair of ill-fitting blue jeans and a grey tracksuit top which she pulled defensively across her. She smiled pleasantly with her lips, but her eyes were cold and unwelcoming.

'Good morning. I'm Jim Wakefield from the British Transport Police Major Investigation Team based in Camden.' He produced his warrant card, which Wood glanced at in a slightly dismissive manner, as if she'd seen dozens before. She stood back from the entrance and waved him in. As he entered the small reception hallway, he noticed a leather travel bag, packed and ready to go, at the base of the stairs. He was shown into a room at the front of the house.

'I hope I'm not interrupting your plans for your day off, Mrs Wood.'

'It's Miss and yes you have, in all honesty. I was meeting a friend for lunch but I've managed to delay her for an hour so can we get on with whatever brings you here.'

There was no offer of tea or coffee and she obviously didn't do small talk—well with him anyway. Just a quick return to the no-nonsense attitude he'd picked up on the telephone. He glanced back into the hallway to the travel bag—a strange thing to take to a lunch appointment.

Wakefield looked around the room—it was quite old-fashioned—glass ornaments and brown furniture—and lacked a personality. There was an absence of any magazines, books or family photographs save for one, face down, on a side cabinet next to the morning's post.

'Have you lived here long Miss Wood?' Wakefield was struggling to get any sort of rapport going. He liked to have a chat with a witness before taking a statement in order to relax them a little. Wood matched the young officer's eye contact, her mouth curled in a contemptuous manner.

'Shall we just get on with this, Constable? I've got to leave within the hour. What's this all about? I presume it's got something to do with work. You said you're from BTP. I'm sure it could've waited until I'm next on duty. When you first rang, I thought you were from the local police. I got burgled a few weeks back. They sent a forensics guy around who dusted the front and back doors and I never heard a bloody thing since.' Wakefield made a few conciliatory um's and ahh's, and an apologetic shake of his head.

'I hope you didn't lose too much property.'

'Some cash, cheap jewellery, a few personal items, photographs that I can never replace.'

Wakefield realised he just needed to get on with his enquiry and opened his notebook.

'How long have you worked for London Underground, Miss Wood?'

'About twenty-six years. I started in 1989 as a station assistant.' Her tone of voice was verging on a bored arrogance as she rattled off her work history. 'I qualified as one of the first women tube drivers and worked on the Bakerloo and Central lines. But I got fed up with the monotony of it, and it was a man's world in those days. I got bored with the sexist comments from the morons I worked with so I left for a year or so and came back as a station assistant. I'm now at St John's Wood, which is nice and quiet, apart from a couple of weeks a year, when you get a load of tossers, in ridiculous ties, passing through to watch some twat throw a ball and another twat hitting it.'

'I take it you're not a cricket fan?'

'Well done Constable.' She allowed herself a half smile. 'One day you might make a detective.' Wakefield blushed ever so slightly, which seemed to please her.

The telephone in the hallway rang. Wood stood with an annoyed look on her face and marched from the room to answer. Wakefield could hear whispered conversation. He got to his feet and turned the photo-frame over to reveal an image of a much younger woman with a strong resemblance to the homeowner, arm in arm with a dark-haired male of a similar age. They were both smiling and seemed genuinely happy, standing on the promenade of a coastal resort Wakefield didn't recognise. He replaced the photograph and quickly rifled through the mail. A familiar brown envelope, from HMRC addressed to Miss E.M.C Wood, was of interest; her middle names didn't appear on her staff records.

Wood ended the call. She returned to the room, glancing quickly towards the over-turned picture and her post. She stopped in her tracks and looked at the young officer; just for a moment Wakefield suspected she'd guessed he'd been snooping around and could feel himself going a slight pink colour for a second time.

Wood sat down without any apology for the interruption. He made a quick note of her initials before he continued.

'Everything OK?'

'I've been getting some nuisance phone-calls over the past few weeks. I can hear somebody at the other end but they never speak. I should just put the phone down. Can we just get on with this?' Wakefield saw that Wood was shaking slightly and quickly moved on.

'I want to talk to you about an incident at Lambeth North station back in 2000 when the booking office was burgled. I believe you were on duty at that time?'

'Is that a question, or are you stating a fact?'

'I'm asking a question, and to be perfectly honest Miss Wood it would be in both our interests if we just got on with it. I know my presence here is not exactly welcome, however I've a job to do, and I really don't wish to keep you any longer than necessary.'

'Nice to see you do have something between your legs. I was beginning to doubt it. Yes I was on duty that evening. I finished work at just gone midnight. The booking office usually shut at around 10pm, if I remember correctly. We had very little passenger traffic coming into the station after that time, just people returning from a night out in the West End and going home. I spent most of the last hour of my duty at platform level making sure that everything was secure. I would've got a train south to Elephant and Castle and picked up a northbound Northern line train home to Burnt Oak. I assume the break-in took place after the station had shut or I would've been aware of it before I went home.' Wakefield was a little concerned about her detailed memory of an incident that happened twenty years ago. He wrote the word 'rehearsed' in his notebook—underlined it and added a question mark.

'How well did you know Liam Brennan?' Wood hesitated. Suddenly her memory had become a little sketchy. For the first time, since he'd walked into Elizabeth Wood's house, he sensed that he had the upper hand as she dropped—only for an instance—the veil of confidence, to reveal certain vulnerability. Wakefield had struck on an uncomfortable cord. After a short pause, in which she seemed to get herself together, she answered.

'He was one of the station supervisors at Lambeth North. I was transferred to the Jubilee Line a few weeks after he'd cleared off with all that money. I've never seen him since. He was a bit weird—something about him.' She seemed to be reluctant to go on but Wakefield added a little pressure by saying absolutely nothing. Wood fidgeted in her seat and looked at her watch.

'He was a bit of a pervert.'

'Go on.' Wakefield remembered the black and white images found in Brennan's bedsit.

'I couldn't put my finger on it, but he was always lurking about. I would turn around and he would be there—he did this thing where he would lick his lips all the time like some salivating beast waiting to feast.'

Wakefield saw that this was making Wood uncomfortable. If this had been an interview of a suspect, he would have her just where he wanted and would drill down until he got the truth. But this was a witness, not a suspect; although unwanted sexual advances—if indeed that was what she was suggesting—could be a motive for murder. He changed the subject.

'Why did you leave Lambeth North?'

'Travelling really, I wanted somewhere a little closer to home, but not on the Northern Line—too dirty. So a vacancy came up for the Jubilee line. It'd only been open for a decade or so, and I was successful.'

'How's that closer to home?'

'It's not that bad a journey. I get a train from Burnt Oak to Golders Green and then a No.13 bus to St John's Wood. It takes about thirty-five minutes *if* everything is running to time. Have you found Brennan after all these years? I suppose he was sunning himself on a beach somewhere or did he get nicked for something else?'

'Brennan is dead.' Wakefield watched carefully. Did she already know that? Was that genuine surprise on her face or just bravado?

'Well, I can't say I'm upset. Where was he found?' Wakefield ignored the question.

'Can you remember the names of other staff members who you worked with around this period?' Wood dropped her gaze to her lap and fiddled with a solitaire diamond ring on her right ring finger. Was she trying to remember names or gaining a little time to compose herself?

'This was twenty years ago. Can you remember, officer, who you worked with twenty years ago? Of course you can't. You were still having mummy's milk and wearing nappies.' The sudden aggression was a diversionary tactic, Wakefield guessed; he actually enjoyed the snipe and just smiled at her—he was getting under her skin.

'Well, at least try, anyway.'

'There was a black guy, who I think operates Victoria line trains now, and a Nigerian woman. She had a name that often appeared in a TV ad for something— I know, Comfort. Yes, that was her name, quite a nice lady. I got on alright with her—probably dead by now.'

'Anybody else?'

'No, that's about it. A few people came and went, mostly covering holidays, sickness or days off, but I can't remember names.'

'Going back to the day of Brennan's disappearance, you said that you finished your duty just after midnight. We know that the Nigerian lady, who you rightly remember as Comfort, was early turn. Brennan and you were late turn. Can you remember if there was anybody else on duty with you that evening?' Wakefield noticed Wood return to the ring on her right hand. There was a pattern emerging, every time she was asked for specifics. She answered his question rather too quickly this time, with annoyance rather than aggression.

'As I said, officer it was twenty years—a lifetime—ago.'

'Okay, Miss Wood, I won't keep you any longer. I can see that you're anxious to keep your lunchtime appointment. I may have to come back and take a formal statement from you; will you be available?'

'Why wouldn't I be?' Wakefield looked back into the hall.

'You look as if you're going on a trip.'

'Is that against the law as well?'

Both rose to their feet. Wakefield moved towards the door and stepped out into the late morning sun.

'Just one more question, Miss Wood. It almost slipped my mind. Can you recall working with a man called Patrick Mullen?'

Elizabeth Wood stood in her front room watching the young detective heading back in the direction of the tube station. She fiddled with the ring on her right hand and picked up her mobile telephone.

Chapter Twenty-Nine

Detective Superintendent Nigel Plummer closed McNally's office door and took a seat.

'How did the briefing go this morning? I read the briefing note. Do you think this former Para will get us any closer to what happened, and more importantly, an arrest?' Plummer crossed his legs, sank further into the seat, and waited.

'It looks like a hostile relationship had developed between Brennan and Mullen, mainly around the situation in Northern Ireland. As you've read in the briefing note, Mullen served in the Province with the Paras and we already knew about Brennan's views on Republicanism. I believe—although I have no solid evidence to prove this—Brennan and Mullen got into some sort of altercation, in which Mullen either struck Brennan to the back of his head or pushed him, sustaining the injury when he has fallen. We are at a disadvantage that the initial incident was investigated as a burglary. Brennan was set up to look the likely suspect, to cover his disappearance, therefore the other areas of the station were never forensically examined and the CCTV was rather conveniently missing, again blamed on our victim.

'Hayhurst, the guy we had in last night, was a close friend of Mullen's and also a former Northern Ireland veteran. He confirmed the belligerent nature of the relationship between Mullen and Brennan, even admitting that he had had his own run-ins with Brennan over the same topic.'

'Did forensics get anything back from the booking office?'

'Nothing of use, there were no unaccounted fingerprints found. They did take elimination prints from the regular staff members who would've all, at one time, been in the office, so that wouldn't have taken the investigation any further. Sam Hodge spoke to a former employee—Comfort Ikande, who's given a verbal statement over the telephone. She remembered seeing Mullen coming out of a local pub as she came off duty on 6th February 2000—the day we are fairly certain the murder took place. She said he was in a bad mood, looked dishevelled and had obviously been drinking. We know Mullen was about to go on duty. If he'd turned up stinking of booze Brennan may well have confronted him and it might have kicked off from there, culminating in his death sometime after 10pm. We know he was alive when the booking clerk left just before 10pm, as he informed Brennan that he had to get away a little early as his wife had gone into labour.'

'We have yet to interview another member of staff that was on duty with Mullen and Brennan that night, a woman called Elizabeth Wood. Jim Wakefield is visiting her this morning. She might be able to shed some light on the atmosphere that night.'

'So where do we go from here?'

'Well, we have a victim, a main suspect no longer of this world, no CCTV or forensics to link Mullen to Brennan; even if we had, we know they would've been forensically in contact with each other throughout the day, so any fibres, DNA or fingerprints would be worthless. We have no weapon; the pathologist is suggesting it was a blunt heavy object; that could be a description of several articles of railway equipment that can be found on any underground station. Unless anything comes from the interviews of the two remaining staff members, or any other witnesses come forward as a result of the recent publicity, I think the only way forward is the submission of a full report to the coroner prior to the inquest.' Plummer nodded and pushed back his chair.

'Sir, there is something I need to bring to your attention.' Plummer plonked his backside down again.

'It's a difficult one and I've been wrestling with how I can best explain it to you.' McNally recalled the conversation with Ben Scrivenor in detail. Plummer listened without interruption. McNally concluded his account.

'I've had Marie Relish do a few enquiries with the London Underground's coroner's officer and also asked her to try and find any connections between the three alleged victims. That's what the meeting was about when you knocked on my door.'

'So you, Frost, Blendell and Relish are the only ones in the know at this moment?'

McNally nodded. 'So far we can come up with no evidence that the claims by Scrivenor are true.'

'Let's be up front here.' Plummer got up from his chair and took a few paces over to the window facing down onto Camden Road.

'This reporter is claiming that we have a serial killer prowling around the tube system identifying victims, who all seem to be women in their late twenties and blond, before pushing them to their deaths under the wheels of a train, melting back into a hysterical crowd of fellow passengers and making good their escape.'

'DS Frost and I have looked at the witness statements in relation to the three deaths. There is no evidence to back up these claims, not one account of even the slightest suspicion of foul play. But when you then look at the evidence from close family and friends the pendulum swings in the opposite direction. All these women had a reason to live: embarking on new careers, impending holidays; they all had appointments in their diaries and not one of them left any indications with their loved ones of what they intended to do.'

'No suicide notes—nothing?'

'No, sir.'

'Okay. It looks as if this Lambeth North murder is coming to a point where it's unlikely, at this stage, a suspect will ever be charged. I want you and your team to start a full investigation into this reporter's claims. I'll bring the chief constable up to date with the situation so far. Have the team here for a 5pm briefing; we need to move fast on this.'

'There is one other major complication. I received a message from Scrivenor, via voicemail, just before I started the meeting. He's intending to go to a Sunday newspaper with the story. He wants me to ring him back and discuss it.' Plummer paced between the office door and the window deep in thought. He glanced at his watch.

'Okay, Ryan. Invite Mr Scrivenor in here, let's say 3.pm. We'll have to sit down with him and try and sweet talk him into giving us some more time. If he believes we are taking his allegations seriously, it may buy us a bit longer. If this story hits the tabloids in the next few days, there will be mass hysteria on the public transport network and that wouldn't do either of our careers any good at all.'

Chapter Thirty

Ryan McNally's team knew something was afoot when Nigel Plummer settled down at the front of the briefing room alongside the boss. It was Plummer who rose to his feet first.

'I would like to thank you all for your efforts in getting to the bottom of the Brennan murder. In all probabilities, it looks as if the man responsible—although we will never be in a position to prove it—is dead. DI McNally and I have concluded that a detailed report will be sent to the coroner so that an inquest can be conducted into the death of Liam Brennan. So I need you to complete any of your outstanding actions in relation to this enquiry and submit them to Marie Relish and Ray Blendell as soon as possible. I believe there are two members of London Underground staff still to be traced and interviewed?' Jim Wakefield raised a hand.

'Sir, I interviewed Elizabeth Wood this morning. She wasn't exactly over helpful. She was on duty on the night of Brennan's murder but her memory is a little sketchy. She remembers leaving about midnight; the booking hall break-in hadn't occurred before that. She recalled two other members of staff, who worked at the station around the time, who we know about already: Devon Lorne, a Victoria Line train operator, and Comfort Ikande. There is definitely something more to her than meets the eye. The strangest thing of all was when I asked her, on my way out, if she knew our main suspect, Patrick Mullen. She denied it outright. Why would she lie about that?'

'Ok, Jim thanks, it's been a few years, and I've certainly forgotten people I've worked with in the past. You've been allocated the action to speak to the train driver as well?' McNally asked.

'I have, guv. He's on annual leave for the next few days. I tried to contact him at home but looks like he's gone away, so I've left messages on a mobile number his depot has for him and with his supervisor to contact us on his return.' McNally nodded and handed back to Plummer.

'Ok, I want you to tie up those loose ends quickly. Jim, you and Marie Relish put together all we have so far on the Lambeth North enquiry. Ray, construct a full report for the coroner's inquest, which, I believe, is the end of next week. We have a major enquiry starting as of now which will be treated with the utmost confidentiality.' Plummer looked around, making eye contact with each of his officers in turn, ensuring that he had their full attention.

'It has been reported to us, initially through DS Frost and DI McNally, and confirmed during a meeting in my office this afternoon, that a story is going to hit the Sunday papers this weekend that a serial killer is on the loose on the London Underground system. The source of this story is a freelance investigative reporter called Ben Scrivenor.

'DI McNally and I met with Scrivenor this afternoon. He provided us with a dossier of what he called "compelling evidence". From an investigative point of view, it is a mish-mash of fact, presumption, theory and personal motivation, without one shred of evidence to substantiate his claims. But due to the absolute hysteria a story like this could cause on our public transport system I reported to the Assistant Chief Constable Crime following that meeting, and he agreed with me that we should scale up a major enquiry immediately to investigate these accusations. So, if this shit should hit the fan, we're in a position to confirm we're ahead of the game and investigating. Please let me reiterate the sensitivity of this investigation. I'll hand you over to DS Blendell and Marie Relish, who have put together a full briefing of what we have so far before urgent actions are allocated. If you had any plans for the coming weekend, cancel them.'

Plummer took a seat at the back of the room as a wave of whispered conversation spread around the room. Blendell loaded his prepared briefing onto a large screen. Relish handed out prepared bundles, containing photographs and witness statements, to each officer. McNally called for order and gave a brief outline of the initial meeting between him, Frost and Scrivenor. Relish then gave the room an update on the results of her enquiries into Ben Scrivenor, whose face flashed up onto the screen.

'Scrivenor is ex-military. He served with distinction on two tours of Iraq with the Royal Engineers before being discharged on medical grounds. He received injuries during a roadside IED, whilst on patrol, took most of his right leg off. Following his recovery he worked for a number of tabloids as a war correspondent before going it on his own. He is married with two daughters, aged seventeen and nineteen, and lives in Islington. He has been arrested on one occasion for drink driving three years ago. He pleaded guilty and offered, in mitigation, the fact that he had suffered PTSD, on his return from the Middle East, and had a drink problem, which he was addressing, but he still received a twelve months' driving disqualification. Other than that he hasn't come to notice. There are no warning signs on PNC. His wife is a beauty consultant in premises just off Islington High Street. His social media profile is quiet extensive, particularly *Twitter* and *Facebook*. Mostly about the conflicts in the Middle East and the plight of Northern Ireland veterans being investigated over historic incidents going back to the 70s and 80s. One really interesting piece of information I did pick up, whilst trawling through his posts minutes before this briefing commenced, was his sister-in-law allegedly committed suicide on the London Underground and this is her.' A picture of a blond-haired woman replaced Scrivenor's image.

'Her name is Cheryl Meade.' McNally and Frost looked at each other; things were starting to fall into place.

Chapter Thirty-One

'Cheryl Meade is possibly our first victim, married with two children.' Blendell looked around the room to make sure he had everyone's attention. 'She worked for the NHS in the Sexual Health Clinic at St Bart's Hospital. Her husband is a financial advisor for a major bank in the City of London. In your bundle, you'll see a statement from him. Their relationship was strong; they were financially secure. The pathologist report says that she died of multiple injuries consistent with the circumstances of her death. She was also three months' pregnant, a fact that the husband was aware of. No suicide note was left.'

'When she left the family home that morning, the 29th May this year, she was in good spirits, reminding her husband to sort out the travel insurance for the holiday they were to take. We have witnesses, but only to her falling from the platform to her death. CCTV is inconclusive, as the platform was extremely crowded. The coroner's inquest—much against the husband's protests—recorded death by suicide.'

'Did anybody speak to her colleagues at work and search her locker?' asked Frost.

'Her line manager was interviewed when they were informed of her death; she was just as shocked. She'd worked for the department for four years, never been any problem. Her yearly reviews were glowing and she was up for promotion and a wage rise, imminently.' Frost looked over to McNally.

'I don't understand why Scrivenor didn't tell us that Cheryl was his sister-in-law, sir.'

'Well it explains what sparked his interest in this case. Obviously his brother has convinced him that she would never commit suicide. She had no reason to, on the surface, but as we all know, through our own experiences, you think you know somebody well until something as tragic as this happens, you then start to question yourself as to why you didn't pick up on their mental state.' McNally nodded to Ray Blendell to continue.

'Our second possible victim is Ruth Ward. You will recall that her apparent suicide at London Bridge station was the same day that Liam Brennan's body was discovered at Lambeth North.' Blendell moved to the next slide, a dated picture of Ruth Ward taken three years previously, when she had dark hair. 'Uniformed officers dealt with the incident as a standard suicide, of which they get around sixty or so a year. Our team was on call that weekend and obviously tied up with the Lambeth North incident but the Counter Terrorism Command, SO15 reserve, got a call on the terrorism hotline from a lady called Felicity Wright. Wright was a regular caller to the line and often reported spurious incidents that usually could never be verified. It appears that she is a lonely old lady who just rings up for a chat. But on this occasion she did have something interesting to say. Marcia went and interviewed her...'

'She was lonely, loved a chat, and mentally as sharp as a razor. She'd told the SO15 officer that she'd witnessed Ruth Ward's death, and was sure it wasn't suicide. She saw Ruth Ward walk passed her on the platform several minutes before the arrival of the next train. She commented that she looked so full of life and had a big smile on her face as if she were looking forward to the future and certainly not contemplating ending it. By the time the train arrived, the platform had filled up considerably, with mainly young people returning home from a Saturday night out. She walked a little further towards the back end of the platform, but didn't see Ruth Ward—she wasn't looking for her, just a gap in the crowd so she could board the train. She was completely shocked when she realised this young, happy, girl had apparently committed suicide and decided to call her friends at SO15 to pass on her concerns.' Blendell continued.

'Ruth Ward was naturally a brunette; she changed her hair colouring to blond three or four months before her death. Her father, who she worked for, said she'd lost a huge amount of weight and the change of hair colour was part of the new image. Sadly it probably contributed to her being targeted. She'd been to Canary Wharf to meet up with some school friends whom she hadn't seen for some time, and met her death at London Bridge on the Northern Line as she travelled back home.'

Frost added 'I spoke with one of the group that she met up with that night— Alice Harrison; incidentally, she was the person approached by the reporter Ben Scrivenor. She received a text message a few minutes after they'd gone their separate ways. The message was very upbeat.' Frost referred to her notebook. *Thanks for meeting up, really enjoyed seeing you all again, looking forward to meeting up again in the near future.* 'That text message was sent from Ward's mobile seven or eight minutes before she went under that train.'

'Again we have appointments in her diary for the near future,' Blendell pointed out. 'She was about to take her final accountancy exams, which she'd have passed, as her course work had been exceptional. Finally, we have our third possible victim.' Blendell waited as those present turned the pages of their briefing notes before continuing.

'This is Laura Marston, who died at Putney Bridge station, following a Fulham football match, which she'd attended with her husband. Laura Marston's death is being treated as manslaughter, which obviously differs from the previous two. I spoke to John Atwood, the DI whose team picked up this job. They have some good CCTV coverage of the platform, which he emailed me just before we started this briefing. They interviewed Laura Marston's husband. His account is verified by the camera footage. He got split up from his wife at the ticket barrier. She tried to wait for him at the base of the stairs leading up to the eastbound platform, but the pressure of the crowd meant she had to move on ahead. The husband said they always got on the train at the same spot on the platform, which allowed them to alight at Earls Court and dive down onto the Piccadilly Line.'

Blendell tapped a few keys on his laptop and loaded the emailed CCTV footage. 'Laura Marston can be seen working her way along the back of the platform, which was filling up very quickly, away from the camera.' Blendell froze the footage and identified Laura Marston to the team. 'We lose sight of her the further she progresses along the platform.' Blendell freezes the footage again. 'What I want you to look at is this group here, about a dozen Fulham fans and this group here, a similar sized group of away supporters. There'd already been a few skirmishes between these two groups on the way to the station.' The CCTV moved on. 'Laura Marston is in close proximity to the away supporters, when a fight starts between the two groups just as a train is entering the platform. You can see the utter panic caused as bystanders try to get away from the fracas. It's at this point we can see the train making an emergency stop. A statement from the train driver—who was pretty shaken up—suggests that she fell backwards onto the track in front of him and that she was pushed. John Atwood is not convinced of the reliability of the train driver's observations. He has changed his recollection of the event several times and has now told them that he may well have been mistaken. Atwood is still keeping an open mind as to the cause of Marston's death but what's plain for all to see—this was not suicide.'

'Why are we including this death in our enquiry?' Graves questioned.

'Because Ben Scrivenor is convinced she meets the victim profile that he's come up with, in relation to sex, age and the fact that she is blond. I agree, as does DI McNally, that on the face of it, if it were not for Scrivenor, we probably wouldn't connect this death with the previous two.' Blendell took his seat, handing over to McNally.

'Right, we have a lot of work to do before this breaks over the weekend. I'm still hopeful that I can persuade Scrivenor to delay going to print. I would imagine the Sunday tabloids will be lining up to publish. I wasn't aware of his personal connection to the first death, so I need to speak to him again urgently. It may be something we can use to get him to delay—well spotted, Marie.

'I want every next-of-kin, of these possible victims, to be re-interviewed. I want to know if there is any connection between them. I want all the CCTV footage from the three incidents re-examined in order to identify any common denominator or possible suspects. Also seize any CCTV footage, in relation to the last two incidents, of our victims entering the Underground system at Canary Wharf and Putney Bridge. Were they being followed? The CCTV, in relation to the Cheryl Meade incident at East Finchley, would probably have been destroyed by now. Ray, allocate those actions as soon as possible.'

McNally looked in the direction of Plummer. 'I think we're going to need some more feet on the ground for this one boss.' Plumber nodded his agreement and picked up a nearby telephone.

'Anybody got any questions?' McNally asked.

'Have we got a press officer on board this yet, guv?'

'One will be here for the briefing tomorrow, Marcia.' McNally looked around at a sea of tired faces. 'Okay if that's all, everybody here for 8am sharp tomorrow—no exceptions.'

Chapter Thirty-Two

The incident room buzzed with activity—everybody knew what they had to do. Computer keyboards beat a rhythm, appointments were made over the telephone, voices raised in order to be heard, office banter kept spirits up, printers churned out paper.

The aroma of food from several of Camden High Street's plethora of take-aways, hung in the air: pizza, kebab, fish and chips and curry. Familiar faces from other teams arrived, got their heads down, and got to work. The excitement of a new job, a new challenge, was palpable.

Most of the detectives took turns to seek out a quiet space to telephone husbands, wives or partners to give advanced warning they were not going to see each other too much over the next few days. Every officer on the Major Investigation Team regularly made these calls; most partners accepted the reality of their jobs. Children were the most difficult, knowing that Mum or Dad wouldn't be attending their birthday party, Christmas school play or their debut in a school team event. Most of these conversations ended with: "I'll make it up to you", which was normally dismissed. McNally was no different as he took five minutes away from the madness to speak to Kate.

'So you won't make it back up to Norfolk then.' McNally recognised the animosity in her voice. If he'd had a ten pound note for every similar call he'd made to her over the years, he would be able to clear his desk and retire.

'How are Ava and Max?'

'They're OK. Max is missing his dad. I've had a long talk with Ava. She is definitely being bullied. I've made an appointment to see the headmaster on Tuesday next week. I spoke to work. They've given me a bit more time off. The boss isn't very happy, but she's got kids of a similar age, so sort of understands.

'I got a call from one of the girls from that art class I joined a few weeks ago, Shirley. Remember, I told you about her; her husband's an accountant, got that big house just off Ballards Lane next to Victoria Park.' McNally mumbled an affirmative but hadn't got a clue who she was talking about.

'Well, she's invited us out to dinner on Saturday, with a couple of other local people. I thought it would be a good chance for us to meet new people in the area. She's got a daughter of a similar age to Ava. They met once before, and seemed to get on really well.'

'A born again artist and an accountant; sounds like a right laugh.'

'Ryan, why be such an arse about this? I'm trying to build a few ties in the area, not for you, you already have your little clan at work, but for me and the kids for God's sake.'

'Yeah, I know. I'm sorry, just got quite a bit on my plate at the moment. It's all going to kick off here quite soon. I'll try my best to be there and I promise to be on my best behaviour. I'm just hoping that the other couple aren't computer geeks or born again Christians.'

'Very funny, just for once forget you're Sherlock Holmes' incarnate, or maybe in your case a Doctor Watson, and be nice to people.' He could sense her smile through the telephone.

'Look, I gotta go. I love you. Say hello to the kids for me and don't eat too much homemade cake and ice cream while you're up there; you're getting a bit podgy. I might have to swap you for a younger, thinner model.'

'You cheeky bastard, Dr Watson; see you soon, I love you too.'

McNally lent back into his chair and opened his decision log. He had a lot of writing to do. If this investigation went tits up, he was creating the stick with which he would be beaten. The *Big Brother* theme tune rang out from his mobile. Cursing Max for the hundredth time, he answered the call from the unrecognisable caller.

'DI McNally'

'Hey, dude. How's it hanging?' McNally initially thought it was a crank call and was about to hang up when the caller continued 'It's me, dude, Sally Cook, your friendly crime scene examiner or to people of your age a SOCO.'

'Hi, Sally, bit busy at the moment. If it's about Lambeth North, can you speak to DS Frost?'

'I need to speak to you. I have tried Marcia but she's engaged. It's pretty important.'

'OK, Sally, fire away.' McNally looked at his watch as he shut the decision log and reached for a notepad.

'A few days ago Marcia contacted me about a couple of suicides that she wasn't happy with and asked me to make a few enquiries. Obviously, it's not something that me or my lot would attend, unless there is an element of suspicion that it might not be as it seems you know, a straight forward one under, a jumper.'

'Yes, I know what a one under is, Sally.'

'Yeah, right. I know you're not from this part of the world, not sure if you're up with the lingo; lingo means…'

'Get to the point, Sally, please.' McNally pinched the bridge of his nose between thumb and forefinger.

'Anyway, I made a few phone-calls. All seemed straight forward suicides until now. I'm at Mornington Crescent station, about half a mile from where you are. The call initially went out as a woman had been pushed under a train and a male suspect detained. Paramedics were called and attended. Uniform officers and the medics recovered the body from the tracks. The suspect was chased and detained by two passengers as he fled the scene, and then arrested by two Euston BTP officers who responded to the call first, he's been taken to our Central London police station.'

'Did the witnesses see her actually being pushed?'

'I'm not sure if they saw the incident, or put two and two together, thinking he must be involved somehow if he's running away. But dude, there is no doubt this was murder—not an accident or suicide.'

'What d'ya mean?'

'She was stabbed in the back before she fell.' McNally took a brief moment to consider what he'd been told. 'She has been cut up badly by the wheels of the train but the stab wound is pretty evident. I've got a couple of local CID lads here already and they have sealed the station off as a crime scene. We're just about to move the body to St Pancras mortuary.'

'OK, thanks for the call. Will you be examining the scene?'

'Yes, but obviously I can't deal with the suspect or the victim at the mortuary. I'll get some help for that. A young female officer, not sure of her name, will accompany the victim to St Pancras for continuity.'

'I'll send DC Graves down to you immediately to deal with the exhibits—I think you met him at Lambeth North recently.'

'Yeah, I remember him, bit of a wanker if I recall—sorry if he's your best mate, dude, but I say as I find.'

'We can discuss that one another time. Was there any weapon retrieved at the scene?'

'I've had a quick look around the platform area and on the track, but nothing as of yet. I presume, well at least hope, the suspect would've been searched by the uniform bods before they took him away. They didn't inform me if they did find a weapon.'

'Is either of the local CID officers there at the moment? If so put one on please, Sally.'

'OK. Will you be coming down here?'

'Yeah, we'll be taking this on. Just one thing before you go, what colour hair did the victim have?'

'Hang on. I'll have to have a closer look, because at the moment it's blood red.' McNally could hear the unzipping of a body bag before she returned. 'It's pretty hard to tell if I'm honest, as half her head is missing, but she had some ID, a driving licence, as far as I can tell she is blond—is that relevant?'

'Bloody right it is.'

*

'Marcia, get in here now.' From McNally's tone, Frost expected a bollocking, for what—she hadn't a clue.

'Make sure no one goes anywhere. I've just had a call from Sally Cook. She's been called to a suspicious one under at Mornington Crescent station…'

'That's just down the road from here.'

'…the victim is blond and has a stab wound to her back and we've a male in custody detained by two witnesses as he ran from the scene.' McNally walked along the corridor and knocked on Plummer's door. He got no answer, the door handle was locked. He tried his boss's mobile and was instructed to leave a message. He glanced at his watch—18.15. 'Lazy bastard's gone home,' he mumbled to himself. 'He'll be on the tube for the next half hour.' He waited for the bleep and left a message that he urgently contacts him.

McNally marched into the incident room. This is why he joined the police service; the adrenalin rushed through him. This was a proper job. He could see the excitement on his team's faces, the weariness had disappeared. They were up for this as much as he was.

133

'Within the last hour, a young blond woman fell in front of a southbound Northern Line train at Mornington Crescent station. She has a stab wound in her lower back, inflicted before she fell to her death. She falls into the profile of our other victims. If you had any doubts in your minds that the incidents we were discussing just half an hour ago were criminal, then banish them. As far as I'm concerned this is now a full-blown hunt for a killer, whose latest victim is on her way to St Pancras mortuary. Put all the actions you've been allocated on the back-burner for now we've a murder scene, a victim and a suspect to deal with. Stuart I want you down at Mornington Crescent station as exhibits officer and liaise with Sally Cook, the SOCO. Ray, organise a Police Search Advisor and search team to be on standby, the murder weapon is outstanding. Marcia I want you and Sam Hodge to deal with the suspect at the nick; full forensic retrieval of his clothes. Jim Wakefield.' McNally looked around the room.

'Here, sir.'

'Jim, take one of the new lads and arrange for the downloading of the CCTV from the station, if it hasn't already been done, and make enquiries within a couple of hundred metres, for now, of businesses that have CCTV in the surrounding area. I want to see if we can pick up our victim before she enters the station. With a bit of luck, we may see our suspect as well. Stuart find out where the victim's ID documents are now, Sally Cook had a driving licence but has probably put it back in the bag with the body. We need a picture of her without the gaping hole in her head, get it photocopied and a copy to Jim, first of all, and then copies back to Ray and Marie here. Ray, the media are going to be all over this and of course our friend, Ben Scrivenor; get that press officer in here tonight and fully brief them. I'll need a Family Liaison Officer on board as quickly as you can. Contact 'B' Division; this is on their patch, use one of theirs and get them up to the mortuary to liaise with the uniform officer there. The FLO can deal with next of kin and identification and make sure the coroner's officer has been advised. I'll go to the crime scene first. I want to have a look at the layout of the station. The two witnesses are still there, but the local CID had the brains to separate them and transporting them to the witness suite separately. I want their statements recorded visually and audibly. Marcia once our man has been tucked up for the night in a cell, you and Sam take one witness each. I'm waiting for the boss to ring me back. Once I've been to Mornington Crescent, I'll liaise with you and Sam at the nick. Does everybody know what they're doing? Good Luck everybody.'

Chapter Thirty-Three

Police Constable Sayeeda Malik was coming to the end of her probation period with the British Transport Police. Her parents wanted her to enter the veterinary profession, but she wasn't comfortable with the sight of blood, not quite Haemophobia, but a fact, her father ironically pointed out, that wasn't going to be a great attribute in the police service. Her family eventually gave her their blessing to join.

At training school, she was told she would struggle to make an effective police constable, due to her inability to 'stamp her mark' on any given situation. She was shy and kept herself to herself during the initial weeks of training, but studied hard. She proved them all wrong—blossoming into a confident young officer, who was well respected on her team.

The day she passed out from training was the proudest of her life. Standing in line on parade with her colleagues, she could see her parents sitting in the crowd of onlookers, her father beaming with pride. She had big ambitions—she wanted to be a detective working in a sexual offences unit—she knew she could make a difference to people's lives.

Although the ambulance was cruising along at no great speed, she started to feel a little bit queasy. She was not the greatest passenger, always preferring to drive. She'd fight tooth and nail to avoid the backseat of any vehicle. Travelling in the back of an ambulance, accompanying a corpse, that, although contained in a body bag, smelt of burnt flesh, was beginning to summon her lunch from the depths of her stomach. She'd been to a 'one under' on a previous occasion but the 'jumper' had survived with relatively minor injuries.

'You okay?' The paramedic asked.

'Yeah, sure I'm fine,' she lied.

'Is this your first one?'

'My first dead one.'

'The dead ones are a lot easier to deal with, you know. They don't bleed and they don't answer back.' Sayeeda gave half a smile and examined her mobile. She wasn't in a mood to talk.

The ambulance pulled up outside St Pancras Coroner's Court. The young P.C leapt out of the back and took a few gulps of fresh air. The driver backed the ambulance up to a set of grey metal doors, which slid open. They were met by a mortuary assistant in overalls and protective gloves. He smiled at Sayeeda before conversing with the ambulance crew.

'Back again so soon?'

'Yep, second time today, a suicide on the underground to go with the road traffic accident from earlier. This one is a right mess, make sure you search the body bag well or you might miss a piece.' All three laughed.

Sayeeda knew about 'gallows humour.' Indeed she enjoyed the banter with her colleagues as much as anyone, but she drew the line at complete disrespect for the dead. A young woman, full of life two hours ago, who has family: a mother and father perhaps a husband and children—lay a few feet from them. This was not pure banter but something a lot darker—some sort of male macho crap being used to intimidate her. She wasn't having it.

'When you three have finished fucking about, shall we get on with the job?' The gobby paramedic, who'd been in the back of the ambulance with her, looked as if he were about to say something, but had second thoughts when he saw the anger etched into the young police officer's face.

The remains were wheeled into the mortuary and placed on a steel examination table. The examination room itself was brighter than she'd expected and, although there was a distinctive aroma, it wasn't wholly unpleasant. During her training she and her classmates attended a post-mortem examination. On that occasion, there'd been several cadavers lined up on tables awaiting examination, including that of a man and two young children, who'd perished in a house fire. The smell had been horrendous, masked slightly by a small smear of decongestant vapour rub they'd been advised to apply on their upper lip.

The paramedics turned to leave. The driver glanced at Sayeeda with an apologetic smile on his face. The body bag was unzipped. Sayeeda tried to avoid taking a deep breath, unsure if she was ready for this.

The mortuary attendant was joined by another, and piece by piece the remains were removed: a severed right foot which had a small butterfly tattoo just above the toes. Sayeeda bizarrely thought how much that must have hurt.

This was followed by a severed arm, the main torso, the remaining limbs and the head. Sayeeda forced herself to look. She was aware she wasn't there to make the tea, but to observe. In a couple of months, she could be explaining her actions in a coroner's court.

The remains were covered in blood and a black sooty muck. It was hard to differentiate between clothing and body tissue. The mortuary assistant removed a small leather rucksack—the victim's property—from the body-bag. Sayeeda was handed some gloves, which she eventually managed to get on her, now, sweaty hands, whilst trying to control her nerves. It was the second assistant that realised the young officer was struggling and guided her to a nearby table, on which he laid the rucksack, and asked if she'd like a drink of water. She declined with a grateful smile and a shake of her head.

The flap of the rucksack was a challenge; the congealed blood had stuck the leather material together. Inside were several items of gym-wear, together with a paperback about a double murder in Victorian England, a metal water container and a black, zip top purse.

She glanced back to the examination table and watched as the men stripped the remnants of the woman's clothing from her body with little or no respect. She focussed on the job at hand, examining the contents of the purse she'd emptied on the table top. She quickly found what she was looking for and walked back over to the body and compared the bloodied mish-mashed facial features to a picture on a driving licence in the name of Valerie Huxley. It took her a few moments of concentration before she was satisfied they matched, before returning to the table.

Sayeeda retrieved several property bags from her jacket, handed to her by colleagues as she entered the ambulance. The driving licence was placed into a self-sealed property bag, on its own, through which the victim's name and address and date of birth could be clearly seen and photographed. She then continued to bag the remainder of the property.

The contents of the purse included: bank cards, a membership card to a gym just off Camden High Street, a business card in her name, stating that she was a legal secretary for a local solicitor's firm and a small passport sized photograph of Valerie with a dark-haired woman, who was obviously a close friend or maybe a lover.

'Who are you?' Sayeeda whispered to herself, as she looked at the other woman in the photograph. 'Whoever you are, you're in for a big shock.' She stared at the photograph for several more seconds becoming aware of another presence close by. She turned and was met by a friendly face.

'Hi, I'm P.C Julie Barber, family liaison officer.' They both looked at the congealed blood on Sayeeda's gloves and decided against offering each other a handshake. 'Everything OK here?'

'I'm Sayeeda Malik, based at Central London police station. I've seen you about the place.'

'Yeah, I work on the sexual assaults team, mainly nine to five.'

'Really, I'd love to do that one day. That must be a really interesting job.'

'It's OK. I like the hours but the work can be a bit grim sometimes, especially the serious assaults. It can drag you down a bit until you arrest and convict the offender, which puts a smile on my face—fucking perverts. I hate them.' Both officers looked over at the mortuary assistants and smiled at each other.

'So, have we got an ID and address that you're happy with, as I've got to deliver the death message?' Malik nodded and handed over the driving licence. 'Have you searched the clothing on the body yet?'

'No, that was next on my list. Her face is a mess by the way, but she does have a small butterfly tattooed on the amputated foot, that will probably mean something to somebody.' She glanced again at the photograph.

'Nice job, Sayeeda. Let's search those clothes before those two throw them away. The coroner's officer is on his way and then I'm off to…' Barber glanced at the driving licence again.

'…Clapham. You wanna come?' Sayeeda couldn't keep the excitement from her face. She had a new role model, as well as a lift back into the land of the living.

'Yes, please.'

*

McNally was pleased to see the whole station had been shut down on his arrival at Mornington Crescent. A few disgruntled commuters were protesting to the uniformed officer on the Bostwick gates. He showed his warrant card and entered the booking hall, making his way to the stairs, noting a blue plaque on the wall marking the life of Willie Rushton, a comedian and actor, who McNally vaguely remembered appearing on a number of 1980s quiz shows.

He took the stairs down to platform level. The train had been removed and taken to Golders Green depot, where it would be sealed off, awaiting forensic examination. McNally recognised the Police Search Advisor—Inspector Neil Williams. They'd worked together before. McNally trusted him, knowing he was very thorough.

'Good to see you Neil, found anything yet?'

'Not so far, Ryan. We've searched the platform and the route the suspect took before he was detained, we're just starting on the track. I've sent a couple of the team up to Golders Green to search the train once the SOCO has finished.'

'OK, mate, but I don't want all our eggs in the one basket. Can you search upstairs: the booking hall area and any bins or drains outside the station, just in case our prisoner is not the killer?'

'Sure, Ryan, I'll radio the PC on the front gates to extend the cordon and get some help from the local police.' McNally, ducked under the inner cordon, having given his details to the officer for the scene log. A clearly marked path, that'd already been searched and forensically examined, led further up the gloomy platform. Intermittent flash light from the crime scene photographer's digital camera seemed to make the posters on the wall eerily come to life.

'Hey, dude, over here.' He really had to have a word with Sally Cook. He wasn't a big *Yes Sir, no Sir* man, but a little respect in front of junior officers wouldn't go astray.

'Hi Sally, anything of interest so far?'

'Not really. There is quite a bit of blood on the tracks—she was pretty badly cut up. I'm not sure if we've got everything in relation to body-parts or soft tissue. The train is being examined at the depot as we speak. I doubt if we'll find any more traces of our victim, as the train was travelling fairly slow, but sometimes blood or human tissue can get mangled around the wheels. We'll look for fingerprints on the outside of the first couple of carriages, but as you can imagine, with half of London likely to have touched it, it's unlikely we'll get anything from that.'

'Anything more about the stab wound?'

'Not a lot at this stage. The paramedic who confirmed life extinct, agreed with me that it looked like a stab wound, but we'll have to wait for the post mortem tomorrow for the definitive answer.'

'OK, keep me up to date. I'm going to Central London police station if you need me.' McNally traced his steps along the platform and back up the stairs.

'Excuse me, sir, are you a police officer?' McNally turned to see a diminutive figure dressed in London Underground uniform.

'Yes, I'm DI McNally. Can I help? Are you OK? You look a little shaken.'

'It's a nasty business. I've heard the two witnesses say that the lady might have been pushed so we're talking murder—right?'

'We're still trying to establish what exactly happened Miss…?'

'It's Mrs…O'Shaughnessy. Katie O'Shaughnessy.'

'Is something worrying you Mrs O'Shaughnessy? Have you any light to shed on the events here?'

'I want to show you something, Inspector. She directed McNally back to the lifts and pushed a button, which illuminated. They waited patiently for the arrival of the lift and stepped inside—McNally followed, trying to disguise his aversion to lifts. She pointed to one of the lift's inner walls. 'There,' she pointed at a poster warning passengers to be alert, and report anything suspicious to the police. O'Shaughnessy stepped closer to the poster that was covered with a thin Perspex sheet and pointed to a red stain. 'I think that's blood, Inspector.'

McNally took a closer look and agreed.

'Were you here when the suspect was detained downstairs, Mrs O'Shaughnessy?

'Yes I was.'

'Can you remember how the police officers got the suspect up to this level?'

'They walked him up the stairs; there were still quite a few passengers making their way out of the station using the lifts.'

'Yes, that's what I thought. Can you take this lift out of service immediately, madam? I need to go back downstairs for a moment. I'll use the stairs.' O'Shaughnessy nodded her head.

'Thank you for your help.'

Chapter Thirty-Four

Police Constables, Sayeeda Malik and Julie Barber sat in an unmarked car in Jedburgh Street—a few metres from the junction with Clapham Common North Side—outside the address recorded on Valerie Huxley's driving licence. It was a substantial Victorian house with views over nearby Clapham Common.

The pair had been chatty during the drive across central London. But since they'd arrived Julie Barber had gone into business mode, and Sayeeda Malik respectfully kept her silence, aware her colleague was weighing up, in her own mind, how to tell Valerie's family that she wouldn't be returning home that night—or ever.

The silence was broken by the FLO's mobile.

'Yes, OK. I've got all that…, yes…, thanks…, brilliant, bye.' She finished making some notes and turned to Sayeeda. 'The electoral register has two other occupants—Valerie's parents. There are no flags or warning markers on PNC against the address.'

'D'ya want me to come in with you?'

'Yes, of course, no point sitting out here. I don't usually deliver the death message as FLO. That's normally done by a uniformed officer.'

'So what's your role after that?'

'Well, as FLO, I'm the link between the family and the SIO. I'll deal with the formal identification of the victim and assist the family wherever I can, by keeping them updated about the coroner's inquest and any later court proceedings if anybody is charged with Valerie's murder. But most importantly, I'm an investigator. I cannot become too attached to the family members. Often they hold vital information that the SIO will need and on occasions one or two of the family or close associates of the victim will be suspects.

'Many police officers think the role of FLO is visiting the family for a cup of tea and a biscuit every now and then, but it's a lot more complex than that, and can be quite stressful. One of the first things we have to establish is ground rules as to when I'm available to be contacted, otherwise you'll get calls through the night, which isn't on as far as I'm concerned. You gotta have a life outside this job.'

Julie Barber reached over to the backseat and grabbed the FLO log.

'I have to record every meeting in this log I have with the family, including any contact by telephone. In a complex case, I might fill two or three of these logs over the course of an investigation. But obviously today it's all about establishing a relationship and obtaining as much information about the victim as possible which is always difficult in these circumstances, as you can imagine. Emotions are going to be running high. Okay you ready, partner?' Sayeeda Malik nodded.

Chapter Thirty-Five

A large platter of bacon rolls sat in the middle of the incident room accompanied by two large urns: one filled with coffee, the other with hot water for tea. Most of the detectives and incident room staff had started at 7am, writing up their actions and submitting them into the office manager's 'in' tray. Small huddles of weary-looking detectives were spaced around the room. Graves went through his exhibit books with a detective drafted in as an assistant, making sure he knew what he had to submit to the forensic labs in order of importance. Frost and Hodge discussed and cross-referenced statements they'd obtained from the witnesses, who'd detained their main suspect, and planned an interview strategy for later that morning. McNally updated Detective Superintendent Plummer in his office.

Pictures of all four victims adorned white boards around the room, with a large map of the London Underground in the centre, on which red pins marked the murder sites: East Finchley, London Bridge, Putney Bridge and Mornington Crescent.

McNally and Plummer walked into the incident room, signalling to the rest of the team that the briefing was about to get started. The ripple of conversation gradually reduced to a silence. McNally grabbed himself a cup of coffee and eyed the last bacon roll.

'Good morning, everyone. I know most of you worked into the early hours of this morning and I thank you for that, but today is going to be another long one. For the benefit of the extra officers that have joined us, yesterday afternoon we had a briefing which commenced an investigation into the claims of a freelance journalist, that a serial killer was active on the London Underground. As we learnt yesterday, the journalist in question—Ben Scrivenor—is related to the first victim, who died at East Finchley station a few weeks ago. About half an hour after the ending of that briefing I received a telephone call from SOCO, Sally Cook.' McNally quickly scanned the room.

'For those who don't know Sally, she's at the back of the room.' Cook raised a hand. 'She'd been called to, what was first thought to be, a suicide at Mornington Crescent station. This was quickly changed to a possible murder. A suspect running from the scene was stopped and detained by two fellow passengers. They were interviewed yesterday evening and I'll get DS Frost to update us all. The victim is a young blond woman—significant in relation to our investigation—called Valerie Huxley and early indications are that she was stabbed in the back, before falling in front of the train. We'll know more detail after the autopsy.

'PC Julie Barber, the designated FLO for the Huxley family, will give us an update on the victim and her family setup.'

'Thanks, sir. Valerie Huxley was divorced, aged thirty-one and a legal secretary for a small solicitors' firm located in Oakley Square—a two minute walk from Mornington Crescent station. She'd visited a local gym and CCTV cameras recorded her leaving at 17.27pm.'

'She entered the station at 17.31pm,' interjected Ray Blendell.

'She lives with her parents in a nice Victorian built house, just off Clapham Common.' Barber continued.

'Her father is an accountant, the mother, a retired teacher. I visited the address yesterday with PC Sayeeda Malik and broke the bad news. I went to the mortuary first, as I wanted to see for myself the condition of the body in order to advise relations. I haven't raised the subject of formal identification with them yet as Valerie's face is a bit of a mess. She has a brother living, in Manchester, who's on his way down to London. I'm meeting him at Euston in forty minutes, so I might have to leave shortly.' She glanced over to McNally. 'I'm hoping he will agree to carry out the formal identification later today. I did take a statement from the father—the mother was too upset—he gives a full description and supplied me with a recent photograph. Valerie had a small tattoo on her right ankle, which corresponds to one found on her severed foot in the mortuary.'

'OK, thanks Julie. Slip out the door when you need to and keep me up to date with the formal ID. I'll try and get down to see the family later today. I'll ring you first. Ray, we need to allocate an FLO to each of the other three victims' families.'

'We might have to beg, steal or borrow from other divisions, but I'll get straight onto that after the meeting.'

'Sally, where are we in relation to the post mortem?

'Just got a message from the coroner's officer, it's due to take place at 15.30hrs, so you have plenty of time.'

'Stuart, I'll need you with me for that.' Graves raised a thumb in the air.

'DS Frost can update us all regarding the witnesses and the suspect in custody.' Marcia Frost weaved in and out of a few desks and chairs until she reached the front.

'The two witnesses work together in a bedding store on Camden High Street. Sam Hodge and I took a statement from each. Not surprisingly, their versions are pretty close together apart from the obvious discrepancies you would normally expect in relation to distances and timings. They left work around 4.30pm and dropped into the Lyttelton Arms for a quick pint. They entered the tube station just before 5.30pm and went down onto the southbound Northern line platform. One of them lives in Walthamstow and was changing at Euston onto the Victoria Line; the other travels south to Waterloo and onto Kingston on the mainline service. The Northern line was running a bit slow. They waited about halfway along the platform for between six and seven minutes for a train, by which time the platform had gotten fairly busy. As the train entered the platform everybody started to move forwards, and jostled for position. Neither of the witnesses saw Valerie Huxley fall beneath the train, as they were at least three or four feet back, with a number of fellow passengers in between them and the edge of the platform.

'The train entered the platform at its usual speed, when both witnesses say they heard a woman scream and a second or two later the train's warning signal blasted out. Their accounts differ slightly here. One saying it was the train warning signal first followed by the scream, the other in reverse order. They were then aware of everybody in front of them backing off from the platform edge. They then see our suspect burst through the mayhem, knocking one of the witnesses to the ground and running towards the platform exit. They assumed something pretty bad had happened and gave chase and caught up with him on the stairs leading to the booking hall and station exit. One of them turns out to be a special constable with Surrey police and arrests him. The suspect was pretty abusive and gave them a hard time, kicking, spitting and trying to head butt them both at every opportunity until BTP arrived and handcuffed him.'

'When the suspect was under control which way did they take the suspect— up the stairs or into the lift?' McNally asked. Frost quickly turned the statement pages over.

145

'They took him up the stairs, sir.' Sam Hodge assisted. 'There were still passengers on the platform and lift levels and our suspect was being pretty abusive, so they walked him up.'

'Alright, what about the suspect, Marcia, do we know any more about him?'

'He gave the arresting officers a false name, but has come back on prints as Daniel Edward Corbell. I've got an address in Pepys Road, New Cross. He has a number of previous convictions for pickpocketing, drugs, violence and assaulting police and is currently wanted on warrant for non-appearance at Southwark Crown Court. He's been inside off and on for the most part of his adult life. All his family are villains; his father is serving sixteen years for armed robbery, and his mother has convictions for cheque fraud. They're just a family of shitbags.'

'Should all be put up against a wall and shot. What do they contribute to society?' Nobody wanted to be associated with Stuart Graves' remarks, but, probably, most agreed.

'I've bagged all his clothes up. Property wise not a lot on him, an Oyster card...'

'What's the world coming to—an honest criminal,' Graves' offer this time resulted in a subdued wave of laughter. Plummer wasn't so amused and turned to face him.

'DC Graves, if you make one more comment like that you'll be back patrolling some god forsaken station in the middle of nowhere, in a top hat with a nice shiny badge on the front. Do I make myself clear?' With Graves suitably admonished, Frost continued.

'...a lot of cash and a mobile phone, which he apparently tried to ditch on the stairs. He was strip-searched on his arrival in custody. A bag of cannabis was found in his sock but other than that nothing.'

'Did he have any blood on his clothes?' Frost looked across the room at an officer she didn't know.

'None that I could see with the naked eye, but he did have a bloody nose as a result of falling face first on the stairs. According to him, it was down to police brutality and has made an official complaint. We've got his brief coming in for 10am, and have prepared the initial disclosure notice; we hope to start the first interview about 11am.'

'Let's move on to CCTV. Jim Wakefield.'

'Sir.'

'How'd we get on with our trawl of local CCTV?'

'I walked the victim's route from Oakley Square to the gym she used, and then on to the station. I identified four possible CCTV systems that may have picked her up and I'm arranging for the downloading of it this morning. The CCTV from the station has been secured, confirming she entered the station at 17.31pm and took the lift down to the platform level. There were half a dozen or so passengers in the lift with her. Once she gets on the platform it's harder to pick her out, as she positions herself in between two cameras. What can clearly be seen is the braking of the train, the panic of fellow passengers as they back off from the area of the incident, and there's a very nice shot of our suspect— Corbell—running towards the camera.' Wakefield looked over at Marie Relish and nodded. The wide screened monitor at the front of the room played a short sequence of footage, Corbell could clearly be seen.

'This was our man just before he leaves the platform, heading towards the stairs. You can see one of the witnesses chasing him. What's interesting is the article he's carrying.' Everybody's attention was drawn to an unidentifiable dark object in the suspect's right hand. The footage then changes to another camera.

'We lose sight of him for, what I estimate to be, three or four seconds before this camera, positioned at the base of the stairs, shows our man being caught by the Surrey special but look at his right hand—nothing—whatever was in it, he's ditched or concealed on his body.'

'I'll speak to the search team. I'm sure they would've covered the stairs. Marcia could it have been the mobile you mentioned he tried to ditch?'

'No, sir. He still had the mobile on the stairs, that's where he tried to ditch it. When he was searched at the nick, he wasn't in possession of anything like the object in his hand on the CCTV.'

'Jim, I want you to supervise the viewing of the CCTV footage. I'll give you a couple of extra pairs of eyes to assist. I want sightings of Valerie Huxley's every move from the time she left work and before she arrived at the station via the gym. Liaise with the technical support people, start putting together a gallery of images of fellow passengers and anybody else that can be plainly seen in her vicinity before she enters the tube, during the lift journey to the platforms, as she enters the platforms and the passengers as they are evacuated from the station after the murder. Once that is done, we need to do the same with the limited CCTV we still have for Ruth Ward at London Bridge and Laura Marston at Putney Bridge. My understanding is the footage for Cheryl Meade at East

Finchley has been deleted. It's a lot of work, Jim, but if Daniel Corbell is not our man, then somewhere on those tapes is our murderer.'

Chapter Thirty-Six

Michael Brewster sat in his shabby, one-bedroomed flat in Stepney, East London. He'd been home for an hour, but sleep evaded him. The early morning sun was streaming through thin cheap curtains. The noise of London going to work was deafening.

Brewster worked nights in London's docklands. He normally stopped off for a coffee and a chat in a small cafe en route from Limehouse station to his second floor flat in Salmon Lane. He had no friends. The café stop was the only human contact outside work; he wouldn't speak to another living soul until he returned to work at 11pm.

He examined the deep cut on his right thumb. Blood seeped through the makeshift bandage; the wound might need stitches he thought. He would re-dress it before going to bed.

He surfed a few channels, knowing he was going to have to get some sleep at some stage. A television presenter was delivering his usual diatribe, disguised as an interview. The subject was about dysfunctional families. The government minister managed only one or two sentences in reply to a barrage of questions, and was fast losing patience at not being given the opportunity to finish a sentence.

Michael Brewster cared little for families. His father cleared off when he was eighteen months old. His mother had been a drunk and incapable of looking after him. He was put into care as a two-year-old and spent most of his adolescence being pushed from pillar to post, suffering abuse and neglect. Eventually he'd been fostered out to some good people, but he could never settle and was disruptive and sometimes violent.

He was eventually adopted by an Essex couple who'd lost a son in a car accident. He even started to think of them as Mum and Dad until the patriarch died in a work related accident when Michael was fourteen. His schooling became non-existent, mainly due to his disruptive behaviour and was expelled more times than he cared to remember.

He was rescued by the Royal Navy, enlisting on his sixteenth birthday. He enjoyed the life, especially the routine and the discipline, something he'd rebelled against throughout his childhood, both at school and at home.

He travelled the world for a couple of years before applying for a transfer to the Royal Marines. His first deployment, as part of 40 Commando, was to Afghanistan in November 2001. Two more deployments would follow, ending in a medical discharge in 2010, following a battlefield injury and suffering from PTSD.

He had very few memories of his mother; a grainy black and white photograph was the only proof she'd ever existed. He remembered more about his social worker, a woman called Sam, who'd often visit him, but even she died when he was nine or ten.

When not at school, he'd got into a little trouble with the police, receiving a caution for shoplifting. He started to drink at an early age; his adopted parents never suspected, or at least never revealed they did. He would steal from them to buy booze and fags, just a few pounds here and there and what he couldn't afford he stole from supermarkets and off-licences. He was a good thief.

He blamed his natural parents for his loveless childhood, especially his mother, whom he often dreamt of killing. The dreams were vivid; his hatred of her grew with every misfortune he experienced through his childhood and teenage years. The only role model he'd ever had, before joining the Royal Navy, was his adopted father, who died too young.

When he reached his late thirties, curiosity took over and he decided that he needed to try and find his natural parents. He returned home to Romford to ask some difficult questions of his adopted mother. She had no information on his natural father. He learnt that his mother had died of liver failure when he was seven or eight years of age. What the paperwork did reveal was Michael Brewster wasn't his real name, and that he had an older sibling.

*

Frost and Hodge entered the custody office at Central London police station, armed with an interview strategy that wasn't usually worth the paper it was written on. Interviewing a suspect was an art some detectives were brilliant at,

150

others pretty average, but all were flexible. Neither Frost nor Hodge had ever conducted an interview that went perfectly to plan. Your opening question and, more importantly, the answer, if you got one, could take the interviewer off on a completely different tangent.

Frost had disclosed, to Corbell's solicitor, as much as she needed to—no more. She had several subjects she wanted to cover in this first interview, and had disclosed the relevant facts covering those subjects.

Police Sergeant Tom Mackie sat behind the raised custody sergeant's desk and gave her a big smile.

'Hi, Marcia, long time, no see.' Frost was happy to see a friendly face. It'd been a while since she'd set foot in this place. Most of the faces had changed.

'Hi, Tom, you're looking well, seeing as you never see the sun in here. Thought you might have sorted yourself a cushy job, sitting on your arse all day—oh look, you have.' They both laughed. 'This is DC Sam Hodge. Tom was my first sergeant when I joined this firm.'

'Is that the time—it's my smoke break, little buggers. I can't get by without them. The solicitor is still in with your man. Let's pop out into the yard and you can tell me how your mum and dad are doing.' Frost was keen to get on but saw Mackie flick his eyes up at the CCTV camera and followed him out, with Sam Hodge in tow.

'What's up, Tom? I'm too young to go out with an old goat like you?' She smiled.

'Yeah, I know, but I could still teach you a thing or two. Listen, Marcia, the guy you are interviewing…' Frost nodded, she knew that serious look from the past. What he was about to say wasn't going to be good news. '…he's an arsehole and his brief—who wouldn't know how to spell legal aid—is a *smart* arsehole. I've dealt with Corbell before. He's a nasty piece of work. The last time was about two years ago, he got nicked for GBH on a dip squad officer. He gave her a right kicking. He knows the law back to front, he will probably give you loads of verbal from the start to try and put you off your stride, just a warning—be careful. Come on. I'll book him out for interview. The Brief should be done with him by now.'

*

151

'Well, well, you lot are really scraping the bottom of the barrel. You run out of proper detectives? What have we got here then?' Daniel Corbell turned to his solicitor, 'An escapee from London Zoo and her boy wonder, who looks like he's going to shit himself.' Frost had expected an aggressive opening gambit, based on what Tom Mackie had warned her of, but she wasn't quite ready for such a personal attack, she kept her cool and remembered that he was here on her terms. She bit her tongue and was impressed Sam Hodge hadn't taken the bait either.

Hodge placed the DVDs into the recording equipment and both detectives waited for the signal to commence the interview. Corbell sat back arrogantly in his chair, placing one hand down the front of his police issue tracksuit bottoms and grinned at Frost. His greasy matted hair covered a spotty forehead. Sunken eyes and sores around his nostrils and mouth and yellowing teeth, were signs of a hard drug addiction. His personal hygiene wouldn't have improved with the night he'd spent in the cells.

'I'm Detective Sergeant Frost from the British Transport Police Major Investigations Team and my colleague is…'

'Detective Constable Hodge.'

'Blimey, the boy wonder speaks, does he?'

'Can you state your full name for us please?'

'Daniel Corbell.'

'You have exercised your right to have legal representation present during this interview—sir, if you could introduce yourself.'

'Adrian Harper, Seymour solicitors.'

'Mr Corbell, we are in an interview room at the BTP Central London police station and the time is 10.55hrs. You've already been cautioned on your arrest but I wish to remind you that you do not have to say anything, but it may harm your defence if you do not mention, when questioned, something which you later rely on in court. Anything you do say may be given in evidence. Do you understand that?'

'My client fully understands the caution as given, officer.'

'If at any time during this interview you require a break to consult with your solicitor, please let me know.' Frost, playing it by the book so far, looked directly at Corbell, interview plan ignored; she decided to go on the attack from the start.'

'Why did you stab that woman in the back at Mornington Crescent underground station yesterday afternoon?' Frost feared that she was going to get a "no comment" interview. She was taking a gamble that this loudmouth wouldn't be able to keep his gob shut when challenged full on. She wanted him angry—it worked. Corbell was up on his feet, hands slamming down flat on the desk; his face inches from Frost's.

'I ain't stabbed nobody, you black bitch.' Frost raised a hand to Hodge to stay where he was.

'Sit down, Mr Corbell. The smell of your breath is making me want to vomit.' Adrian Harper grabbed his client's arm and pulled him back.

'DS Frost, insulting my client was not listed on your disclosure notice. Maybe we could concentrate on the evidence you have against him.' Frost knew she had Harper's respect at least, and had put Corbell exactly where she wanted him.

'Maybe we could start with why you were at Mornington Crescent London Underground station yesterday afternoon?' Corbell glanced at his solicitor, who gave a slight nod of his head as he noted the question.

'I was going to Camden Market.'

'A bit late in the day to be going to a market wasn't it?'

'I was going to meet some friends there and go for a few beers.'

'Can I ask you the names of these friends?'

'You can, but I ain't telling you.'

'You were first seen on the southbound Northern line platform. How were you going to get to Camden Town from there? You were heading in the wrong direction.'

'That's why I left the platform when those two thugs jumped on me.'

'Those "two thugs" caught up with you at the base of the stairs leading to the exit from the station.'

'I decided to get a bit of fresh air and walk. I get a bit claustrophobic on the tube. Suddenly, I've got these two geezers chasing me, and shouting at me to stop. I didn't know what they wanted with me. For all I know, they were going to turn me over; it's a dangerous place the underground, officer, you should know that.' Corbell—pleased with his answer—sneered at the two detectives.

'How did you get to Mornington Crescent station?'

'What d'ya mean?'

'It's a simple enough question Mr Corbell, even for you. Do you want me to repeat it?'

'I got a train from New Cross to London Bridge and then up on the Northern line.' Frost opened a folder in front of her and a retrieved photograph, which she passed first to Harper and then to Corbell.

'This is a still photograph marked exhibit MF/15 showing the northbound platform at Mornington Crescent station. As you can see, from the date in the top right-hand corner, this was recorded yesterday evening at 17.24hrs. Do you recognise anybody in that image, Mr Corbell?'

'No comment.'

'Well let me show you another image. MF/16 shows you entering New Cross station at 14.25hrs yesterday. Could you tell me where you were between 14.25 and 17.24hrs?'

'No comment.'

'It always amuses me when suspects pick and choose what they want to answer. Let me point out somebody in that first image I showed you, just in case you have missed it. That's you there, Mr Corbell, alighting from a northbound train some ten minutes before a young woman is murdered and thrown in front of a train on the southbound platform. You had no intention of travelling to Camden Town. You were on the underground station to steal from passengers, weren't you?'

'No comment'

'What happened? Did your intended victim fight back? You stabbed her in the back, before running away, like the coward you really are?' Corbell's face was red with rage. 'I think we'll take a short break, there Mr Corbell. You look as if you may need it. Have a chat with Mr Harper, mull over what we've said and think about telling us the truth.' Frost nodded at Sam Hodge to end the interview.

Chapter Thirty-Seven

It had taken Michael Brewster a couple of years, but he eventually tracked his sibling down. He'd spent another few months deciding what he should do next. Did he approach her and say, 'Hi I'm your baby brother?' Or maybe write, or just leave the past in the past and get on with his life. In the end, he did a bit of detective work to find out where his sibling lived, worked and socialised.

One morning he decided to pay a visit to her home address. He sat outside the house for the best part of two hours. He felt no emotion, no love, just curiosity. He wanted to find out if she'd had a better life than he had.

He eventually approached the house. There were no signs of life. He couldn't remain in the car any longer; he'd driven around a few times, but before long he would attract attention. Having prepared a cover story to use if he didn't like what he saw he tentatively knocked on the front door, but there was no reply. If he didn't find out now, he would probably never return. He slid down the side of the house. The backdoor was securely locked but he noticed the kitchen window was slightly ajar. Checking that nobody was watching, he unlatched the window and climbed through. What he was about to discover would change his life forever.

*

Frost and Hodge sat in the CID office, plotting the next stage of the interview when Ryan McNally joined them.

'How did it go you two?'

'OK. I think. He *is* a top-grade arsehole. We left him with a few things to think about and discuss with his Brief. If I'm honest with you, sir, and I think Sam will back me up on this, I really don't think Corbell is our man. He has never used a knife before, or been in possession of one during any previous arrest. If he had a knife, where is it? Everywhere has been thoroughly searched

155

and we know he never left the station. The only thing he tried to ditch was his mobile. He's got a big gob, a temper and contempt for women but I don't think he's our killer.

'I think you're right, Corbell isn't our murderer. But he may well have seen our killer. There were fresh blood stains on the inside of the lift, they've been sent to the lab for analysis. If it's our victim's blood or even our killer, it rules him out of it, as we know Corbell didn't enter the lift after Valerie Huxley met her death. He ran from the platform and was detained at the base of the stairs. When police arrived, he was arrested and walked up the stairs, as he was being so abusive. Get back in there and put him under a bit more pressure. Keep winding him up and see if he lets anything slip.'

McNally travelled back to his office from the police station. Nigel Plummer stuck his head around the door looking pleased with himself.

'Ryan, I've enlisted the services of an offender profiler. Her name is Doctor Sara Hallam. She's on her way over to Camden, should be here later this afternoon. What's with the facial expressions? We need all the help we can get with this, unless you're a bloody expert on serial killers all of a sudden.'

'I worked with a profiler on a series of rapes we had in the north west a few years back, sent us off on a completely different course of investigation—waste of bloody time. I just think it's a bit early; we haven't even, definitely, linked any of these murders together yet.'

'Well give it a try. When we get the inevitable outside force come in, and review the investigation, I don't want them asking why we didn't get a profiler on board early.' Plummer turned and left before McNally could make any excuses.

'Fucking typical, all he wants is to cover his own arse.'

Chapter Thirty-Eight

Hodge gave Frost the thumbs up that the visual and audible recording equipment was playing ball.

'This is the continuation of an interview with Daniel Corbell at Central London police station.'

'The time is 12.45. Mr Corbell, I must remind you that you are still under caution. Do you understand that?' Corbell nodded.

'I have in front of me a still from a CCTV camera on the southbound platform at Mornington Crescent station labelled MF/20, which shows you running from the platform just after a woman called Valerie Huxley was stabbed and thrown under the wheels of a train. Do you acknowledge that the person in this image is you?'

'No comment.'

'It appears that you are holding an object in your right hand. Can you tell me what that was and where is it now?'

'Well it obviously ain't a knife dripping in blood is it, Sherlock?' Corbell sat back in his chair, tipping it onto its back legs, a clever smirk spread across his face.

'What do you actually find funny about all of this? Is it that a young woman has been stabbed and pushed under a train, or indeed, the fact that you find yourself in this police station under arrest on suspicion of committing that murder? You tell me?'

'You're struggling. You've got nothing on me—no blood on my clothes, no weapon, and by the sound of it, any eye-witness. I'm a thief. That's what I do for a living. I don't carry a knife and I don't kill women, just steal from them.'

'So you're telling me that you were at Mornington Crescent station for the purposes of stealing from passengers, is that it?' Corbell looked at Adrian Harper, who nodded.

'Yeah that's right.'

'I'll ask you again—can you tell me what the object is in your hand as you fled from the scene?'

'It's a purse.'

'I presume it's not yours. Where did you get it from? Just tell me the whole story and stop playing silly buggers and wasting our time, whilst a murderer is still out there.' Harper whispered into his client's ear. Corbell nodded his agreement.

'I usually work between Leicester Square and Tottenham Court Road stations.'

'When you say *work,* what do you mean by that?'

'Thieving, you know, dipping—stealing. Anyway I saw this woman at Leicester Square. She was obviously loaded, nice clothes and shoes—really classy. She had this fastened shoulder bag over her right shoulder. I moved behind her as a train came in. I had the strap fastening half undone, but she felt the movement of the bag, I suppose, and started to turn around to look behind her as she boarded the train. Normally I would back off, but she was perfect— rich and foreign. If they're foreign the CPS don't usually go with the job, because it costs too much money to drag a witness back for any trial.'

'I followed her on for a second go. It took a couple of stations, with people getting on and off, before I could get right behind her again. I got my hand under the flap of the bag, but she turned around and fronted me out. I just backed off and jumped out at the next station, which just happened to be Mornington Crescent; just my fucking luck, the same station that some lunatic was stabbing people.'

'Go on.'

'Well at first I thought, where the fuck *am* I? I followed the signs to go back south. When I got on the southbound platform, to return back to Leicester Square, it was quite crowded and I picked up on another punter. I got a couple of feet behind her and the train came into the platform. By now, I had tunnel-vision, nobody else existed, just me, her and her bag. Next thing I know I heard a scream from my right and the train slamming on its brakes—perfect for me as it caused a load of confusion. I was in her bag and out with the purse in a split second. I weren't going to hang around so I scarpered. As I left the platform I put the purse down the back of my trousers. I don't know the station that well, whereas Leicester Square and Tottenham Court Road I know all the escape routes. That's why those two blokes caught me. I hesitated about which way to go and bang they were on top of me. Then one of them said he was a copper. I thought fuck it. They searched my outer clothing quickly, as did the uniform bods who turned up.'

'Did you see the incident to your right? You must have looked that way when the woman screamed?'

'No, not really, I told you, when I was happy there were none of your lot around, I zeroed in on the bag. I wasn't looking at anything else.'

'So why did you run?' Hodge asked.

'Well, why do you think? I got a purse in my hand, I'm wanted on warrant and I knew the "old bill" were going to be all over the place in minutes. It's just my luck that some plod from Surrey put two and two together and come up with ten—wanker.'

'How do we know this just isn't some story you've made up in the cells last night? You said you stuck the purse down the back of your trousers before you were detained. The purse wasn't on you when you were stripped searched, and your clothes removed in the custody suite, so if your story is true, where *is* the purse?' Corbell looked at his brief, unable to keep the smarmy look off his face.

'Your lot didn't have a proper wagon to take me to the nick, so they put me in the back of a patrol car on my own. I was handcuffed behind me. I got the purse out and stuck it down the back of the car seat; it's probably still there.'

Chapter Thirty-Nine

He stood in the middle of the small, dated, kitchen holding his breath, listening to his heart pounding in his chest. Confident he was alone in the house, Brewster slowly moved into the living room, using the stealth and balance he had relied on in the Royal Marines. He picked up a copy of yesterday's *Daily Mirror* from an armchair before replacing it where he had found it.

He walked into the hallway and saw the safety chain on the door was not secured, giving him confidence that his sister was definitely not at home. He was tempted to shout 'hello' but thought it absurd, what if somebody returned his welcome? What would he say then?

The smell in the house was not unfamiliar to him, taking him back to the age of two, when he last had any contact with her. He looked around for photographs of her and maybe of his birth parents. He was frustrated at the room's bareness. Brewster wondered if she'd ever given him a thought over the years. She had a comfortable life. He had few prospects, a dead-end job and a rented one-bedroomed flat.

He looked at the stairs leading to the first floor, within three strides he was at the base with a hand on the banister. He willed himself to climb, but something was stopping him. An invisible barrier that was sub-consciously saying this was wrong.

He returned to the living room and started a search for information: photographs, letters, anything that connected his dismal existence to a sister, a family, and a sense of belonging. He found a framed photograph, in a draw of a dresser, of a woman—who he presumed to be his sister—sharing a smile with an unknown man. They looked happy. He recorded the image on his mobile and moved on. He opened a cupboard and removed a lid from a box which contained an amount of correspondence. He felt a little sick. Among important documents, including house insurance and title deeds, was a letter. It took him some time to read its contents. It was evident that it was a letter addressed to him. A letter she'd never sent, or ever intended him to read. It simply started: *Dear George.*

Chapter Forty

Two uniformed police constables, who'd taken Daniel Corbel into custody from the Surrey officer, stood rigid in front of Ryan McNally's desk, hands strategically clasped in front of their genitals, anticipating that they were about to get them chewed off—they weren't wrong.

'Why the hell was the car not searched when the prisoner was taken into custody?' Both PCs looked at their feet. Making eye contact with the detective inspector was not an option either of them considered. 'Well, one of you, offer me an explanation. Is that not standard procedure or have things changed so dramatically since I was in uniform?'

'It was my, fault, sir' offered the younger of the two constables, who glanced in the direction of his partner. 'I was the passenger and placed the prisoner in the back seat. We couldn't get proper prisoner transport; all were on other shouts. The prisoner was pretty aggressive, so I decided to use our vehicle to get him down the nick ASAP. I took him into custody and should have returned to the vehicle straight away to search the backseats, but I got carried away a bit, having arrested somebody on suspicion of murder.'

McNally picked up the sealed property bag containing a purse, recovered from the patrol car. He sat back in his chair, manipulating the bag until he could examine the purse's contents. He threw the bag back onto his desk and looked at the two PCs directing his next question at the older one.

'Is your mate right? About what happened?'

'Yes, sir, but I take just as much responsibility. My colleague took the prisoner into custody. I could've easily searched the back of the car myself.'

McNally sighed and swivelled his chair around, so he was looking out of his window, and rubbed his face with his hands, as if trying to wash away this disaster. He returned back to face the officers.

'This, I would imagine, is a big learning curve for you both. If you'd come into my office with some bullshit excuse, I would've had your jobs.' Both officers nodded. 'Go and give this bag to DC Graves. Make sure you sign the bag for continuity before you do so, and fuck off out of my sight.' He waited for the relieved officers to shut the door behind them, before he dialled Frost's number.

'Marcia, are you still in the custody suite?'

'Yes, guv.'

'Can you talk?'

'Yep.'

'I've just had the uniformed officers in my office—they found the purse. It was stuck right down behind the backseat.'

'Looks like Corbell *is* telling the truth. What d'ya want me to do with him?'

'Charge him with the theft of the purse and the bail offence. Speak to Graves and get the victim's details, she has probably already reported it. He'll appear before Southwark Crown Court this afternoon. See if you can contact the victim. She may well be a witness to the murder. She would've been standing only a few feet away.'

'OK, sir, will do. I'll see you back at Camden in about an hour.' McNally rubbed his temples in a circular motion before opening his desk and retrieving some *Paracetamol*, which he swallowed with the dregs of a cup of coffee. He lay back in his chair with his eyes closed for a moment, when he heard the *Big Brother* ringtone of his mobile phone.

'Ryan, its Neil Williams. I got some good news for you.'

'I could do with some, mate.'

'My search team had all the drain covers up within one-hundred metres of the station. We got lucky, one of the last we were going to search on Eversholt Street, about fifty meters from the station, was blocked with leaves just under the grate. When we removed it, we found a blue handled knife with a 15cm curved blade. It appears to have bloodstaining on it. One of my team used to be a butcher. He says it's a boning knife, used to fillet meat and fish; looks like we might have our murder weapon. Sally Cook is on her way to package it up and get it off to the lab.'

'I don't suppose our luck runs to a CCTV camera in the location?'

'There are a few big houses around the area and a hotel a few metres down the road. I'd get your enquiry team down here to knock on a few doors. You might just strike a bullseye. That's us done here, Ryan. I'll get the officers who found the knife, to make statements and get them over to the incident room. We got another job on so it'll probably be tomorrow—good luck, mate, anything else we can do give me a ring.'

'Thanks, Neil, catch up soon.'

*

DC Jim Wakefield sat in the CCTV viewing room, just off the main incident room, reviewing dozens of DVDs collected in his sweep of CCTV systems in the local area surrounding Mornington Crescent station and the station cameras themselves. He had other officers reviewing footage from London Bridge and Putney Bridge half an hour before and after the incidents resulting in the deaths of Ruth Ward and Laura Marston. They were looking for a suspect—somebody present at all three locations.

On instructions from McNally, Wakefield deployed one officer to liaise with Inspector Neil Williams by telephone, and conduct a search for CCTV cameras that may cover the area of Eversholt Street, where the possible murder weapon was dumped. Whilst balancing so many spinning plates, Wakefield's mobile rang.

'Yes.'

'PC Wakefield?'

'Yes. How can I help?'

'This is Devon Lorne.'

'I'm sorry, sir, the name rings a bell but…'

'You left me a message to ring you. I've been in Jamaica for the last couple of weeks. When I booked on duty today, I was told by my supervisor to ring you urgently. I believe it's something to do with an incident at Lambeth North station. My boss wouldn't elaborate further. I haven't worked there for twenty or so years so I'm not sure if I can help. Can you tell me what it's all about?' Wakefield moved back to his desk in the incident room to find his notebook, and turned a few pages.

'Mr Lorne…yes…sorry about that, sir. I've been moved onto another enquiry and I've got lots of names spinning around in my head. Could I make an appointment to see you—if possible—later this afternoon?'

'Just a moment please' Wakefield heard the muffled sound of conversation through a hand covering the speaker.

164

'This is my first shift back and I'm running spare, so my boss is happy for me to help you. When and where would you like to meet?' Wakefield looked at his wristwatch. It was already 1.30pm. Lunch had been and gone, a rumbling stomach reminded him of the fact.

'You're based at Seven Sisters, I believe. Would you be able to travel down to me at Camden Town as soon as you can?' Muffled voices followed again.

'Yes. I'll be there within the hour.' Wakefield thanked him and gave directions. He needed to eat before his arrival; otherwise he would be good for nothing.

Chapter Forty-One

McNally bought Frost and Hodge up to date with the latest developments on the investigation.

'Marcia, speak to Sally Cook. Make sure she is fast-tracking the analysis of the blood on the knife. I want to know if it belongs to our victim, also the blood found in the lift. Is it our victims? In the meantime, get Marie Relish to make some enquiries into the knife itself: who manufactures it, where in London it can be purchased? I know I'm jumping the gun on this a bit. We can't be sure if this *is* our murder weapon yet, it could be from a gang stabbing—we've got enough in London at the moment—but from what Neil Williams said, it sounds like a specialist knife, probably used in the food trade. I want to get ahead of this.' A knock on the door interrupted McNally's thought process. He beckoned Ray Blendell in.

'Sorry, guv, just to let you know Sara Hallam is here...the offender profiler from City University. I've given her a coffee and sat her with Marie Relish, who's bringing her up to date with what we have so far.'

'Thanks, Ray, I'll be out in a minute.'

'An offender profiler—really? Frost looked at McNally. 'An academic, whose read a few crime novels?' This brought a smile to McNally's face.

'I know Marcia. I've worked with one before and the experience wasn't great but I'm always up for somebody else's perspective on what we've got here. Sometimes we think we've got every angle covered, until somebody else points out the blindingly obvious. Grab her Sam and show her in? Get Marie Relish to come in as well.'

McNally took a moment to read a message from Kate: *Back home kids OK don't forget Saturday for the works meal. I really want to go. Hopefully C U later x.*

The last profiler McNally had worked with was short, fat and needed to get out more. Sara Hallam was a breath of fresh air. McNally stood and offered his hand. She responded with a firm grip. She was a little shorter than him, about 5'10, with straight red hair, pulled back and fastened. Her nose was slightly off centre, her eyes bright green and very alert. She was dressed in a smart dark brown business suit covering a crisp white open-necked blouse. McNally invited her to sit down. He guessed her age to be about thirty to thirty-five and she radiated confidence.

'Thank you for coming so quickly, Miss Hallam. I'm really pleased that we've got you on board so early in the investigation.'

'Why, Inspector! I would hope you're a better liar in court, but sorry, of course, policemen never lie.' She smiled, showing slightly uneven white teeth. 'Call me Sara please and by the way it's Doctor; years of studying and a thesis as long as a novel qualifies me for that honour, so I might as well use it. Here's my card.' McNally turned the crisp white business card over in his hand.

'That's a lot of letters after your name. I believe you lecture at City University?'

'Yes. I'm currently lecturing on the Criminology and Psychology course to second and third year students; it's an interesting job, but this is what I love, being out in the field practising what I preach—it also looks good on my CV. That doesn't sound like a London accent. You're obviously not from these parts, Inspector.'

'Please, it's Ryan, and you're right. I'm from Manchester; been down here for about a year now, still haven't got my head around the *apples and pears* dialect yet—probably never will.' A knock on the door signalled the arrival of Marie Relish.

'Sorry, sir, I had a couple of phone calls to deal with.' She pulled up a seat, notebook at the ready.

'Have you had a chance to look at what we have so far?'

'Marie has given me a quick summary, but I would obviously like to study witness statements in more detail and visit the crime scenes.'

'Of course, I'll sort you a desk out somewhere. I'd appreciate you attending the 5pm briefing tonight to keep you up to speed—things are starting to move pretty quickly. Have you any initial thoughts?'

'I'd prefer to have a look at some more material before I commit myself to anything that's going to come back and bite me.' McNally liked the psychologist and saw her as a person he might be able to bounce ideas and theories off, to which, he would receive an honest answer.

'Have you ever led an investigation into a serial killer before…Ryan?'

'It's not something we come across frequently in this country is it—especially on the railway network. Is that your early impression that we've a serial killer on the loose?'

'Well firstly, what is a serial killer? We see them bandied around on our TV screens often enough. The academic definition is: a person or persons that kill more than three victims in a period of over thirty days. This differentiates them from say a killing spree that has little or no planning, such as some of the recent terrorist knife attacks we have seen around the country. The murders you're investigating are thought out and planned, as far as I can see. The different geographic locations are a problem for me, and you, I would suggest. Is there a specific reason the killer chose each particular station? I also need to look at the victims; ethnicity, age, gender are all going to be important. Marie mentioned that they all had blond hair. Were they connected by interests, professions, occupations or social activities?'

'I asked Marie, initially, to look at connections between the victims along the lines that you've mentioned—nothing particularly stands out, except rough age and hair colour.'

'The victim's gender and the locations of the murders are also relevant. I think the best approach would be to consider the location as the 'London Underground' rather than the individual stations. That's something I'll have to consider.' McNally nodded his agreement.

'How long will it take to give us a summary of your initial findings and a profile of our killer?'

'I would hope to give you some direction by tomorrow. As for your first remark about serial killers on public transport, the case that really kick-started offender profiling in this country was the railway rapist case back in the 1980s, when a number of rapes and murders on or in the vicinity of railway stations took place. But I would imagine you were still in school uniform then, Ryan.' Relish let out a squeak, which she tried to muffle with a hand over her mouth, but her eyes gave her amusement away.

'Okay, Sara, that's fair enough. May be we can get our heads together after the briefing. In the meantime, Marie will make sure you have everything that you need.'

McNally re-read the message from Kate. He would make an effort to get out of here after the briefing and get home—he needed to see his family. His mobile vibrated. It was Graves.

'Guv, I've got a car in the yard. The post-mortem is set for 15.30. We need to get a move on.'

'Be right down.' He thought it best not to text Kate back with a time he hoped to be home—she wouldn't believe him anyway.

Chapter Forty-Two

P.C Jim Wakefield was glad of a break from CCTV screens. He grabbed a tea and a coffee from the canteen, and went down a couple of floors to the ground floor level and into a small interview room off the reception area.

Devon Lorne was a big man with square shoulders and a clamp-like handshake, which Wakefield tried to reciprocate. He had a welcoming smile and looked immaculate in his London Underground uniform. His hair was short and grey, with a well-trimmed, grey, goatee beard.

'Hi, Mr Lorne thanks for coming down to see me. We're rushed off our feet at the moment. I have tea or coffee. Which would you prefer?'

'Tea would be great thanks. It's not a problem. Having spent a few weeks in Jamaica I wasn't particularly looking forward to getting back into the cab of a tube train and not seeing the light of day for eight hours. I work on the Victoria Line—all underground.' Wakefield nodded. 'Are you working on this murder at Mornington Crescent—terrible business? I feel for the lady, but also the train driver. I've had a couple of jumpers in my time—not a nice experience.'

'Yes, it's pretty hectic at the moment. The reason I asked you to come in to see me is, a body was found at Lambeth North station a couple weeks ago. You probably wouldn't be aware of its discovery, as you've been out of the country. It'd been buried under some railway ballast in a tunnel, a few metres from the lift shaft and been there for, we believe, twenty years. We've now identified the remains to be those of a former station supervisor—Liam Brennan. Did you know Mr Brennan?' Devon Lorne took a sip of his tea before placing it back on the table; the smile had disappeared from his face.

'Liam Brennan?' Wakefield got a picture of the deceased and showed it to Lorne who was thinking hard. He removed a pair of silver-framed glasses from a case, and put them on.

'Yes, I think I did know him, briefly. I was a station assistant back in the early 2000s and worked mainly at Elephant and Castle on the Bakerloo line, but would often cover shifts when people were on holiday or sick. I think I only worked directly with him on a couple of occasions.'

'Do you remember, what was originally thought to be, a burglary of the station's booking office, in which Brennan was the main suspect?'

'Yes, I have a vague memory of that. When was it?'

'February 2000.'

'I'd moved onto the trains in September 1999, so I must've read about the burglary and Brennan's disappearance.'

'What was he like? Did he get on with the rest of the staff?'

'As I say, it was a long time ago, but I remember he was a bit weird. He got on better with male staff. He could be quite antagonistic to the ladies. I think he was a bit of a misogynist.'

'Can you remember a male staff member called Patrick Mullen?'

'Yes I do—Irish guy. I met him at Elephant and Castle. He was there for a bit. Funny, now you mention his name. He and Brennan never got on, always arguing about Irish politics, nearly came to blows one late turn. I had to split them up. Have you spoken to Patrick? He will obviously be able to help you more than I can?'

'Sadly not, Patrick Mullen died of a heart attack in 2004.'

'Oh, that's really sad. I heard he'd got married the year before I think it was. He married a female member of staff he met somewhere.'

'Can you remember any of the women who worked regularly at the station?' Wakefield asked.

'There were two women. One was a lovely Nigerian lady; she used to bring food in. I remember a dish called *Jollof Rice*. She said it was a culinary symbol of her home country—rice cooked in a tomato sauce. The following night I returned the favour with a goat curry, nearly blew her head off.' Lorne laughed, his huge smile filled the room.

'What was the other woman called?'

'Elizabeth Wood—blond hair, quite attractive. Yes, that was her, but she didn't use the first name Elizabeth because it was the same as her mother's, who she apparently hated.'

'What name did you know her by?'

'I remember her telling me that her middle name was Charlotte; her mother had a thing about naming her kids after kings and queens.' Wakefield again glanced at his notes recalling the initials on the letter he'd seen at Wood's house:

E.M.C Wood. 'Charlotte was a bit of a mouthful, so she liked to be called Charlie. I remember her telling me that she had a younger brother, who'd died. He was called George.

Chapter Forty-Three

McNally and Graves got to the mortuary with fifteen minutes to spare. They were met at the door by Family Liaison Officer Julie Barber, who was standing next to a man in his sixties, who looked gaunt and was smoking like a chimney. They were accompanied by a younger man, who bore a strong resemblance to the other.

'Hi, Sir, this is Jeffrey Huxley—Valerie Huxley's father and her brother Tom.' McNally introduced himself as the Senior Investigating Officer and offered his condolences.

'The formal identification of Valerie has just taken place. I was about to take Mr Huxley and his son back home to Clapham.'

'Thanks, Julie. Mr Huxley, I will make sure that I pass on as much information about our progress with the investigation into your daughter's murder via Julie as often as I can and, I assure you, that you are at the forefront of my officers' and my own thoughts in relation to everything we do. If you've any questions, please speak to Julie and she'll report to me.' Jeffrey Huxley looked as if he was about to speak but was unable to get any of the words out.

'Have you got any suspects yet Inspector?' McNally turned to Tom Huxley. 'I heard reports that you had a man in custody.'

'Yes, we did have Mr Huxley, but he has been charged with other offences not relating to your sister's death. We are scanning CCTV footage of the scene. The killer must be on tape somewhere. We've also discovered a possible murder weapon, although I must stress, this has not been confirmed yet. So we've a lot of leads to follow. We'll be issuing a press release, either tonight or tomorrow, as well as utilising social media outlets for witnesses to come forward.'

'Are you going to be present as they cut my sister up?' McNally tuned into the emotion and simmering anger the brother was trying to keep a lid on.

'A post mortem is a necessary procedure to allow the coroner and indeed you, the relatives, and us, the investigators, to ascertain the exact cause of your sister's death.' He thought, as he said it, that it sounded like some sort of managerial sound-bite from a training course that people, like Plummer, would use; but he meant every word.

'Julie will notify you when the coroner is prepared to release your sister, so that you can make the necessary arrangements.' Julie Barber led the two men away back to her car.

'The brother was a bit touchy, guv.'

'Stuart, don't ever consider putting in for a FLO course in the future will you. I'm not sure you could even spell the word *empathy*. Come on. Let's get this over and done with.'

*

Hodge turned the volume of the car radio up a notch. He and Frost were heading south to St Paul's Cathedral. Frost had hardly spoken a word throughout the journey. Hodge decided it better to leave her to stew rather than offer her any words of wisdom, not that he could think of any at that precise moment. The lyrics of *Queen's—I Want to Break Free* weren't helping her mood so Hodge pushed the mute button. The silence was deafening.

'What you up to at the weekend, sarge?'

'The same as you, I would imagine: work, sleep, work, sleep.'

'We'll probably get one day off, I should think.'

'You're ever the optimist, Sam.' Hodge swerved to miss a black cab pulling out of a turning to his left and sounded his horn. He got the standard London reply—a middle finger pointing to the heavens.

'Fucking cabbies think they own the bloody road.' This brought a hint of a smile to Frost's face.

'He got right under your skin didn't he—Corbell?'

'He was an arsehole. At least, he won't be going anywhere for a while. Sometimes I wonder why we do this job, Sam. Doesn't the abuse, we get, ever bother you?'

'Sometimes, I suppose. The personal stuff doesn't bother me much, but it can grate a bit when someone calls your mother a whore or your wife a slag— not that I'm married. The racial stuff was a bit out of order. I thought you handled that really well. In the end, you got out of him what you wanted. I think we both knew early on he was no killer—just a piece of south London shit.'

'Hey, you—I'm from south London,' she protested with a devilish smile on her face.

'Yeah, but you're south west that's a bit posher than south east.'

'True.'

'What did this witness sound like to you—genuine?'

'Yeah, I think so. She works in the Club Quarters Hotel on Ludgate Hill. She sounds like she's Romanian, or something, when I spoke to her on the phone. She didn't want to meet in the hotel, said her boss was a bit funny about having the police around—not good for business apparently.'

'Why was she at Mornington Crescent station?'

'She's got a boyfriend, who lives on Crowndale Road a few minutes from the station—she spent the day with him. He works in a local restaurant. She was on her way to work for a night shift on the hotel reception.' Hodge turned left onto Ludgate Hill. The unmistakable dome of St Paul's dominated the skyline.

'Not sure I've ever been inside the cathedral. Have you?'

'I went on a school trip once. All I can remember is the schools liaison officer, who showed us around, had a voice like a trumpet. You should go in with the girlfriend, Sam—might bring the inner Christian out in you.'

'Where we gonna park. We can't just dump the car outside?'

'Park in the taxi rank for now while I go and speak to the City cop—don't piss the black cab drivers off while I've gone.'

'Given half a chance it would be my pleasure.' Hodge watched Frost present her warrant card and then wave a beckoning arm in his direction. The uniformed officer moved a bollard and directed them to an area on the north side of the cathedral, where a number of works vans were parked. Hodge put a blue police sign on the dashboard, locked the car up and joined Frost at the top of the stairs leading down to the crypt.

A man-mountain of a security guard carried out a superficial search of Frost's handheld leather document case and asked them both to undo their jackets. Once satisfied they weren't about to blow the cathedral up, he allowed them to continue down into the crypt.

Frost took a seat at a table, allowing a view of the stairs leading from ground-level. Hodge went and bought a couple of hot drinks.

'Bloody hell!' Hodge returned with two takeaway cups. 'Have you seen the prices in here? Glad you didn't want something to eat—if she turns up she can buy her own.'

'I suppose your idea of a treat for your girlfriend is a McDonald's and a take away coffee. Anyway the last time we were out together, I bought *you* breakfast—remember?'

'Yeah, I remember. The same breakfast that half an hour later was heaved up and sprayed all over the bonnet of the car.'

A large group of rotund, breathless, American tourists entered the crypt, led by a guide holding a closed yellow umbrella high in the air. One couple in the group were exasperated that Christopher Wren hadn't built the cathedral nearer the tube station. The group followed their guide deeper into the bowels of the crypt, which was surprisingly well-lit and airy.

Frost saw a dark-haired women looking around, before their eyes locked on each other, realising they had found who they were seeking.

'Madalina?' The young woman nodded and took a seat. She was aged between twenty five and thirty, Frost guessed. She was dressed in a smart uniform. Her makeup and hair were immaculate. She looked around inquisitively and relaxed as she saw they were in no one else's earshot. Frost looked at Sam Hodge, who was having trouble keeping his lower jaw from hitting his chest.

'You must be detective Frost—yes?'

'Yes, that's me. Please call me Marcia. My colleague is called Sam,' they both showed their identification. 'It was very good of you to firstly call in, and then to meet us at such short notice.'

'That's OK, I a little nervous. In my country, Romania, you don't sit down with two police officers and share drink.' Frost nudged Hodge in the ribs.

'Of course…yes…would you like a drink Madalina?' His faced reddened as he fumbled in his pocket to find some money, before nearly tripping arse over tit as he returned to the counter, looking back as he did. Both women smiled at each other.

'Madalina, you told me on the telephone that you were at Mornington Crescent station at the time a young lady was murdered; her name was in fact Valerie Huxley.' She nodded her head and took a deep breath.

'Are you OK, do you need a moment?'

'No, I'm fine, Marcia, just knowing young lady's name brings it a little home more—makes it a little bit more personal. I woke up last night, asking myself, if I really saw what I did. Hearing her name, make it very real for me.' Marcia covered Madalina's hand with her own. Her English was very good and Marcia loved the vulnerable naivety of it.

'How long have you been in this country?'

'Nearly five years now,' she eyed the detective suspiciously. Maria tightened her grip a little.

'Don't worry. We are not here to check on your immigration status— honestly. Watch out here comes your number one admirer with your coffee.' They both giggled and looked at Hodge, who again went the shade of a tomato.

'In your own time, please tell us what you saw. Do you mind if I record it at the same time?'

'I not suspect, am I?'

'No, of course not.'

'I spent day with my boyfriend, who works in local pub. He normally starts work at 6pm. I left his flat at 5.20pm—I was due to start work in the hotel at 6pm as well. I catch a train from Mornington Crescent, sometimes I walk up to Camden Town but time was bit tight. I change at Tottenham Court Road onto Central Line to get here. I was standing about halfway along the platform, just behind the yellow line, and reading a book. I think it was five minutes before the next train. I was aware of people behind me and to each side. Most regular passengers know where they need to stand to get off at their next stop.' She took a few deep breaths and received encouragement from the detectives.

'The train started to approach platform and I heard woman, who died, shouting out "What are you doing?" I looked at her, she seemed frightened. Behind her stood man with left arm around her waist. I first thought they together, but as train entered platform I saw him look towards it and I saw his right arm thrust forward towards her and the woman screamed and then disappear in front of train. Sound will live with me for the rest of my life.' Madalina placed both hands in front of her face and wept. Marcia grabbed a couple of serviettes from the table and passed them to her.

A very smart looking man with a ramrod straight back and shoulders, adorned with a red sash, and a St Paul's Cathedral guiding badge, approached the table.

'Everything OK here?' he enquired in perfect public school English. Sam Hodge stood, showed his warrant card and guided him a few feet away. The volunteer looked back pitifully at the poor young woman.

'I'm sorry for your loss, madam; would you like to speak to a priest?'

'That won't be necessary, thank you.' Marcia answered. Madalina looked oddly at Hodge, who just shrugged his shoulders.

'I had to tell him something.'

'Okay, Madalina. The worst part is over, getting that off your chest, sharing it with somebody else. What we need now is a full description—as much as you remember. Let's start with his physical appearance. I know you only had a quick glance, but just close your eyes, take a few deep breaths and try and put yourself back on that platform and play the whole thing again in your mind. Go on. I promise you it works.' Madalina did as she was asked.

'He was white, about mid to late forties, a little taller than me so 5'9" to 5'10".' She opened her eyes. 'Sorry I can't recall anything else.'

'Did you hear him speak to the victim?' Madalina turned to Hodge and shook her head.

'Okay, Madalina, what about his clothing or anything distinguishable about him?' She thought about Frost's question for a few minutes. Neither detective spoke, not wishing to interrupt her thought process.

'He had hat covering his head, which came down to above eyes, it was very tight-fit.'

'Did it have a bobble on top?'

'No it didn't. At least, I don't think so.'

'What about colour, can you remember that?'

'Dark, maybe dark blue or black; sorry I need go to toilet.' Madalina walked further into the crypt to locate the ladies' toilet. The detectives looked at each other.

'Sam, I want you to go upstairs,' Frost quickly glanced at her mobile. 'You won't get a signal down here, and speak to Ray Blendell. Firstly, give him the description of our suspect and get him to pass it onto Jim Wakefield and his CCTV team and secondly, after you have taken a statement, arrange for an e-fit for Madalina. I think she finishes work at 6pm today. We need it doing tonight— you stay with her until it's done.'

'It's a shit job, sarge, but I suppose somebody's got to do it; what about the 5pm briefing?'

'I'll be there for that. I'll bring you up to date later on, when the e-fit has been done.' Both detectives looked at their witness as she returned to the table. She smiled gingerly at them.

'I think I have remembered something else about him. As he passed me, I thought I smell fish.'

Chapter Forty-Four

Ryan McNally and Stuart Graves filled their lungs with a sharp intake of London air as they left the mortuary, flushing away the smell of death from their nostrils.

'Don't matter how many of these examinations you attend, guv, you never really get used to that smell do you?'

'No, not really, the body on the next slab, found floating in the Regents Canal for a few days, didn't help did it?' McNally looked at his watch. 'I'll drive Stuart. Give Ray Blendell a ring will you, put the briefing back to 5.30pm, we should just get back in time for that. It's been a long day. I'll try and get the troops off at a reasonable time. I don't want anybody falling by the wayside.' Five minutes into the journey back to Camden, McNally's phone rang, transferring it onto the hands free; he answered.

'Guv, its Jim Wakefield. Can you talk?'

'Yes, Jim, it's just me and Stuart in the car.'

'Got a break on the Lambeth North enquiry; the train driver, Devon Lorne, contacted me this afternoon. He's just come back from a few weeks in Jamaica. I interviewed him at Camden. He didn't spend a great deal of time at Lambeth, just covering shifts now and again but he can remember Liam Brennan and Patrick Mullen and that Mullen had married another member of LU staff.' McNally turned the car onto Euston Road.

'Go on.'

'He also remembered Elizabeth Wood, but she used the name Charlie, short for Charlotte, one of her middle names. When I interviewed her last week, the last thing I asked her was if she knew Patrick Mullen. If you remember, she categorically denied it. When I was snooping around her front room, when she was on the telephone, I saw a picture of her and a man in one of the only photographs anywhere in the house. In that image, she was wearing an engagement ring, the same one she was wearing when I interviewed her. I called up a contact at London Underground and asked if they still had a picture of

Mullen—they sent one over. I then did a few enquiries with the Burnt Oak registry office. The man in that picture was Patrick Mullen. They were married in 2003.'

Chapter Forty-Five

The incident room was rammed full. Personnel filled all the available chairs, sat on desks and filled doorways; a lot had happened in the last twenty-four hours. Nobody wanted to miss out on this briefing. McNally and Graves had just made it back to Camden in time. McNally took a huge gulp from a lukewarm cup of coffee, before addressing his staff.

'Before I get on with the briefing, I want to welcome those who have joined us since yesterday including POLSA Neil Williams, offender profiler Doctor Sara Hallam and the additional divisional CID officers pulled in from various places around the country.'

'I know you've all been working extremely hard, but there are areas I must cover tonight before a few of us *might* get the chance to go home. I want to start with the post-mortem examination of Valerie Huxley, carried out this afternoon at St Pancras mortuary, which Stuart and I attended. The pathologist confirmed the presence of an upper thrust stab wound to the lower thorax just below the rib cage, piercing the kidney, which, he said, is basically a blood sponge. There would have been a considerable, instant, amount of blood emanating from the wound which, the pathologist believes, would be evident on the weapon and most likely on the offender. The knife, in his opinion, had a thin blade about four inches in length with a serrated edge. There is some bruising around the entry point, indicative of the blade being inserted up to the handle with great force. He was unable to say if this wound had been the cause of death, as she was struck by the train so quickly after the initial attack, but the wound would've been fatal in its own right, if she had lived any longer.'

McNally looked around the room before taking another gulp of coffee to give all present time to take in what he'd just said—many scribbled notes for later reference. He continued.

'The injuries, that Valerie Huxley suffered, under the wheels of the train, were catastrophic. We've all seen similar injuries in our careers, so I see no need to expand on those. The pathologist was of the opinion that the killer either got extremely lucky when administering the blow or more likely knew what he was doing. It worries me, and I'm pretty sure some of you are thinking the same, that if the deaths of Ruth Ward, Cheryl Meade, Laura Marston and now Valerie Huxley are all connected, why has our killer progressed to using a weapon? He could have just pushed her, as he did with the others.'

There was a silence in the room, as each and every person present pondered the very same conundrum. It was Sara Hallam who offered an explanation.

'On that point, Ryan, I would suggest that the use of a weapon was borne out of frustration. Frustration with the person these women represent, wanting to hurt them, to violate them more and more. Or even frustration, with you—the establishment—for not firstly recognising that these women were actually murdered and secondly, in his mind, you are no closer to catching him. It's possible he is irritated about not reading details of his crimes in the media. It's possible that he *wants* to be caught.'

'A lot of if's and but's there Professor.' Graves smiled.

'Agreed, arsehole, but they are possible explanations for suddenly using a weapon.'

'Hang on, I'm *no* arsehole.' Graves objected.

'And I'm *no* Professor.' The room erupted with laughter. Even Graves bowed his head in congratulatory gesture, knowing he had met his match.

'Alright,' McNally glanced at his watch. 'Let's calm down and go around the room, starting with Sally Cook our SOCO—Sally.'

'The knife found in the drain has been submitted to the lab for examination. Initial results confirm that it's human blood on the knife but blood grouping and DNA are going to take a little longer. I've asked them to fast-track it. I hope your budget can take it, dude?' A few sniggers circulated the room. Cook continued.

'There is some good news, and some bad news on the blood found in the lift at Mornington Crescent. The good news is that not only is it our victim's blood but also mixed with probably our killer's, who, I assume, must have cut himself on his own weapon. The lab techs have managed to create a DNA profile. The bad news is there is no match on the DNA national database. Hopefully by this time tomorrow, I'll be able to confirm, one way or the other, if the knife found is definitely our murder weapon.'

'Thanks, Sally let's stay on the knife found in…'

'Eversholt Street.'

'Thanks, Neil. Marie, any update on the knife?' Marie Relish brought up a picture of the recovered knife, which lay next to a ruler showing the blade to be four and a half inches in length.

'The knife does have a maker's mark '*Sabatier*' on the handle, quite hard to see on this particular image. *Sabatier* is a French company with a long history of making some of the best quality knives in the world. However the *Sabatier* brand name appeared well before the first French legislation concerning intellectual property rights, which means, in my understanding, everybody and their aunty can replicate the knife and mark it as *Sabatier*, which obviously doesn't help our efforts to pin down likely locations of purchase. Of course, for tracing purposes, it would have been better to have a specialised British make that can only be purchased in a handful of shops in the UK, but it still is a quality knife, not something you could buy in any hardware shop.'

'As I said to you on the phone, Ryan, one of my search team was a butcher in a previous life and recognises the shape and balance of the knife, which he believes would have been used for filleting meat or fish.'

'It's done a good job on the victim's kidney.' Graves was on a roll.

'Sally, any chance of finding fingerprints on the blade or handle?'

'I'm waiting for the knife to come back from the lab; obviously the fingerprint examination will have to take place last to preserve the DNA. The handle is quality wood, the blade, although long and thin, has potential for at least a partial print—I'll keep you updated on that.' McNally nodded his thanks.

'Marcia, you and Sam interviewed an eye witness this afternoon?'

'Yes sir. She is a Romanian national with excellent English.'

'I hear she made quite an impression on young Sam Hodge?' Ray Blendell shared.

'Yes, but of course let's all keep that one a secret shall we?' A few jeers went around the room. McNally enjoyed the break in the tension but needed to get back on track.

'Okay, quieten down, Marcia go on.'

'She was at Mornington Crescent station and witnessed what she thought at first was a row between two people who knew each other. She then heard a piercing scream before she saw Huxley fall in front of the train. There was a lot of pandemonium. The suspect passed her, he didn't run, just walked quickly, following other passengers leaving the platform and she lost sight of him. She's with Sam at the moment making an e-fit.' Marcia glared at Stuart Graves, daring him to make any inappropriate comment. He obviously thought better of it.

'She gave as good a description of our suspect as she could but he was wearing a tight "Beanie" type hat, which came down to just above his eye-line. One important point she belatedly remembered, as he brushed past her, his clothes smelt of fish.'

Chapter Forty-Six

Brewster parked the stolen car where he could see his sister's home clearly. It wouldn't be dark until gone 8pm. He looked at his watch, another forty-five minutes to go. There'd been no movement inside the house for the past hour.

He hadn't stolen a car since he was fifteen; he'd forgotten the adrenalin rush it gave him. Luckily he'd never been caught, otherwise, probably, no military career and would now be languishing in a prison cell somewhere. Taking the night off from work had been easy. He'd gone sick, telling his boss that the wound on his hand, that he had carried the night before, had gone septic and he needed a few days off.

An earlier visit to Silverman's army and navy surplus store on Mile End Road had provided him with a new knife. He slid the *Fairbairn Sykes* fighting knife out of its leather sheath, gripping the ring grip patterned handle firmly. Brewster rolled his sleeve up and pricked his forearm with the needle sharp end of the knife and watched a trickle of blood criss-cross the contours of veins and muscle, imagining that it was his mother's blood. He'd last held such a weapon in Afghanistan. The 7" blade reflected the orange light of the street lamps that flickered into life.

Since reading the letter he'd found addressed to him in this very house, his focus had changed—curiosity had been replaced by pure hate. This was a very special weapon for a very special person. He sank back in the driver's seat, listening to dusk birdsong and the constant flowing of a nearby stream and waited.

*

McNally looked at his watch again, time was passing fast. The likelihood of him getting home to see Ava and Max before they went to bed was diminishing. He turned to Jim Wakefield.

'Jim, CCTV.'

'I've gone through the images at Mornington Crescent, following the description given by Marcia's witness.' Wakefield produced a compilation of five images on the incident room's TV screen. 'This, I believe, is our man. The first image shows him entering the station at 17.15hrs. He is wearing the hat described by the witness and a distinctive blue tracksuit top with a white stripe down the sleeve.'

'That's bears out my theory about being organised and an element of planning,' Hallam pointed out. 'This was no random attack. He was on that platform a good fifteen to twenty minutes before he identified his victim, which suggests he was looking for a little more than a woman with blond hair. She had to be a certain type, possibly in relation to age and build as well as hair colour.'

Wakefield continued. 'The second has him walking on the platform, so I assume he walked down the stairs, as he doesn't appear on the camera emerging from the lift. The third is him leaving the platform after the incident with several other passengers. The next shows him with his head down in the lift as he travels to the booking hall; again the lift is packed but you will notice that he is standing next to the poster the boss found the blood on. He probably used the lift because of the commotion going on at the base of the stairs. Lastly, we have him leaving the station at 17.42. These are stills I have just taken from the CCTV footage with the limited equipment I have. I'll get the tapes over to the tec guys to see if they can enhance the images.'

Wakefield was enjoying himself and struggling to contain his enthusiasm. 'In relation to the weapon, found on Eversholt Street by the search team, I decided to go down there myself, late this afternoon, when the briefing was put back, and struck lucky.' Wakefield inserted a DVD and loaded some images onto the screen. 'This is footage from a camera inside the reception of the Crescent Hotel looking out onto Eversholt Street, about fifteen metres from the drain where the knife was discovered. When I first viewed it, there was nothing of interest until the security manager informed me they hadn't forwarded the clock on the security system in late March, so I went forward one hour. You'll see a figure coming from left to right. The time on the sequence is 16.45hrs which is obviously 17.45hrs.' Wakefield froze the footage; everybody looked at the image in complete silence.

'It's the same blue tracksuit top, with white stripe running down the sleeve, as our man in the beanie hat. Unfortunately the angle of the camera doesn't give us an image above the shoulders.' He ran the tape onto 17.47hrs. 'Here he is again, returning towards Camden High Street and the station two minutes later.'

'Well done, Jim' McNally said. 'We'll need to look at what CCTV we have available for the other murders, see if we can pick him up at those locations.'

'We'll make a detective of you yet,' Graves added sarcastically.

'I think he's building up to something—a final act, an end to what started all this madness for him.' Everybody turned to face Sara Hallam, after her put down of Stuart Graves earlier, everybody wanted to hear what she had to say next.

'Go on, Sara.'

'I've been looking at all the evidence, you know, statements from witnesses, scene photographs and, of course, the CCTV. The geographical locations of the murders, spread all over London, puzzle me. These are not random sites he has picked. I believe there is a reason behind each location, and he has carefully selected each one in turn. Does he have a quarrel with London Underground as an organisation? Another question bothering me is why did he choose such a public place? He must know that he will feature on CCTV footage. We've just seen him arriving and leaving the crime scene, although his choice of headwear does suggest some thought has gone into disguising himself. He is a loner, with very few social skills. There is something in his past in relation to the colour of the victim's hair—could be his mother, a former teacher, when he was at school that spurned his advances or ridiculed him in front of his peers, or a bad relationship with a former girlfriend.

'There are two categories of serial killer: organised and disorganised. I believe our man fits in the first of these two. He has a relatively orderly life with a regular job. He plans his crimes in relation to location and escape routes. All the murders were planned, including that of Valerie Huxley. In this case, he thought about a weapon and how he was going to carry out the murder. He just needed to find a victim that fitted his nemesis. Valerie was in the wrong place at the wrong time. It would seem that he didn't panic, but just walked away from the scene with other passengers and then had the wherewithal to ditch the murder weapon some distance from the station.'

'Will he kill again?' Frost asked the question on everybody else's lips.

'Without a doubt.'

*

187

McNally tapped out a quick text telling Kate that he would be home within the hour. He called Frost, Wakefield and Hodge into his office and told them to shut the door. Wakefield brought both detectives up to date with the interview of tube driver, Devon Lorne, earlier that afternoon, and the discovery of the relationship between Elizabeth Wood and Patrick Mullen.

'What do you think, Marcia?' Frost was beginning to enjoy the trust McNally was starting to place in her judgement.

'Well, the fact that she denied knowing Patrick Mullen—our main suspect in the murder of Liam Brennan, when in fact she was married to him, points to her knowing what had happened that night. I think she'll probably be one of the women featured in the images found at Brennan's bedsit, which gives her, and her husband, a joint motive. We know that she was on duty with Patrick Mullen that night—she's got to be elevated to a suspect. We need to pull her in.' McNally nodded his agreement.

'Jim, you OK?'

'When I was at her address, she had an overnight bag packed and ready to go—I think she might have cleared out already.'

'Marcia, you and Sam pay her a visit, early tomorrow morning. Take a couple of uniform with you. Pick up an out of hours search warrant tonight, just in case she isn't there.'

'What if she is there?'

'Bring her in on suspicion of the murder of Liam Brennan.'

Chapter Forty-Seven

Michael Brewster relieved himself in some bushes next to the stream and zipped up his trousers. He ducked down as a car's headlights lit up the quiet road. He got back into the car and pulled his Beanie hat down as far as it would go. It had been a long night and, although the sun was breaking over the horizon, he felt pretty cold and was frustrated that his intended victim was a no-show.

He had drunk the last of his coffee from a thermos and was feeling hungry. His sister's house was still in darkness, as it had been since his arrival the previous evening. He settled back down, he'd spent many nights like these, waiting and watching, fighting for his country in more hostile surroundings than Burnt Oak—that was for sure.

He could tell the car, which pulled up a few yards down the road, contained police officers, and instinctively knew, from their position and body language, it was his sister's house they were paying attention to. The interior light flickered on—a woman was driving, a man sat in the passenger seat with a mobile phone held to one ear. Both of them were drinking from take-away cups. Brewster weighed up the odds—if he drove away now, at this time of the morning, it was likely they would see him. A quick check on the vehicle would show it was stolen, and his cover would be blown, before he'd finished what he had to. He decided to stay put and wait for them to make the next move.

*

By the time she'd got home, following last night's briefing, and had a large glass of white wine, Frost had fallen into bed totally exhausted. The alarm on her mobile, waking her at 4.30am, had not been welcome. Frost picked Hodge up on the way through central London and travelled up an almost empty Edgware Road arriving in Burnt Oak just as the sun broke from behind grey clouds. A local café, which had opened its doors at 5.30am, provided much needed coffee.

'What time did you get finished with Madalina last night?'

'About 9.30, I dropped her off home. She estimated the e-fit to be about a 75% to 80% likeness. I took it back into Camden and gave it to Ray Blendell. I must've just missed you. He said the briefing went on a bit.'

'Yeah, but it was entertaining. Graves finally met his match in Sara, the profiler. I left about 9pm and got home, via a friendly magistrate, about 10.30.'

Frost checked the search warrant and calculated that No.17, Silkstream Road, was the fourth door down from their position. The street was deathly quiet, as you would expect on a Saturday morning. Hodge's airwave radio crackled into life.

'Bravo four zero, just pulling up behind you now.' Frost looked in her rear view mirror and saw the uniformed carrier, headlights extinguished, slowly approaching them and park within a few feet. The detectives jumped out of their car and quietly closed the doors. Frost went and spoke to the senior of the three officers.

'Hi, Marcia Frost from Major Investigations at Camden.'

'Morning, Sgt Dan Wait. Where d'ya want us?'

'Can you deploy two of your officers around the back with Sam? You and the other officer stick with me at the front door. I'm not expecting any problems. We have a search warrant for the address. If the woman, we're after, is inside, she'll be arrested by me on suspicion of murder.' Dan Wait nodded his understanding and whispered his orders to the rest of his team. As Frost approached the front door of Elizabeth Wood's terraced house, nobody took any notice of a Ford Escort, with one occupant, slowly drive past.

Chapter Forty-Eight

It was an early start for the rest of the team as well. Two images sat side by side on Ryan McNally's desk. The e-fit compiled by the Romanian hotel receptionist, and an enhanced image of their suspect leaving the platform at Mornington Crescent station—the scene of the latest crime. McNally compared the two and looked up at the other three occupants of his office.

'Do we go live with these images?' McNally directed his question to DS Ray Blendell and the BTP press liaison officer Shirley Tresidder. It was the office manager, who offered an opinion first.

'Obviously, we have to be careful about compromising any later identification evidence when our suspect is eventually arrested. But I see no reason why we can't put the e-fit out on TV news channels, newspapers and social media. What do you think, Shirley?'

'I can get you a spot on lunchtime news bulletins, Ryan, probably do it outside Mornington Crescent station. You can produce the e-fit then with an appeal.'

'I can't see any reason not to release the image from the CCTV as well. At the moment, we don't really have any eye-witnesses, apart from the hotel receptionist. I think we need to put everything out there that we have, before our man decides to murder again. I'll have a word with Plummer, see what he says but in the meantime, Shirley, let's get the media interviews up and running for say 11.30. Does that give us time to get it on the lunchtime news bulletins?'

'Yes, that's fine, are you going to read a prepared statement to them?'

'No, I think I'll just wing it for now. It always looks so unprofessional when somebody, who is supposed to be on top of the investigation, has to read from a piece of paper. Jim, do you have anything on this logo on the hat?'

'Yes, sir, it's a British brand called *REGATTA. GREAT OUTDOORS* appears under the maker's name. It's a very common brand within the UK, available at most outdoor retailers. I have contacted the company to explore the possibilities of tracking down points of sale for this particular design, but I don't hold out much hope it will be of any use—too many.'

'Ray, allocate that action out to one of the others, will you. I want Jim to concentrate on the CCTV from the other crime scenes. I'll put the incident room number out when I do this appeal as well as *Crimestoppers*, so also arrange for staff to be here manning the phones. We'll bring the briefing forward to 5pm. OK that's all for now, Ray ask Sara to pop in will you.'

*

Marcia Frost rang the doorbell for a third time before peering through the letter box into a dark hallway. She could make out a large pile of post lying on the varnished wooden floor. Her airwave radio blurted out like a megaphone in the still of the morning. Sam Hodge had gained entry through an open window. Frost waited patiently for the front door to be opened from the inside.

Stepping into the hallway, she directed one of the uniformed officers to check upstairs, with instructions to leave everything untouched.

'Jim Wakefield was right; looks like she scarpered after his little visit.' Hodge said as he walked through into the hallway. 'I'll go and get some property bags from the car.' The officer came down the stairs shaking his head.

'Nobody upstairs, sarge.' Frost turned to Dan Wait.

'Thanks, Dan. Sorry to waste your time, but you can stand down. We've got a search warrant, so we'll stay and go through the house.'

'We can stay and help you look, got nothing else on this early.'

'No, that's fine thanks; to be honest we're not sure what we're looking for. We'll know when we find it.' Frost shut the front door and turned to Hodge. 'Let's start in the living room and find that picture of the happy couple.'

*

The stolen Ford Escort took a circuitous route around Burnt Oak before turning, lights off, back into Silkstream Road. Brewster knew that he should just clear off and come back another day. He knew that his sister wasn't at home, but curiosity got the better of him. The police carrier had disappeared, but, the now empty, unmarked car he'd first seen was still parked nearby. He drove slowly passed his sister's house and saw several rooms illuminated. He wondered what they could want with her. He briefly considered it might have something to do with his break-in. He'd removed a few items of cheap jewellery and left a few drawers open to cover his own tracks, but it was a mistake not to take the letter with him, when he'd had a chance to do so. He quickly dismissed his own reasoning. They wouldn't turn up at her house with a van full of uniform coppers and enter the property when she was not there, just to discuss a burglary that happened weeks before. He put the car in first gear and drove slowly away. He had to find her before they did.

*

To be honest Sara I was thinking about using the 'daughter of a friend' angle but thought you probably wouldn't fall for that one.'

Hallam smiled, 'We've only known each other for a day or so Ryan but I think we're both people who like to get to the point, so why don't you get what's bothering you off your chest.'

'I don't even know if this is something that you could advise me on, it's a personal matter. My daughter Ava has never settled since moving down from Manchester and now we believe she is probably self-harming.'

'How's she doing that?'

'I'm not sure, her grandmother noticed some injuries to her forearms, and they look like cuts. She asked Ava what they were; she said she had scratched herself. When my mother-in-law tried to talk to her about it further, she just went off on one—did the same thing when I was up there a couple of nights ago. I've never seen her so angry.'

'How is she doing at school?'

'Not great, her teachers are concerned, she says she has no friends and keeps on going on about going back to Manchester. She even tried to get a train back there from Euston the other night. God knows where she thought she was going to stay.'

'I can't really comment without seeing her, and to be honest, I'm probably not the best to do so anyway, what with my involvement in this case. But unofficially it sounds like it's a bit of a cry for help. The self-harming is worrying. It's her way of dealing with the situation. She has no control in relation to where she lives or goes to school. Self-harming is one aspect of her life that she *is* in control of.'

Chapter Forty-Nine

Both detectives stretched latex gloves over their hands. Frost started the search with an Oak Welsh dresser, against the far wall, adjacent to the front room window, through which the early morning sun was bursting.

Hodge stood by with an exhibits book and a wad of property bags ready to record and package anything of interest. One of the drawers contained various utility bills, including a recent itemised bill for the addresses landline which she passed to Hodge for bagging up. Finding nothing of further interest they then moved to a sideboard on the other side of the room.

'Well hello Mr Patrick Mullen, we've been looking for you.' Frost held a silver-framed photograph removed from a draw. Hodge placed it carefully into a property bag. She returned to the same sideboard cupboard and removed some old curtains to reveal two boxes. The first contained a Northern Ireland campaign medal; Mullen's name and service number were engraved around the edge. The second container was an old Christmas card box containing some personal documentation together with an envelope addressed simply to 'George.'

She sat down and began to read.

*

This was the first news conference he'd taken part in since he moved down to London from the north-west. McNally had appeared on TV and radio several times, even a two minute slot on *Crimewatch* about a series of armed robberies in Greater Manchester and Cheshire, but this was his first in London and he was more aware of his Manchester accent than at any other time since his move. Trying to imitate a cockney accent wasn't an option, so he just tried to be himself. Shirley Tresidder convinced him that it had gone well and he hadn't made a complete arse of himself.

Having discussed the matter with Plummer, McNally decided to release the CCTV image of their main suspect, as well as the e-fit, with details of the brand of hat he had been wearing. Now it was a waiting game and fingers crossed that the incident room telephones would start to ring.

*

Dear George,

I hated you the first time I saw you. I'm not ashamed by that fact. It was an emotion that drove me to do some terrible things to you and to our mum.

The first line of the letter was explosive. Frost shuddered, as an image of her own brother, and their non-existent relationship, fleetingly crossed her mind. She read on:

Why have I decided to write all this down now? Doctor's orders! Apparently, it might allow me to come to terms with what a bitch I've been. I know that you'll never ever read this, as you're probably dead. That is not its purpose. It is to allow me to face what I have done in my life and hopefully move on.

It started the first day they brought you home. I was always her favourite; she even gave me the same name—Elizabeth. You drove a huge wedge between Mum and me. Dad was never going to stay around. He worked away from home, shagging anything that moved. They were always arguing and Mum was hitting the gin bottle every night. I was only ten or eleven but I came up with a plan to get rid of you.

I never ever let Mum sleep. I would wake you at all times of the night driving her to exhaustion until she believed she couldn't cope with us both. When a social worker came around for a visit (I think it was the next door neighbour who contacted them. I used to constantly bang on the wall screaming all times of the day and night), I made sure Mum was drunk and the place was looking filthy. My favourite scam was putting your dirty nappies behind the cushions on the sofa. It worked, they took you away and we never saw you again.

Everything went to plan for the next few years. I think I was about fourteen when she was drinking more than eating and the money was drying up. We hadn't heard a thing from our father for years and the benefits only went so far. I used to go out and steal a few things, like her gin, but she decided to start

195

pimping herself out. I used to come home from school and she'd be 'entertaining' one of her 'friends' as she used to call them.

One day she was so pissed she offered me to one of them. She stood and watched as this fat pig molested me, but luckily he couldn't get it up again. She must have had second thoughts because she slung him out, but I never forgave her for that.

That incident seemed to be a turning point for the next couple of years. I'd turned sixteen, she was still pissed every day, but things were a bit better. That is until one particular day, I came home feeling pleased with myself. I had a few weeks until I finished school and I'd gotten a job at a local supermarket. When I got in, she had a man with her who was beating the shit out of her. I grabbed a knife from the kitchen and threatened him with it. I chased him out of the house.

When I returned to see if she was alright, she grabbed the knife from me and threw me onto the bed and held the blade against my throat. She told me she knew what I had done to her and how I had gotten rid of you. She was going to kill me, of that I had no doubt. She was frail. I was a lot stronger and managed to get her off me. I ran out of the house, the neighbour had heard all the commotion and called the police. She was arrested and I never ever saw her again. I was taken into care until I was eighteen.

A few months after my eighteenth birthday I got a visit from the social worker who had responsibility for us. Her name was Samantha Kirwin she liked to be called Sam. She told me Mum had died from liver disease and offered to take me to the mortuary to see her. I was glad that she was dead and wasn't going to miss the opportunity of telling her so.

It was a strange day. I didn't really recognise her. Her skin was yellow and haggard. I had no other emotions for her but hate. Kirwin had great pleasure in telling me that Mum had told her everything before she died. She had even left a note to pass onto me it simply read 'Fuck you.'

Kirwin left me there laughing her head off as she walked away. As far as I was concerned she'd signed her own death warrant. I pushed her under a train at Hendon Central station six months later. Her death was recorded as suicide. She knew that it was me. She looked up from the track a split second before she was cut to pieces our eyes locked and I smiled at her.

After her death, I started to use the name Charlie—one of the middle names that cow gave me.

There you have it all, dear George. I hope you had a shit life.

Your darling sister,
Charlie.

Marcia Frost placed the letter on top of the coffee table. Hodge came back downstairs.

'Nothing of interest up there, just some clothes and a spare room, how about you?'

'Sam, you need to have a read of this letter. It's addressed to somebody called 'George' and signed by 'Charlie'. Didn't Jim Wakefield say the train driver he interviewed told him Charlie was the name Elizabeth Wood liked to be called?'

'Yeah, I think it was.'

'So this letter is written by Elizabeth Wood to a brother called George. I don't know if this is all just total fantasy, written by a woman who is stark raving bonkers; or it's a serious account by a manipulative, evil, murderess. Okay, I don't think there is anything else for us here, leave a copy of the search warrant on the table we need to bag this letter and get back to Camden.'

'You okay, Sarge?'

'Sam, we came here thinking she may have been involved in the death of Liam Brennan.' Frost looked up at Hodge with disbelief etched over her face. 'This letter is a confession to a murder she claims to have committed maybe thirty years ago.'

Chapter Fifty

Graves was in a bad mood. He'd been given the shitty end of the stick as far as he was concerned, stuck in the incident room to answer telephone calls from half of London's nut cases. He'd tried to worm his way out of it, protesting that he had exhibits to submit to the lab and a handful of actions he had to complete. But McNally wasn't having any of it, probably payback time for opening his big gob once too often. He knew who was behind it—Frost. She would get it back in spades one day.

So far he'd avoided answering any calls, letting the other muppets, drafted in, deal with the 'it was me; I'm the killer.' calls. He took a large gulp from a soft drink can when the phone on his desk rang. He looked around waiting for somebody else to answer it but they were all engaged. He lifted the receiver.

'Incident room, can I help you?'

'Yes, maybe you can. I saw the detective on television at lunchtime. I couldn't ring in any earlier as I had to return to work. The more and more I think about it, I'm sure it was the same man.' Graves flicked the lid off his biro and reached for his notebook.

'Who do you think you saw, sir?'

'The man in the…what do you call it nowadays…an e-fit?'

'Yes, sir, that's correct, we've moved on a bit from *Photofits* on *Police 5*.'

'Yes, quite. Then when I saw the CCTV image, although it's not very clear, I'm fairly sure it was the same man on my bus on the way home from work.'

'A bus! Are you sure about this, sir? I'm not sure any self-respecting murderer would make his escape by bus.' Graves tossed his pen aside and took another mouthful of drink before stifling a yawn.

'Look, young man, I'm not sure if you are taking this seriously. I am a consultant anaesthetist at St Mary's Hospital, Paddington. I assure you that I wouldn't waste your time if I wasn't fairly sure of what I saw.' Graves could see a complaint coming his way and pictured himself walking around Kings Cross station with a big hat on. He changed his attitude quickly.

'Sorry, sir, it's been a long few days, and we've had our fair share of timewasters since the broadcast went out. Let's start again. Can I have your name?'

*

He knew the signs of an impending migraine: semi-blindness in one eye, nausea and disorientation, followed by the mother of all headaches. Michael Brewster had dumped the stolen car a few streets from his own, nearer than he'd intended, just managing to set foot in his own dingy flat before he violently puked the contents of his stomach into the toilet. Now he lay, naked, on his bed, curtains drawn and head under a pillow trying to block out the sun. Sleep was a long way off. The memories of gun fire and exploding IEDs that haunted him every night, along with the agonising cries of his mates blown to bits, pushed the sanctity of sleep far out of his reach. He wanted this all to be over. He wanted out of life. It held no purpose for him anymore. All those women he'd killed in an attempt to try and erase the memory of his mother.

He *had* left clues for the police; he didn't want to kill any more innocent women. But now he needed more time—time to kill the one evil that remained, his sister. They were closing in. His photograph, which he saw on the news, would be on the front of every newspaper by tomorrow. He was confident they didn't know who he was, yet, and hadn't connected him with his sister, but that would only be a matter of time.

He still had no idea why the police were looking for her. But they were both now looking for the same woman, but for different reasons. It was now a race as to who could find her first.

His mind cleared a little as the *Ibuprofen* kicked in. His staged burglary, weeks earlier, had given him a head start. He pushed the play on his mobile voice recorder and listened to the only message stored on his sister's ansaphone.

'Hi, Elizabeth, it's Doctor Gillian Forsyth here from North Lodge. I'm just following up on our conversation the other day. You sounded pretty upset. I know you are approaching another anniversary of Patrick's death. If you need to talk just ring me on my mobile 24/7. If it gets really bad and you have the urge to

self-harm or develop suicidal tendencies, get in a taxi and come here straight away. We've got through worse, Elizabeth; we will get through this as well. Bye.'

Pleased that he had had the foresight to wipe the ansaphone tape clean, he started to plan how and when she would die.

He watched some pointless quiz show on the television. He pulled his knife from its sheaf and ran the razor sharp blade along the length of his penis. How easy it would be just to slide the knife into his chest and end this hell. His sister's words emerged from the fog of his migraine *'Dear George, I hated you the first time I saw you.'* His attention returned to the television screen. If that twat says 'thank you very much indeed, Richard,' one more time he was going to put his foot through it.

Chapter Fifty-One

Events had moved on at such a pace. Ryan McNally sat at his desk—yellow post-it notes covering three quarters of the available space relegating the framed photograph of Kate and the kids to the window shelf. As each decision was entered into his log, a yellow sticker was binned.

He glanced at his watch and calculated that he needed to be out of here by 7pm to get home and get changed in time for the meal with Kate's arty friends. He ran a few excuses through his already cluttered brain, without success. The scenarios he'd come up with were never going to cut it—make it home or face the probability of divorce.

With ten minutes to spare before the afternoon briefing, he looked through the SIO's copy of the *Dear George* letter, seized at Elizabeth Wood's house that morning. It threw up more questions than it answered. Did she really kill a social worker or are they the ranting's of a mentally unstable woman, as she alludes to in the letter? Why does she believe her brother—whom she hasn't seen for years—to be dead? Has she killed him? McNally put his head in his hands to try and stop his brain spinning as fast as it was. He was hoping that he could've put the Lambeth investigation to bed and concentrate on a serial killer. His mobile rang, it was Sally Cook.

'For fuck's sake,' he mumbled, 'that's all I need.'

*

Graves had been busy. Several phone calls had secured him CCTV footage from Euston station and the No.205 bus route from Paddington to the east end of London. He opened up the attachment from Transport for London, e-mailed to him in the last few minutes. He had a little time to view it before the 3pm briefing. He fast forwarded the footage of the bus and smiled as he saw Dr Rufus Marston board at St Mary's Hospital. He clicked on another email to double-check the photograph the doctor had helpfully sent of himself earlier. Happy it was one and the same; he fast forwarded the footage and pressed play as the bus pulled into Euston Station.

Chapter Fifty-Two

McNally loved this part of the job. As far as he was concerned it was like a footballer walking out at Wembley stadium or a singer performing to a live audience. The incident room was the arena for ideas—good and bad, for detectives and civilian staff to put forward notions and solutions, to blow off a little steam, to make sense and clear the muddied waters they faced.

Different fragments of evidence: witness testimonies, CCTV footage, forensic analysis and offender profile, were pulling in different directions and threatening to rip the investigation apart. It was, ultimately, McNally's job to pull it all together into a coherent, evidential bundle. But what he was about to reveal to his team was going to blow this investigation apart.

*

Her room was comfortable, with a bar-less window, facing out onto the beautiful gardens of North Lodge Hospital. Birds flocked to and fro between surrounding trees and several bird feeders; Robins, Blue and Coal Tits, Blackbirds and Chaffinches. She smiled as the territorial Robin chased the other birds away, strutting around with his red breast prominent.

She'd asked for the same ground floor room she had first occupied in 1998 and several subsequent stays—the familiarity gave her a sense of security that she rarely enjoyed elsewhere, even at home.

This was her most vulnerable time of year. Two anniversaries were on the horizon: the deaths of her brother and her husband within calendar days of each other, although separated by six years. She'd made the phone call within minutes of the police officer leaving her house. She had packed her travel bag days before, just in case it was needed, believing, that this year, she might be able to cope. But the mention of Patrick Mullen's name had destroyed any hope of doing so.

A knock at the door made her jump, even though she knew who it was. It was nice to see the familiar face of Dr Gillian Forsyth and she relaxed for a moment.

'Hello, Elizabeth. It's good to see you again.'

*

'Before we start the briefing regarding the on-going investigation, I want to mention some important developments in the investigation regarding the murder of Liam Brennan. For those of you who have recently been drafted onto our team, this is an investigation that we've been conducting into the murder of a former London Underground station supervisor, an investigation that was running independently of this one.

Brennan's skeletal remains were found at Lambeth North station a few weeks ago. For the members of my team, I take it you've all had a chance to at least browse through a copy of the *Dear George* letter, taken from Elizabeth Wood's house early this morning?' McNally saw a few nodding heads and continued.

'For the benefit of the others in the room Elizabeth Wood, aka 'Charlie', is now a suspect for this murder. I believe that her former husband Patrick Mullen, who died of a heart attack in 2004, killed Liam Brennan following, either an argument about politics and religion or the pair had discovered that Brennan was covertly taking pictures of female staff in compromising situations in the staff toilet. A number of these images were found in Brennan's belongings when his bedsit in Brixton was searched.'

'Both Wood and Mullen were on duty the night Brennan disappeared. After they'd concealed the body, which would lay undiscovered for twenty years, I believe they staged a burglary of the booking office, knowing that people—including detectives—would assume Brennan had carried out, before going into hiding.'

Frost took over. 'We can't rule out the possibility that Brennan was trying to blackmail Wood by producing one of these images—probably of her—in return for money or sex. She may well have killed him herself and Mullen assisted her to hide the body and fake the burglary. Reading the *Dear George* letter; she is obviously capable of killing.' Many in the room nodded in agreement with Frost's comments.

McNally briefly considered how he was going to paraphrase the news he'd received ten minutes earlier. He looked around the room and was pleased to see Sally Cook at the back who gave him thumbs up, he took a deep breath.

'I can see the confusion in the faces of my own staff as to why I've decided to brief everybody on the developments on the Brennan case at the start of a briefing in relation to our serial killer. Just before I left my office to address you I received a telephone call from SOCO Sally Cook, who has now joined us, Sally, over to you.'

'If I may, to put everything into context, I'll firstly bring you up to date with our serial killer investigation. The lab has confirmed that the blood on the knife, found in the drain in Eversholt Street, does belong to Valerie Huxley, so *is* our murder weapon. Also present on the knife blade is a different blood group—the same as found in the lift with the same DNA profile and most likely our killer's. As we thought yesterday our killer must have, at some stage, cut himself on his own knife. I would guess either when stabbing Valerie Huxley or when hastily concealing the weapon in his pocket as he escaped from the scene. This specialised knife would be part of a set of knives normally kept together in some sort of presentation case. It's likely the knife was being carried freely without a protective sheath; it is extremely sharp and he could easily have cut himself.'

'There is also a partial fingerprint on the knife's blade; unfortunately there is no match on the fingerprint database.'

She waited patiently for the scribbling of notes to finish before delivering the hammer blow.

'When DS Frost returned from Elizabeth Wood's house early this morning, she dropped off the "*Dear George*" letter to me for examination. I lifted two sets of prints from the paper on which the letter was written. I also examined a photograph in a glass-fronted silver photo-frame recovered from the same address. I found another two sets of prints present. I managed to lift a controlled sample of Wood's fingerprints from an envelope containing her tax return. I submitted all these prints to the lab and requested a priority response. About thirty minutes ago I received an update. One of the sets of prints present on the "*Dear George*" letter and photo-frame match the prints on the HMRC envelope which I think, at this stage, we can say are Wood's. The second set on the letter and frame *do not* appear on the database. But when this second set of unident prints were compared against other unidentified marks on the system nationally, it produced a surprising result. The unidentified marks on the '*Dear George*' letter and the photo-frame match the partial fingerprint found on the murder weapon used to kill Valerie Huxley. Whoever handled that photo-frame and the 'Dear George' other than Wood is the killer of Valerie Huxley and probably three other women.'

The incident room went deathly quiet. Sally Cook sat down like a Member of Parliament who'd just made a maiden speech in the House of Commons. McNally stood.

'Now that we know both these investigations are inextricably linked must not deflect from our main priority and that is finding this man.' All eyes in the room settled on the grainy image of their main suspect.

'Sir, can I pick up from there?' McNally nodded at Graves, hoping he was going to say something constructive for once.

'I took a phone call from a Dr Rufus Marston, a consultant anaesthetist at St Mary's Hospital in Paddington. He called in response to your lunchtime witness appeal. He lives in Tredegar Square in east London and travels to and from the hospital on a 205 bus; he won't use the tube as he was on the train at Edgware Road that got blown up in the 7/7 2005 suicide attacks. He's never been on a tube train since.

'On the day of Valerie Huxley's murder, he'd been in the operating theatre until 5pm. He regularly catches the 205 bus that leaves from outside the hospital at 17.12pm; however, he was delayed by a colleague who wanted to discuss the following day's operating list, so he missed it and caught the next one at 17.22pm. He sat on the upper deck on the nearside of the bus adjacent to the stairs from the lower floor.' Graves nodded at Marie Relish; she loaded CCTV images onto the incident room TV screen.

'He's pretty easy to spot. He is the only passenger with a multi-coloured silk bow tie on.' Even McNally smiled; glad of a little light relief.

'The bus travelled as far as Euston station. He remembers a man ascending the stairs and sitting one row in front of him, but to the offside of the bus. He described him as 5'10" tall, aged about forty, and looked in good physical shape. I suppose that's something a doctor would notice. He couldn't remember what he was wearing apart from a dark 'Beanie' type hat pulled down to just above his eyes.' Relish moved the footage on at Graves' direction.

'Here is our man coming up the stairs and taking a seat as Dr Marston describes. Look at the time—18.05hrs. I walked the most direct route from Eversholt Street, where he dumped the knife, to Euston station; it took me just short of ten minutes. The bus travelled on and our suspect gets off at Stepney Green; our good doctor travelled on to Mile End. The reason he remembers our man so well, is the bloodied makeshift bandage he had wrapped around his right hand and the fact that he smelt of fish.'

'Brilliant, well done, Stuart. I want you and Jim Wakefield to concentrate on the Stepney Green area. See if we can pick our man up on any more CCTV as he got off the bus. Also liaise with the local Met police station, supply copies of the stills and e-fit and see if he is known to them. We now have two witnesses who've been in close contact with our man. Both recall him smelling of fish. Sara, you believe our man is organised and probably holds down a reasonably good job?' Sara Hallam nodded.

'Ray, we need to establish any fresh fish outlets or wholesalers in the Stepney Green area and let's not forget that our murder weapon is designed to fillet meat and fish; he must work in that industry. Sara, anything else you want to add?'

'As I stated yesterday, our man is clearly organised and puts a great deal of planning into his every move. The geography of the murder sites still puzzles me. These locations are not random. Everything is planned. It was not by chance that he walked to Euston station, where he could catch the very bus that would take him back home avoiding the tube, which he knew, in all probability, wouldn't be an option for him immediately after the attack. I believe he's trying to tell us something but at the moment I can't figure out what.'

McNally started to get a niggling feeling about the profiler. Was she just recycling the same old information that she'd gleaned from the briefings? He wanted to trust her—in a few short minutes he would be glad he did.

'Marcia and Sam, the two areas I want you to concentrate on are, firstly in the *Dear George* letter 'Charlie', who I think we all agree must be Elizabeth Wood, claims to have murdered a social worker called Samantha Kirwin. It could be the ramblings of a mad woman. We don't know yet. We've got a rough date, so dig deeper into that. Secondly we've got to find Elizabeth Wood aka 'Charlie.' It would appear that she might have disappeared after Jim Wakefield's visit. I don't know how she fits into the death of four women on the underground but she must know who those unident fingerprints belong to.

'There was unopened post at the address this morning dated from the day after Jim's visit, so I think you're right there, guv.' Hodge said. Jim Wakefield raised his hand.

'During the interview with Wood, the landline rang and she answered it. It was a whispered conversation, but I got the impression that she was speaking to somebody she intended seeing after I left. She gave me some cock and bull story about receiving silent phone-calls, so an itemised billing for that day could identify where she was going and who she was going to meet.'

'Ray, make an application to BT for subscriber details on all numbers to and from Wood's landline for a week prior to Jim's visit and present day.'

'We've got her mobile number, as well, I'll get onto her provider and request the same information for calls made and received.'

'The plain fact is we need to find our suspect as a priority, and also Elizabeth Wood. Marie, I want you to delve as far as you can into Wood's past. We know from her letter that she had come from a broken home and was fostered, we know she has a brother who appears to be called George. Where is he now? Is he still alive? What did she do before she worked for London Underground? That information should be on her personal file, including details of family—next of kin, a previous address. Speak to the Financial Investigations Unit. Ask them to look at her credit rating, loans and credit cards; does she have any? Are they being used now?'

'OK, all. Mr Plummer has authorised the working of rest days tomorrow. Yes, I know it's Sunday. Looking at the amount of actions that will be churning out of that printer in a moment, justification of the overtime will not be a problem. Anybody got anything to add? No? Thanks for all your help today we've made some real progress. Let's start afresh tomorrow; next office meeting will be at 9am Monday morning.'

'That's it!' Everybody turned to look at Sara Hallam.

'Sara, have you got anymore to add?' Hallam ignored the serenade of tired groans.

'Marie, can you write the locations of the murders on the white board please.' Relish glanced at McNally, who gave a weary nod.

'Each scene is detailed around the room, Sara.'

'Bear with me please, Ryan. Marie, if you could write each location in date order as a list.'

'Sure—here we go.'

East Finchley

London Bridge

Putney Bridge

Mornington Crescent

'OK, good. Elizabeth Wood, in her *Dear George* letter, claims to have killed her social worker—Samantha Kirwin by pushing her under a train when she was about eighteen years old, a woman she'd come to hate as much as her mother. I know that we've yet to confirm that such a death took place and if it did, was it murder? But she mentioned a location, where she claimed to have carried out this attack. Can anybody remember where that was?'

'Hendon Central, top of the Northern Line.' Hodge answered.

'OK, Marie, please add Hendon Central to the top of the list and highlight the first letter of each station.' Relish did as she was asked.

Hendon Central

East Finchley

London Bridge

Putney Bridge

Mornington Crescent

'There's your connection Ryan.' All present in the room looked at the whiteboard and then at each other and then back at Sara Hallam. Hallam waited for the penny to drop.

'I was always pretty sure that the, seemingly, random locations of the attacks, were a clue in themselves—a message from the killer. When you just thanked everybody for their *help* today, it suddenly fell into place. Our killer is asking for our help. For whatever reason he is killing, he wants to stop, but only when he has achieved his aim.'

'So, what about the last location, the missing word?' asked Graves 'Which I presume is the letter E?' Are you saying that he will kill one more time, at a station location, beginning with the letter E? There must be...'

'Seventeen—I've just googled it, and that's without including the Docklands Light Railway.' Marie Relish confirmed.

'Here is your second link, Ryan.' Hallam continued. 'Yes, he will kill again. But I can safely say that our killer has also read the *Dear George* letter. Indeed he is George.'

'Elizabeth Wood did mention to me that she'd been burgled a few weeks before I saw her,' said Wakefield.

'Probably got through the same dodgy window with the broken lock Marcia and I got through this morning,' Hodge added. All eyes returned to Sara, she hadn't finished.

'The final letter—the letter 'E' doesn't denote a station but a name: Elizabeth. The man we are looking for is Elizabeth's brother and he's last murderous act will be the killing of his sister.'

Chapter Fifty-Three

The mini cab dropped Ryan and Kate McNally outside *De Luca's* Italian restaurant at Tally Ho Corner in North Finchley, with minutes to spare.

'Remind me of their names again?'

'Shirley is the artist. I can't remember her husband's name; she did tell me but you know what I'm like with names.'

'True, you can't remember mine half the time. Anyway who *is* Jake?'

'Jake…I don't know any Jake.'

'You were mumbling his name in your sleep last night'

'Ryan you cheeky…' McNally forgot how sharp Kate's elbows were, especially when they came into contact with his ribs.

'Might be a good time to tell you the bad news; I've got to work tomorrow. This case we're working on is about to crack open right down the middle.'

'Oh well, I suppose I'm privileged to have you to myself for one night.'

'Well, we could have stayed at home and spent the evening in bed with a bottle white wine and a bag of pork scratchings.'

'You romantic, you can take the boy out of the north but not the north out of the boy. Anyway I'm sure our two children would've allowed us the time for that! Listen, you might just enjoy yourself. Shirley is a right laugh, so just smile. They are over in the corner near the window. They've even left a seat so you can watch the door, detective.'

*

Having eaten only half of her dinner, Elizabeth Wood returned to her room. The food at North Lodge was pretty good but she just didn't feel hungry. Her supervisor at St John's Wood had been very understanding when she reported sick a few days earlier, but she knew she would have to go back to work soon; she still had bills to pay.

She lay on her bed and thought of the earlier session with Dr Forsyth. They'd spoken about the events of 1998, which had resulted in her being sectioned under the Mental Health Act and detained at this very hospital. She'd returned several times since then when she felt like she was free-falling back to the dark days of depression and self-loathing; remembering all the bad things she'd done in her life and the people whose lives she had ruined—her parents, her brother.

Dr Forsyth had been a good friend as well as a psychiatrist, especially since she'd lost Patrick in 2004. Maybe this time would be different. Perhaps, when she left here, she could leave the past where it belonged. The visit from the police had been upsetting. The officer had been fishing for information—that was all. If they'd suspected anything she would be sitting in a police station cell not a mental health institution. The truth, as far as she was concerned, had been cremated with her late husband.

*

The restaurant was quite busy and buzzed with the sound of conversation and background music. It was nicely decorated and the staff very attentive. The four occupants of the table, to which they headed, were a few drinks in front of the new arrivals, evidenced by two empty bottles of wine. McNally wasn't really a wine-drinker. His preferred tipple, Guinness, was unlikely to be sold in such a poncy establishment as this; he'd probably have to settle for bottled beer. He didn't really go for these manufactured meetings with people he didn't know, and probably wouldn't like, but this was Kate's evening. He would have to grin and bear it and laugh when he was expected to.

'Hi, I'm Shirley, nice to meet you, Ryan. I've heard a lot about you. This is my husband, Steve, and these are close friends of ours, Mellissa and Roger Knight, who live in Totteridge.' McNally went through a round of handshakes and smiles before sitting down next to Kate.

'I hear you're a detective, Ryan?' Here we go, thought McNally, that didn't take long.

'Yes, Roger. That's what I do. Keep you all safe in your beds. What—may I ask—do you do for a living?'

'I'm a property developer, buy houses do them up, sell them on.'

'Roger bought our house in Totteridge when it was a neglected shell and now it is one of the most impressive in the area.' Melissa added proudly.

'Yes, some big and very expensive properties in our area. I've done up a few myself, sold a couple to some footballers; one was the Arsenal manager, the other a goalkeeper apparently. I don't follow football myself.'

Ryan is a big Arsenal fan, aren't you darling? McNally nodded as he took a mouthful of his starter, not really interested in talking about football to someone who has no interest in it, just to feed one man's ego. He'd taken an instant dislike to Roger from Totteridge.

The evening continued and by the end of the meal Roger and Steve, the accountant, had drunk more and more and were getting louder and louder. It wasn't long until the police-baiting started in earnest.

'Not sure how you get by on a copper's wage, Ryan. I suppose your children go to a comprehensive do they?'

'And what's wrong with a comprehensive, Roger?'

'There's nothing wrong with them. Roger, don't start. You're getting a little drunk.' Melissa looked around, embarrassed at the attention they were attracting from other diners.

'My wife likes to see the good in everything.' Knight sneered.

'I've always found that an attractive characteristic, one she shares with my wife in fact.' McNally gave Kate a smile. 'I do hope you aren't driving home tonight Roger, you look a little worse for wear.'

'Why, are you going to put a sly phone call in to your traffic buddies? Get them to wait for me up the road?'

'You can leave your car here, Roger. Steve and I will drop you off. It's only ten minutes out of our way.'

'Nonsense, I'm perfectly able to drive home; anyway Steve has had as much as me. Do you share your wife's and Shirley's passion for crap art, Ryan?'

'Maybe we can keep the language down a bit Roger?'

'Any more comments like that Steve and you can say goodbye to the £100,000 a year you charge me for my accounts, and you'll be lucky to get employed by some shitty corner shop to do their VAT returns.' McNally could see the atmosphere was upsetting Kate and nodded towards the exit. He'd had enough of this pompous twat and even though tomorrow was Sunday, he had an early start. He summoned a waiter over and asked for their bill and excused himself before heading towards the toilets.

A minute later Roger stood and told his wife he needed a cigarette, before making his way to a small *al fresco* dining area and bar at the back of the restaurant.

'I'm sorry about Roger. He's been under some pressure lately; I'm worried about his drinking. It's getting out of hand.'

'That's OK, Melissa. We understand,' said Shirley, sympathetically. 'I think it's about time we went as well, Steve—before you end up getting sacked.'

'He didn't mean anything by that Steve. He'll have forgotten all about it by the morning.' Mellissa reassured him.

Kate looked over towards the toilets, hoping to see her husband return. She needed to go as well, but just wanted to get out of here. She was just glad that Ryan had kept his cool. McNally returned, they said their good byes, not waiting for Roger to return. As far as McNally was concerned, one more utterance from him might be one to many.

Chapter Fifty-Four

Brewster woke the following morning, the pounding headache of the night before now a dull ache whenever he moved his head from side to side. In all probabilities, the discovery, by police, of his sister's letter and secret violent past meant that his plans for her death would have to be brought forward. He wouldn't be missed at work until late Monday night. By then, he'd have no need for a job.

The sickness of the night before had left him with pangs of hunger. He showered and put on fresh clothes that, for once, didn't stink of fish. He took the short walk to his usual café on Stepney Way. It was pretty quiet for a Sunday morning, so he sat at his favourite table, by the window, where he would normally watch the world go by; but not today. He had a plan that would start this evening with a drive up to north London and a visit to see his dear sister.

*

Graves and Wakefield had made an early start. The area around the bus stop on Stepney Green, at which their suspect had alighted, was mainly residential, with little opportunity of CCTV cameras. Armed with copies of the e-fit and the CCTV image from Mornington Crescent, they decided to walk back in the direction of Mile End Road. The detectives split up and visited any small commercial premises that were open on a Sunday morning, including newsagents and a couple of small Asian mini-markets, dotted around the area.

Graves knew that, sometimes, good old fashioned policing: walking, talking, listening and looking, were just as effective an investigation tool as any computer generated crime model or forensic test. But, on this occasion, having drawn a blank, he met Jim Wakefield back at their starting point. They found a small café, where they sat and discussed their strategy.

'I've googled fishmongers within a two mile radius of here, thinking there might be two or three. No! There are sixteen, and as you would expect, most are closed on a Sunday. Let's be honest, he could work at any of them or none.' Graves tried to keep his voice down as a few other tables were occupied.

'What else we got?' Wakefield questioned himself as much as his colleague. 'We know the killer left his own blood in the lift at Mornington Crescent and on the knife. Dr Marston mentioned that he had a cut on his hand. It might be worth going into the A&E at the London Hospital and speak to the staff there, see if they remembered our man coming in for treatment.'

'We might get a look at their CCTV for the rest of that day,' Graves thought. 'Although I would imagine if he intended going to the hospital, he would've got off the bus two stops earlier near Whitechapel—but it's worth a shot.' Graves went up to the counter to pay for the drinks and showed the vendor his warrant card, the e-fit and the CCTV still.

'Have you seen this man in here or the local area by any chance?' The Asian male glanced quickly over to the empty corner table by the window, on which sat an empty plate and a half full cup of coffee, and shook his head.

Chapter Fifty-Five

Frost and Hodge were having equally little luck in north London as their colleagues in the east. The detectives had failed so far to unearth any information about the death of a social worker twenty five years ago, including searches of their own force's archives. Both of them were starting to think that the *Dear George* letter was a complete work of fiction, some private fantasy world, that Elizabeth or 'Charlie' lived in. As they discussed their next move Frost's mobile rang.

'Hi, Marcia, it's Marie, in the incident room. Made any progress?' Frost turned her phone onto speaker to let Hodge in on the conversation.

'No, not really, have you come to our rescue?'

'Well, actually, I have.'

'Go on.'

'I drew a blank on all our systems in relation to Samantha Kirwin's death, so I did a random search on the *British Newspaper Archive* website.'

'They're at Colindale, aren't they? Down the road from the Met's training school—or what's left of it, apparently a couple of buildings, a parade square with a flag and a statue of Robert Peel, although if he had any dealings with the slave trade he'll be off to a darkened corner somewhere soon.'

'That's where it used to be. The records have now been transferred online. It cost me about £80 to register, but I think it's been worth it. I'll claim it back.'

'Good luck with that. OK. So what you got?' Frost pulled the car over while Hodge pulled out a pen and notebook.

'Two hits on Kirwin. Firstly a couple of paragraphs in a tabloid dated the 13th September 1988, reporting that a female social worker, identified as Kirwin, apparently committed suicide by throwing herself under a train at Hendon Central station. Her line manager, a woman called Jackie Gibson, stated that— and I quote: "Samantha Kirwin had worked with our department for nearly fourteen years and we are deeply saddened to hear of her unexpected death. All of the Social Services Department based at Hendon Town Hall would like to extend our condolences to her family".'

'Two weeks later in a local paper, the *Hendon and Mill Hill Times*, there is an entry of the inquest into her death, which was recorded as suicide. You got all that?'

'Yeah, Sam is writing all this down. Probably not a lot we can do about this today. Barnet Social Services will only have an emergency callout response, so I'll get on it first thing tomorrow. Nice one, Marie. I owe you a large glass of something; anything on Elizabeth Wood?'

'I've been going through her personal file. A couple of things of interest: she was off work for a year in 1998 when she was operating trains, funnily enough, bearing in mind what we've just been discussing, she had some guy walk towards her in a tunnel between St Paul's and Bank stations. She had no chance of stopping; the guy turned out to be some banker from the City who'd been helping himself to company funds, and due to stand trial at the Old Bailey that day. There is some mention of psychiatric help, partially paid for by London Underground—she never returned to driving trains after that.

'There is a previous address recorded for her, a former family home in Burnt Oak, not too far from her present house.'

'Got all that, Marie we were heading back up to Burnt Oak anyway to knock on her door again, just on the off chance she's turned up. We'll have a look at the earlier address and speak to some neighbours. Thanks, we'll see you at Camden in the morning.'

*

It had felt like being back in Afghanistan; the planning, the checking of equipment and the sense of danger. Michael Brewster surveyed the area around the stolen vehicle he'd abandoned that morning, Satisfied there was no police activity, he jumped in and got it started. He had some experience of anti-surveillance and followed a diverse route around Stepney, Mile End and Whitechapel. The close shave, he'd had in the café earlier, had put him slightly on edge. Not because he had a fear of being caught—he'd left them enough clues—but a fear of not being able to end the life of the woman who'd made *his* life, at times, a living hell. The police were closing in; he hadn't expected them to be so close, so soon.

Using his mirrors to observe, he sped down a couple of one way streets, circumnavigated roundabouts several times, indicated one way before veering across the highway and turning in the opposite direction. Once satisfied that he wasn't being followed, he headed north.

*

'Watling Crescent is the second turning on the right.' Frost turned into a small cul-de-sac, parked up and turned the lights off.

'This isn't looking promising, Sam,' the small crescent was made up of six terraced houses, four of which were boarded up. 'What number was Elizabeth Wood's former house?'

'No.4, they're all council houses, due to be demolished once the remaining couple of properties are vacated. Seeing as we are here, we might as well justify our overtime and go and knock on the occupied two. I'll take No.2 you can have No.6.' Hodge received no answer at No.2. Frost was a little luckier.

'Hi. Sorry to disturb you on a Sunday. I'm a police officer making a few enquiries about a family that used to live at No.4 in the mid-eighties by the name of Wood.' The occupant was probably in her mid-sixties and vastly overweight with a cigarette dangling out the side of her mouth. The smell of burning fat wafted from the house and made Frost gag.

'Lenny, turn that bloody telly down, I can't hear myself think.'

'May I ask how long you have lived here Mrs…?'

'Richards, Sandra Richards. People call me Sandy. I think it was about 1978…yeah the year after we got married. We were living in a one-bedroom flat in Hendon and I fell pregnant with twins and the council re-housed us. It used to be a nice little cul-de-sac but the council never spent much on the place and now, after forty-odd years' living here, they've sold the land off to developers who're going to build an old people's home. We're waiting to be re-housed in a smaller place; the kids have fucked off now thank God.'

'Who is it, babes?' The door frame behind the woman was filled by a gigantic West Indian man in a dirty white t-shirt and stained boxer shorts.

'A detective, asking some questions about No.4, can you remember who lived there when we first got here?' Lenny Richards looked over the top of his wife's head at Marcia Frost.

'Not sure I've ever seen a black detective, where you from girl?'

'I explained to your wife, I'm from the British Transport Pol…'

'No, not that, girl—where were you born?'

'South London—Stockwell.'

'Yeah, really, I was born in Kennington, what about your parents?'

'Antigua.'

'Are, so they were a bit posher than mine, they were from Kingston, Jamaica. You wanna come in; got some proper Jamaican rum on the go?'

'That's a tempting offer,' she lied 'but we've got a lot of ground to cover before we finish.'

'OK. I'll leave you to it, keep her talking, babes, I'll get rid of the stolen gear out the back.'

'I wouldn't do that, sir, my colleague, and his police dog, are waiting.' Lenny Richards looked at her and they both started to laugh.'

'You almost had me there, officer; you'll be top dog one day. I'll see you on the news, the first black commissioner.' He let out a roar of laughter, which faded as he went back to his TV and rum.

'Yeah, I do remember the family, they weren't that sociable; they looked down on us a bit with Lenny being…you know—black and me being white. You'd know what I mean. The father wasn't around much, worked away a lot. They had a daughter, probably about ten years old. Not long after we moved in, she had a baby boy, I think it was. They used to argue a lot and after two or three years the old man left her and the boy disappeared. I heard he was adopted. She liked a drink and, if I'm honest, the placed turned into a bit of a knocking shop— you know—men in and out all sorts of times day and night. In the end, she couldn't cope and Social Services took the boy but the girl stayed with her. Well that's until the Mum got nicked, taken off in a police car—never saw her again. The daughter was taken into care and then the council moved some Bangladeshis in.

'Have you ever seen the girl—of course a woman now—in the area since then?'

'No, love, me and my Lenny keep our noses out of other people's business, anyway I wouldn't recognise her now.'

'How long has No.4 been empty?'

'A couple of years ago, I think. It was all smashed up inside by local yobs so was one of the first to be boarded up, although I did see some light in there a couple of nights ago. I was trying to get the fucking cat in about midnight. I called Lenny out but he said it was probably a couple of dossers. We thought about calling your lot but you have to have a knife in your chest around here, before they turn up, so we didn't bother.'

'Have you seen any movement in there since?'

'No, can't say I have.'

'That's been really helpful, Mrs Richards. Can I leave my mobile number with you just in case you or your husband remembers anything else that could help us? Thank you for your time and I wish you luck with your move.' Marcia Frost turned towards the car as the door shut behind her. She could smell the chip fat on her clothes.

Chapter Fifty-Six

North Lodge Hospital was situated just off Muswell Hill Road; its acre or so of grounds backed on to Highgate Wood. Brewster parked the stolen car a few yards from the hospital's main entrance on double yellow lines—he didn't intend being too long. He needed to find out where his sister was located in the two-storey building. If he had a chance, he would take her tonight, and needed the car nearby.

He'd driven past the main entrance a couple of times to look for CCTV cameras and any other security measures. The front door had an out of hours keypad entrance and a security guard sat at reception—feet up, reading the Sunday newspaper, not paying any particular attention to the bank of CCTV cameras in front of him.

Brewster, dressed in a dark combat jumper and trousers, pulled his Beanie hat tight over his head. He felt the *Fairbairn Sykes* fighting knife secured tightly against his torso. He touched the screen of his mobile, his sister stared back at him, smartly dressed, long blond hair tucked behind her ears, standing next to a smartly dressed man, whom he didn't know and didn't care about. Now he was ready to go. Brewster looked up and down the street, making sure the coast was clear and opened the car door.

Accessing the rear of the hospital was relatively easy; clambering over a five foot high wall, with the aid of one of three massive rubbish bins, was no obstacle. He may be in his early forties, but he'd kept himself in good shape.

He froze as a security light, activated by his movement, shone brightly, illuminating an area ahead of him along the back wall of the hospital. Brewster merged into the shadows and hoped the security guard was still ensconced in his paper. He counted to twenty-five before the light went off, information that could come in handy later. He noted two similar lights along the back wall of the hospital and judged that, if he stayed close to the wall, he would avoid the movement sensors.

He reached the first ground-floor window and peered inside. A woman, half-naked, was rocking herself back and forth in her chair, staring, blank-faced, at the plain magnolia coloured wall, which she faced.

The second room was empty, but the third had a light on and the window was slightly ajar. Brewster peered through the partially drawn curtains and set eyes on his sister for the first time in over forty years. He didn't know how long he'd stood there—just staring. The trance was broken by her standing upright, facing a mirror as she combed her blond hair. Brewster slid his hand inside his jacket, feeling the handle of his knife, which he slid silently from its sheath. He pulled the open window outwards when a glint of flashing blue light reflected off the dark trees of the hospital grounds. He replaced the knife, backed off and whispered.

'See you tomorrow night, darling sister,' before disappearing into the darkness of the grounds and Highgate Wood.

Chapter Fifty-Seven

The Monday morning briefing was set for 9am, all the incident room and investigations team were in much earlier, making phone calls to people unavailable the previous day. Graves had arranged for an observation point to be manned by some local crime squad officers set up in an empty flat opposite the café he and Jim Wakefield had visited. The café owner's reaction to Graves' enquiry the previous day hadn't gone unnoticed. He knew who their killer was but was unlikely to say, even if they pulled him in. It wasn't the sort of area where helping the police was top of your 'to do' list.

Graves sat with Wakefield at a desk top and tailing some of their actions, before submission when Graves' phone rang.

'DC Graves.'

'Morning, mate, nice to see it's not only me up at this time of the day. It's DC Sharon Hendry at Bethnal Green nick, you're working on the tube murder, I believe?'

'Hi, Sharon, Stuart this end, what can I do for you?'

'I got an informant who's given me some proper good stuff in the past. He gave me a ring last night, wanted to meet up, so I saw him early this morning. He was still a bit pissed from an all-day bender yesterday, but he's not one for wasting my time.'

'I'm all ears, Sharon.'

'He thinks he knows the guy you're looking for, in relation to the tube killing. He says he's always wearing a dark Beanie hat and the e-fit isn't a million miles away.'

'OK, sounds promising. How does he know him?'

'Well, that's the downer—he doesn't. But he's seen him at a place he delivers to and spoken to him a few times but never got a name, but a third party told my man that this guy was ex-military and's got a screw loose.'

'How do we find him?'

'He works for a company called J and M Seafood.' Graves quickly scanned a list of fishmongers and wholesalers they were going to contact today, but no J and M Seafood appeared on the list.'

'Do they operate from the East End?'

'No, Billingsgate Fish Market in London Docklands.'

*

Brewster had had a fitful night's sleep; a car back-firing outside his bedroom window at 2am, had caused him to panic and dive under his bed clasping his knife; he stayed there until first light. He dragged himself out of hiding by mid-morning and tentatively looked out of the window at the street below, expecting to see police cars sealing off the street. He'd had a lucky escape. Obviously the hospital security officer hadn't been as incompetent or as lazy as he'd thought.

Having sat deep in the woods, praying the police didn't deploy a search dog, he moved off after nearly an hour, knowing that going back to the stolen car was not an option. He found his way to Highgate tube station and travelled home. Tonight he would be much more careful. He knew where his sister was, and he knew how she was going to die.

*

It had taken a few phone calls for Frost to locate social worker Samantha Kirwin's line manager, at the time of her death—Jackie Gibson. Gibson had retired eight years ago and now lived in a cottage in the Cotswolds. Frost knew that a fast moving, time critical investigation like this would not afford her the time for a trip that would take up most of the day. She rang the number she'd been given and it was answered on the second ring.'

'Hello who's this?' It was obvious that Jackie Gibson received very few calls.

'Hello, Mrs Gibson. My name is Marcia Frost. I'm a Detective Sergeant with the British Transport Police.'

'You don't sound like a police officer—how do I know you're not some sort of scammer after what little savings I have?'

'I can give you my number and you can call me back if you like.'

'Don't try that with me young lady. That's what they do, don't they? But all you're doing is contacting the same people.' On the one hand, Frost was pleased to hear somebody very much aware of their personal safety and security, but on the other, she didn't have bloody time for this.

'If I may explain that my enquiry is about a person you used to work with in Barnet, rather than asking you anything about your financial status, hopefully that might reassure you?' There was a silence on the other end of the line, followed by a long sigh.

'OK.'

'I want you to think back to 1987. You were a line manager at Barnet Social Services. One of your team was a lady called Samantha Kirwin. Do you remember her Mrs Gibson?'

'Oh yes I do, such tragic circumstances—threw herself under a train at Hendon Central. I remember my staff and I being very upset as you'd expect, Inspector.'

'It's Sergeant, Mrs Gibson, but please just call me Marcia. What I'm about to tell you would be far better coming during a face to face conversation but the nature of the enquiry means I need to expedite my investigation. We have reason to believe Samantha Kirwin was murdered.' Frost allowed Jackie Gibson to take in what she'd just said. 'Mrs Gibson, are you okay?'

'Yes…yes I'm fine, I think. Please give me a moment to take the telephone and sit down. There, now that's better. Did I hear you correctly say that you believed Sam was murdered?'

'Yes. Can you remember her dealing with a family by the name of Wood? The mother and daughter were both called Elizabeth and a young son called George?'

'Even in those days a social worker's caseload would have been substantial but I do remember Sam mentioning the case to me; it would've come across my desk at some point as one of the children was taken into care—I think it was the boy. But what has this got to do with Sam's death?'

'I can't really discuss too many details with you; suffice to say that we are urgently looking for the daughter, Elizabeth as we believe her to be in great danger. Can you remember anything about George, where he was relocated or anything about the family who adopted him?'

'I remember Sam was very concerned about the boy's safety. She did remark to me that it was one of the most troubling cases she'd experienced so far and she was losing sleep over what actions she should take. On her visits, she got the impression that the mother may have been suffering from *Munchausen Syndrome by Proxy*, as she would always complain of the child's crying, lack of appetite and high temperature. George was taken into hospital on a couple of occasions but found to be in perfect health, if a little under-weight. Sam believed that if he stayed with his mother and sister he would be in grave danger. He was removed from the family home in great haste and fostered with several families. He never seemed to be able to settle—he could be quite a disruptive child if my memory serves me well. I know Sam kept in touch with the case and visited the boy in his early years before she died. You can get access to the file and adoption papers through a court order, I believe. I'm a bit out of touch these days.'

Marcia Frost knew she was touching a sensitive area with her questions but to apply for a court order, and serve it on the council, would take more time than she believed they had. She pushed on.

'Can you remember where he ended up, Mrs Gibson?'

'After Sam had died, I kept a watching brief on the case. I knew it would be something Sam would have wanted. It was out in east London somewhere. The family who took him on his fourteenth birthday were a lovely couple who'd lost a son in a road accident two years before. Mr and Mrs Brewster; lived in Romford. When the adoption went through they changed his first name, with his consent, to Michael.'

*

Two burglaries and a stolen car, not bad for a Monday morning thought Terry Bullen—the early turn Scenes of Crimes Officer. He'd been a civilian SOCO in the Metropolitan Police Service for nearly nine years. It was a job he loved, virtually his own boss, and working alone, most of the time, really suited him.

Both burglaries had been in a domestic setting with the same *modus operandi*, a brick through the back door window and only small items of value taken. Probably the same person responsible for both, he thought, some junkie who only wanted property he could sell on quickly.

He arrived back at Highgate police station and grabbed himself a cup of strong tea, before going down to the underground car park for the final job of the morning. A Ford Escort had been cordoned off with blue and white police tape with: 'DO NOT TOUCH—FINGERPRINTS' scrawled on a piece of A4 paper.

Terry Bullen read his job-sheet, each of the three crime scenes he had to examine this morning, were accompanied by a brief description of the circumstances. The stolen car had been recovered, parked on yellow lines, outside the North Lodge Hospital, off Muswell Hill Road.

Those sorts of places gave him the shivers. Although it was a relatively modern building, he bet they still had a padded cell or two for the more difficult patients.

He took a few gulps of his cooling tea and recalled the old Friern Barnet Hospital, only a couple of miles away from where he stood, which closed after the government of the day came up with its new mental health care policy—closing most of these specialist hospitals and sending patients into the community.

Before this job he'd been a paramedic with the London Ambulance Service and could remember driving along Friern Barnet Road early on a very cold, winter, Sunday morning. The bus stop, outside the main entrance to Friern Barnet Hospital, had a queue of people awaiting the first scheduled bus. As he drew the ambulance up at a red traffic signal, he realised all those queuing were dressed in pyjamas. One man, pyjama bottoms around his ankles, was openly masturbating. He and his colleague's smiled at the spectacle of two male nurses desperately ushering them back inside. Two weeks later, that lack of respect for the mentally ill, caught up with him, when he was called to the hospital for an attempted suicide.

The hospital itself was a Victorian architectural marvel, as many mental institutions of the day were. He was told, as he entered the building, it had the longest continuous corridor in the world. His journey along the full length of this corridor was a walk in hell: patients screaming, the smell of human incarceration, click-clacking of his shoes on the highly polished lino flooring—the sense of fear. His experience had been so profound that, shortly after, he resigned from the ambulance service, realising his lack of empathy with his fellow human beings, was a deep, unattractive flaw in his character.

After hopping from one job to another, he trained as a forensic examiner and here he was, in a job that required very little in the way of empathy.

The interior of the stolen car looked like it'd been lived in: discarded coffee cups and sandwich packets were strewn throughout the interior. He bagged several of these items up for DNA analysis and carefully lifted several sets of fingerprints off the steering wheel and radio display panel. Many of the marks would belong to the legitimate owner, whose fingerprints would need to be taken for elimination purposes, but he was confident of a result. It was time to return to his vehicle and find a nice quiet spot for a snooze.

*

It had been relatively simple to trace J and M Seafood through the Billingsgate Fish Market website. Graves sat impatiently at his desk. The telephone number he'd dialled rang continuously. The market had been shut on Sunday night and wasn't open for trade until Tuesday at 4am, but market traders would start work around midnight tonight, preparing the fish for the early morning trading. After what seemed an age, the ring tone was replaced by an ansaphone, on which Graves left a message to be contacted urgently. He looked at his watch. There was time for a quick freshen up before the 9am briefing.

Chapter Fifty-Eight

McNally had spent much of Sunday in his office reading through statements, briefing notes and completed actions and liaising with Ray Blendell for further actions to be raised; in all honesty he was glad to be at work.

He'd hoped for a pleasant evening with his wife and her friends, but sadly it had all gone rather wrong. When they'd returned home on Saturday night, Kate was quite upset about how the evening had gone but stopped short of blaming her husband, who was clearly not at fault. In fact, McNally had quite liked Shirley and her husband and felt sorry for Melissa, and this softer, friendlier side to her husband's character seemed to cheer Kate up a little before he shot himself in the foot when admitting he'd been tempted to smash his fist through Roger's face.

He looked at his watch and collected his papers for the Monday morning briefing. He'd spent the last fifteen minutes talking to the journalist Ben Scrivenor, firstly updating him on the progress of the investigation as much as he could, and then thanking him for holding back the story for a few more days in order not to compromise the work they'd done so far. He was feeling positive and strode into the incident room; they just needed a couple of pieces to complete the jigsaw.

*

He knew it was only a matter of time before he got the knock on the door. The CCTV footage and e-fit would result in somebody coming forward. They'd found the murder weapon with his blood on it, and they were likely to have found the car he left at North Lodge Hospital, although he was banking on the police not yet putting all these pieces together.

Brewster threw a few items into a rucksack including his knife, a length of rope and a reel of strong parcel tape he'd purchased a few days ago. He looked around the flat he knew he would not be coming back to, checked the street outside, once again, and left.

*

The morning briefing was kicked off by McNally; he could sense the tension, so wasted no time in going around the room.

'Stuart, Jim, how're we doing with the Stepney Green lead on our suspect?' Graves brought the team up to speed with the phone-call from DC Sharon Hendry at Bethnal Green.

I've traced the company he worked for, but I'm waiting for a reply to my call.'

'If you haven't got a reply by the end of this briefing, find an address and get over there—good work. Marie, anymore on Elizabeth Wood's past history?'

'Yes. I dug some old addresses out and passed them onto Marcia. She's got a couple of credit cards and two bank accounts. Neither the credit or bank cards have been used since the beginning of last week. The mobile provider can't give us any updates on the location of her mobile. They believe it's been turned off for at least three days; looks like she's gone into hiding. Somebody, somewhere, must be looking after her.'

'Marie, start to check on hospital admissions or any unidentified bodies turning up, like suicides or unexplained deaths. Have we had the subscriber checks back yet, Ray, on her landline and mobile?'

'Not yet, guv, the weekend wouldn't have helped. I'll chase them up after this meeting.'

'We need to know who she was talking to when Jim was at her address. Okay, Marcia, what you got?'

'I spoke to Samantha Kirwin's line manager—Kirwin was the social worker mentioned in the *Dear George* letter, who Elizabeth Wood had claimed to have pushed under a train. She remembers the Wood family well and that Samantha Kirwin had major concerns initially about the mother, suspecting *Munchausen Syndrome by Proxy* and subsequently Elizabeth; so much so that she instigated the removal of George, the young brother and placed him in care.'

'What's *Munchausen Syndrome by Proxy*? Dr Frost.' Ray Blendell smiled at her.

'Well, sadly I'm no doctor; otherwise I'd be earning a lot more and not having to work with some of you morons.' She returned Blendell's smile two-fold. 'I haven't had a chance to *Google* it yet but Jackie Gibson, Kirwin's line manager, explained it briefly. It's a mental health problem, where a person who's in a position of caring for say the elderly or children, makes up or causes symptoms of illness, such as reporting a high temperature or a person having a fit, when in fact there is nothing medically wrong with them. Well that was my understanding anyway. This could have been George's mother or indeed his sister reading between the lines of the *Dear George* letter. It would appear Elizabeth the younger had quite a bit of responsibility for George's well-being, once the father had left the scene.

'Gibson kept a watching brief over the case, for the next ten or so years, including the fostering and eventual adoption of George after Kirwin's death. She was shocked, but I sensed, not overly surprised, when I told her that we are dealing with Kirwin's death as suspected murder. She was quite talkative about George and the fact that he was adopted by a Mr and Mrs Brewster in Romford, Essex, who changed his name to Michael. I haven't had time yet to search for the Brewsters.'

'I'll get onto that, Marcia.'

'Thanks, Marie. Sam and I visited a former family address of the Woods' in Burnt Oak last night and spoke to a couple of neighbours, who remembered the family. The address itself is virtually derelict and awaiting demolition to make way for a new residential home.

'Marie also mentioned last night that Elizabeth Wood was a train driver in the 1990s and had a year off work, following an incident between St Paul's and Bank on the Central Line, in which a City of London banker was mown down by her train. Her personal file records London Underground funding some psychiatric care for her. Maybe we should include searching mental health facilities as well as hospitals.' A mobile phone rang out.

'Sorry, guv, I gotta take this. I think it's J and M Seafood.' McNally gave Graves the thumbs up.

'Right, let's get together again this afternoon. Keep going, we are getting there.'

*

Staff in the *Costa Coffee* had become a little wary of the menacing male sitting by the window nursing a cup of coffee he'd purchased two hours ago. Michael Brewster knew he was attracting unwanted attention and saw the manager working up the courage to challenge him. He couldn't afford a scene. He still had a few hours to kill before stealing another car. He gathered his rucksack and left without looking back.

Chapter Fifty-Nine

The aroma of Mexican, Caribbean and Chinese food wafted in the air, making Graves' and Wakefield's stomachs rumble. The three-hundred-year-old Berwick Street market stood in the centre of Soho. The detectives calculated there were between twenty and thirty stalls, all preparing for the lunchtime rush.

It took a couple of minutes to locate the stall rented by J and M Seafood. Jack Cousins was the man in charge and was busy shouting at a couple of younger members of his staff, who seemed to be in no rush.

'Mr Cousins?'

'Yep, that's me.'

'DC Stuart Graves, I spoke to you about an hour ago.'

'Yeah, I know who you are.'

'Oink, Oink the pigs are here' commented one of the young lads.'

'Fuck off out the back. Get those salmon and haddock fillets sorted before I sack you. Sorry about that, officers. No respect anymore. What can I do you for?'

'I believe you trade at Billingsgate during the week is that right?'

'Yeah, that's right—you the fish police or something?' Wakefield smiled, Graves wasn't as impressed. Cousins realised the look and thought he might have gone too far and answered the question. 'I trade at Billingsgate Tuesday to Saturday and on Monday I got this plot—mainly to get rid of the fish I had left over from the week before. You know what I mean officers?' Cousins tapped the side of his nose, signalling he was letting them into some secret world. 'So you mentioned it was urgent—couldn't discuss it over the dog.'

'We couldn't discuss it over the phone because I want you to look at a CCTV image and an e-fit of somebody you may know.' Wakefield showed the fishmonger the two images and both detectives watched his initial reaction carefully. Jack Cousins handed the images back and looked conspiratorially out of the back of the stall. When he was happy nobody was listening, he turned back to the detectives.

'I know the geezer; he works for me at Billingsgate. Bit of an oddball, ex-military, looks at you sometimes like he wants to stab you. His name is Michael Brewster. I keep him on because he don't mind working nights; you're lucky to get those two buggers out back to turn up at all—lazy bastards.'

'We need to find him quickly. Do you have an address?'

'What's he done, killed somebody? It wouldn't surprise me. I didn't see him the last couple of nights last week; had a nasty cut on his hand.' The two detectives glanced at each other. 'He rang in sick on Saturday night, said it'd gone rotten. Not sure my customers would be too pleased with him leaking pus all over their fish.'

'Address, Mr Cousins.' Wakefield wasn't sure how the direct approach was going to work, but they didn't have time to play verbal tennis with this twat.

'Okay, hold your horses, mate. I need to get my laptop from the van.' Within seconds, he was back and tapping away.

'Here you go—Flat 6, Bow Court, Salmon Lane, Stepney. I take it he ain't going to be in work tonight?'

'Unlikely.' Wakefield took another picture from his case and showed it to the stallholder.

'Have you ever seen that sort of knife before?'

'Yeah, it's a boning knife. I use that make myself—bloody expensive. I'm actually missing one of...' Jack Cousins facial expression indicated that a penny had dropped into place somewhere deep in his brain. Graves moved in so close that he only needed to whisper.

'I just want to offer a little guidance Mr Cousins, a phone call to Michael Brewster when we walk away from here, by you, would be inadvisable. If you were to warn him, it will be us turning up tonight at Billingsgate to have another word. Have I made myself perfectly clear?' Graves gave the fishmonger an uncompromising stare. Cousins just nodded.

*

The station car park at Mill Hill East Station was small and well hidden from the platforms and the main road. Utilising skills from his childhood and the military he was inside a car and hotwired the ignition within ninety seconds. The car was an old Ford—probably somebody's pride and joy. He didn't want a car that would draw attention. A quick search of the car's boot presented Michael

Brewster with a bonus and an idea. This time he wasn't going to skulk around the back of the building—he was going in the main entrance.

*

It had taken McNally nearly forty minutes to get across central London and into the East End. He'd turned off the blue light and siren half a mile from the address his satnav was directing him to. He saw the BTP uniformed carrier, with at least four occupants, and Graves and Wakefield's unmarked car fifty metres further on. McNally parked up and jumped in the rear of his colleague's car.

'What we got?'

'Bow Court is two-storey, with three flats on each level; our man lives in No.6.' Graves looked up to the first floor. 'We've had a drive past a couple of times. The curtains are drawn and, apart from an elderly tenant walking his dog, nobody has been in or out for the past hour. Marie Relish has done some research for us into his background and come up trumps with Military Intelligence. Brewster served with the Royal Marines and saw action in Afghanistan. He was a bit of a hot head and, in their opinion, would eventually have been *court martialled* if he hadn't been medically discharged. His records show what we already now know, that he was adopted at the age of fourteen to a family in Romford.'

'Have the uniform been briefed?'

'Yes I spoke to them, guv,' Wakefield said. 'Two of them will cover the fire escape at the back. When we give the standby, the other two will wait for us to gain entry through the front communal door, which has a key-fob entry system before they join us.'

Graves dangled a fob in the air, 'courtesy of the building manager. Giving what we know about this man, they will put the front door of the flat through straight away, secure him, and call us in. Are we nicking him for all four murders?'

'No, just on suspicion of Valerie Huxley's murder at Mornington Crescent, we still haven't secured an evidential link with the other three yet—we will; and, Jim, you can do the honours.' Graves tightened his grip on the steering wheel as he looked at Jim Wakefield's Cheshire cat grin in the rear view mirror. 'You both got stab-vests on?' When both his officers nodded McNally picked up the radio, took a deep breath and gave the order to go.

*

She could hardly keep her eyes open, concentrating on the orange sun, flickering through the trees, before slowly starting to disappear for another day. Elizabeth Wood had been frightened by the whispers going around the hospital of a prowler in the grounds the night before. The staff had attempted to brush it off as a local drunk, but she'd sensed somebody near, adding to her anxiety levels, that were already sky-high. The medication, prescribed by Dr Forsyth, helped a little with her nerves. However she knew, as soon as she closed her eyes, the nightmares would return as they did every night. Images of her mother, her tight yellow skin against the grey of the mortuary slab; a man, she'd always believed to be her brother George, smiling at her, as the train she was operating, cut him to bits.

Elizabeth Wood glanced at her bedside clock; she needed sleep. She concentrated on the small passport sized picture of Patrick Mullen as she swallowed two sleeping pills, hoping that the memories of him would banish all her nightmares. As she drifted off, Elizabeth dreamt that her room door opened and a menacing shadow hovered above her, she mumbled Patrick's name as she prepared herself for another restless night.

Chapter Sixty

The three detectives hardly spoke a word on the journey back to Camden, each sensing the others' disappointment. They'd missed their target, probably by a few hours, and now he could be anywhere in London.

'We know Brewster wants to kill his sister so we have got to find her before he does. Let's hope the rest of the team have had better luck than us.' Graves and Wakefield nodded their heads.

McNally, summoned Sally Cook to Stepney to do an urgent examination for fingerprints. He was hoping, as Brewster was such a loner, his would be the only prints in the flat. Two uniformed officers would remain at the location just in case he returned. Most of the team were present when they entered the incident room.

'As you will know already we have identified our main suspect for the murder of Valerie Huxley, his name is Michael Brewster. Brewster's flat was turned over a couple of hours ago. It looks like he was there earlier today but is well gone. Somebody give me some good news.'

'The subscriber checks have come back from the BT landline', Blendell held a sheet of paper triumphantly in the air. 'There were a few incoming and outgoing calls the day of Jim's interview with Elizabeth Wood.' Blendell turned to Wakefield. 'Jim, can you remember the time of the incoming call that you partly overheard?' Wakefield looked in his pocketbook.

'I left the address about 11.30am so it would be 11 to 11.15. I can't be any more specific than that. I just remembered as well, as I walked away she was making a call on her mobile. That was definitely 11.30ish.'

'There are four phone-calls on the landline all in the morning at: 7.30, 10.50, 11.10 and a final one at 11.55. The 10.50 was a minicab firm in Edgware; the 11.55 to London Underground. The first and third are of most interest. The call at 11.10, when we know you were there, Jim, was from the North Lodge Hospital in Highgate.'

'That's a mental health hospital, has a secure unit and a voluntary care centre.' Marie Relish said excitedly. 'That's where she is.'

'Marie, give them a ring.' McNally looked at his watch, 'there must still be somebody we can get hold of if it's a secure unit. Sam, ring the cab firm. See if they have records for that day. She may have an account with them. Try and trace the driver and speak to him' McNally's phone rang. 'Stuart, give London Underground a ring on the number she used, see if you can find out what the call was about. I suspect it's her probably phoning in sick.'

'McNally' he shouted, annoyed with the interruption.

'Hey dude, its Sally Cook, had a bit of a result. I got a decent set of prints from a glass on the coffee table in the flat. I've ran them through the system. There are two hits.'

'Go on, Sally.'

'The first is a match with our mark found on the murder weapon, so confirmation Brewster is our killer, and secondly a match to several marks found in a stolen car, only this morning, recovered outside some hospital in north London. Hang on. I've got the name here somewhere…'

'Let me guess—North Lodge Hospital in Highgate?'

'You got it. Apparently the locals think it belonged to an intruder, seen at the back of the premises. Jumped over a five foot wall but legged it into some woods when the blue lights turned up. The car was originally stolen a few days ago. The owner didn't report it until yesterday afternoon. He'd been in L.A on a business trip.'

'Where was the car stolen?'

'In Bethnal Green, a quarter of a mile from here. One other thing before you go. I've done a proper search of the flat and found a top similar to the one he was wearing on the CCTV, with the stripe down the sleeve, looks like it's got a fair bit of blood-staining on it.'

'Thanks Sally, we might need you in north London. Don't book off.'

Blendell continued. 'The fourth call on the landline at 7.30 is a surprise'

'Who's it from?'

'This will put a smile on your face—Henry Hayhurst the morning after he was brought in by Stuart and Jim.'

'Guv,' Marie Relish looked worried. 'I've just spoken to the hospital. They've got a major fire, everybody has been evacuated; the London Fire Brigade are in attendance.'

Chapter Sixty-One

It had been easier than he thought. He'd been wracking his brains all day, trying to come up with an idea to distract the hospital security guard. The small can of petrol he'd discovered in the boot of the stolen car was the answer. Brewster kept a careful watch on the front door. 7pm seemed to be the finishing time for most staff, so he gave it an extra hour; his patience was rewarded when an additional three people left the building, and the solitary security man locked the automatic sliding entrance doors. He waited another fifteen minutes, as dusk turned to night, before removing the knife and tape from his rucksack and pulling his hat over his head. He popped the boot open, retrieved and shook the red petrol canister. It was probably a quarter full—enough for his purposes.

Brewster crept across the road to where the rubbish bins were stored. He panicked momentarily. Had they emptied them that day? He relaxed when he saw each was full to the brim. He sprinkled petrol over the top of each of the bin's contents and took an old tea towel from one, which he tore into three strips and soaked one end of each in petrol, and placed the can down on the ground. He returned to the corner of the building and glanced up and down the main road—all was clear. He took a deep breath and struck a match.

*

The cars roared out of Camden, blue lights flashing, sirens blasting, and headed north. McNally, Frost and Hodge in one car, Graves and Wakefield close behind in a second. McNally got a text from Ray Blendell '*The mob she rang after Jim's visit was a Dr Gillian Forsyth. Already contacted her she will meet you on your arrival at hospital.*'

*

The bins went up like a bomb had gone off. For a minute Brewster stood, mesmerised by the flames that were scorching his skin. Flashbacks of screaming comrades, gunfire in the distance and the smell of burning flesh in his nostrils.

The flames started to climb up the hospital's exterior wall setting fire to some ivy that clung to the rendering. Brewster shook himself back to reality. He had a couple of minutes at best.

He ran around to the glass entrance doors and banged loudly shouting 'fire, fire.' The security guard meandered over, like he had all the time in the world. Hearing the words being screamed at him, panic spread across his face and he quickly returned to his desk and found the relevant camera. Immediately he picked up the telephone presumably to ring the fire brigade.

'Let me in,' Brewster continued to shout banging on the glass doors. 'I'll help you get people out.' The guard hesitated, returned to the sliding doors and turned a key on the control panel—the doors swished open.

'You need to alert the rest of your staff?' The guard looked in several different directions.

'There are only two night staff on duty, and they are at the far end of the second floor, where the secured patients are.'

'Look. Don't panic. Have you rang the fire brigade?' The guard nodded his eyes wide-open in utter fear. 'You go upstairs and get the other staff and start moving people out I'll do the ground floor. Are the doors locked?'

'No, not on the ground floor.'

'Well go on, get a move on, otherwise people will die.' The guard headed for the stairs to the first floor. To create a little more panic, Brewster smashed the cover and activated the fire alarm. He entered the corridor off the reception area. He opened the first two doors and shouted 'Fire, get out.' He wanted as many people running all over the place, in blind-panic, for his plan to fully work. He could actually smell smoke now, which made him focus.

He reached for the handle of the third door and walked into the darkened room.

*

It was like wading through a thick fog; the sleeping tablets had taken affect quickly and she really didn't want to get out of her bed, but the voice was insistent. Her dressing gown was draped around her shoulders with the hood pulled over her head and she was led by a firm hand into the corridor, where people were shouting and screaming. She could smell smoke and started to cough and pulled the baggy hood of her dressing gown across her face, covering her mouth and nose.

The smoke was worse in the reception area, billowing through the automatic doors every time they glided open; she noticed the piercing sound of what she presumed, in her muddled state, to be the fire alarm. She questioned why she was being led into what seemed a kind of hell; her guide tightened his grip and pushed her through the cloud of toxic fumes until she gulped in fresh air.

*

Brewster dragged his sister across the road to his vehicle. His eyes were stinging from the smoke, blurring his vision. He opened the boot of the car and forced his sister inside. He felt for the strip of tape, he'd torn off the roll before he left the car, and stuck it over her mouth and slammed the boot closed. He fumbled with the ignition wires. He could hear the approaching sirens of the emergency services. The car's engine fired into life and he accelerated away.

Chapter Sixty-Two

The nearest they could get to the burning building in the cars was one hundred metres, where a police cordon had been set up. McNally showed his warrant card and dashed on foot towards the hospital with Frost close behind.

'Marcia, I'll find the Met Police's senior officer and explain what we've got. You find this Dr Forsyth. We need to find Elizabeth, although I think it's probably too late.'

The fire had spread to the roof space but seemed to be under control. Patients mingled around aimlessly as two members of staff tried to herd them into the safety of another part of the building, untouched by the fire. Frost stopped one of them and asked if they had seen Dr Forsyth. She was pointed in the direction of a smartly dressed middle-aged woman who had her arm draped around a patient, who was obviously in great distress.

'Dr Forsyth?'

'Yes, that's me. Are you from the police? I got a bit of a garbled message from a DS Blendell at the same time I was getting phone-calls about the fire, so I'm sorry I'm not sure what I can do for you.' Frost produced her warrant card and had to shout over the noise of the fire-engines as they shed gallons of water onto the burning roof.

'Doctor, we need to speak urgently about Elizabeth Wood. Please don't think I'm being dramatic but this *is* a case of life and death. Can we move away a bit so you can hear me?'

'Elizabeth? I haven't seen her since I arrived fifteen minutes ago.' Forsyth called a nurse, who'd just arrived to help, and handed the distressed female to her and asked if she'd seen Elizabeth Wood. She answered with a shake of her head. Frost guided the doctor away from the burning building until they could communicate without shouting.

'What's this all about, officer?'

'We believe Elizabeth Wood is in grave danger. Has she ever mentioned her brother to you?'

'I will have to make you aware from the start that I cannot discuss anything of a personal nature about Elizabeth. She is a patient of mine.'

'Dr Forsyth, we believe that Elizabeth's life is at risk; she may already be dead. We have got to find her as a matter of urgency. I understand your patient confidentiality but I'm sure in this situation—needs must.' Forsyth looked at the building; her face was pale as she tried to digest what was happening in front of her and what the officer had just told her.

'Elizabeth was referred to us in 1998. She was a tube train driver on London Underground. One early shift she was operating a train which left St Paul's station, a couple of hundred metres before reaching the next station—Bank if I remember correctly—she saw a man walking on the track towards her. She was travelling at about twenty-five miles an hour but she was unable to stop and the man disappeared under her train. She was convinced then, and I'm pretty sure she still is now, that the man was her brother, George.

'The police and the coroner were happy that the victim was a man called Richard Talbot a banker from the City of London who, that morning, was due to stand trial at the Old Bailey for fraud. He had no link to Elizabeth whatsoever, but as I said she has never accepted this. She also lost her husband to a heart attack in 2004. When she is feeling depressed, bordering suicidal, she comes back and sees me and often stays for a few nights under observation; she has been with us for four nights on this occasion. Are you saying that her brother is the danger to her?'

'Yes, we think he was here last night but was disturbed.'

'We did have reports of a prowler in the gardens last night. That is a fact. The police attended but found no trace of the intruder.'

'In the case of an emergency, like this, you must have set procedures—a roll call of some sort?'

'Yes, of course. The senior night nurse is doing that as we speak. She is over there, I'll introduce you, come on.' The rather harassed nurse reported that all patients were accounted for except Elizabeth Wood and one other and that the fire brigade are currently searching each room on both floors. Frost looked around for McNally and spotted him talking to a senior Met police officer.

'Guv, a quick word please.'

'Have they found her?'

'No, she and another patient are still missing, she could still be in her room, and the fire brigade are going through each room as we speak. Any sign of Brewster?'

'No. I've got Stuart and Jim trying to find him. I think he's well gone. He has either killed her here or taken her with him.' They were joined by Graves and Wakefield, who were both shaking their heads at the DI. Frost's phone vibrated in her pocket.

'Hi, is that Sergeant Frost?'

'Yes, speaking. Who's this?'

'My name is Sandy Richards. You knocked on my door the other night, had a nice chat with my Lenny, and you wanted to know about a family that lived in No.4 Watling Crescent years ago.' Frost remembered the smell of chip fat that had clung to her clothes; she felt slightly sick.

'Oh! Hi, sorry Sandy, I can't talk at the moment. Can I give you a ring tomorrow?'

'Well, OK, but they would've fucked off by then.'

'Who are 'they'?'

'You asked me to give you a ring if we saw any more movement inside No.4,' she broke off and Frost heard her ask her husband if they were still there. 'Lenny saw a car pull up outside No.4 about twenty minutes ago. He's a bit nosey, so went outside to have a look, it's quite rare to get any vehicles down here anymore, especially at this time of night. By then, whoever it was had gone around the back and now all we can see is a torch or flashlight beam moving around in what used to be the front bedroom. All these houses are the same love. Hope I ain't wasting your time, probably dossers again, I'll call the locals if you're busy, probably won't turn out, but at least I've done my bit.'

'Can Lenny see the car's registration without going outside, Sandy?'

'Hang on.' She could hear Lenny's deep West Indian voice relaying numbers and letters.

'Yeah! Here you go, he says hello by the way. You got a pen handy—well you would have, wouldn't you.' Frost wrote the details down and the words PNC and handed it to Graves.

'Sandy, that's brilliant. Just leave this with us, say hi to Lenny, but ask him not to go outside. We don't want to disturb anybody in there.' Frost replaced her phone in her pocket and turned to McNally.

'I think I know where Brewster is.'

Graves returned.

'The car was nicked about four hours ago from Mill Hill East tube station.'

Chapter Sixty-Three

Brewster had intended to park the car a little further away, but his eyes were still streaming from the smoke and he couldn't take a chance his passenger wouldn't start screaming her head off. The crescent was quiet. He knew from his previous visit only two of the six houses were occupied.

He collected the rope and flashlight from the back seat of the car, felt inside his jacket for the handle of his knife and popped the boot, dragging his sister around the back of the house, which, for the first two years of his life, had been home. He was a little surprised how compliant she was, he hadn't yet had the opportunity to look her in the eye. He was looking forward to telling her that her little brother was going to end her life where she had *literally* ended his.

*

Marcia Frost gripped her seat, as McNally accelerated along the Great North Way, reaching nearly eighty five miles an hour.

'At least, there's a chance she's still alive. If he'd just wanted her dead, he would have done it at the hospital.' Frost was trying to convince herself more than her D.I. who wasn't listening anyway, as he applied the brakes at a red light before creeping across the junction when it was clear.

'Marcia, try and get us some uniform backup, but tell them to keep well away from the house. We should be there in ten minutes.'

Before she could make the call, her mobile rang.

'Yes, Stuart.'

'Have you got there yet?'

'No, ten minutes away.'

'We've found her.'

'Who?'

'She was hiding in the toilet scared out of her wits. She was moved from the ground floor to the second floor this morning, she got really spooked by the intruder last night, and the security guard got her out. Marcia, he's taken the wrong woman. Elizabeth Wood is standing in front of me. The woman he's abducted was admitted this afternoon. Her name is Susan Crawford.'

*

The front bedroom, of No.4 Watling Crescent, was damp, the wallpaper had peeled away and been chewed by rodents to make their nests. Brewster couldn't remember, but imagined this had been his parents' room.

He sat Elizabeth down on a seat and tied her hands around the back of the chair—they were going to have a little conversation before he slit her throat. He grabbed her by the chin, ripped the tape off her swollen lips and shone the torch in her face. She shut her eyes to the strong light and started to shake and whimper.

She looked different from the image he had on his mobile. But that was probably a few years old. Plus her face was caked in soot from the billowing smoke of the fire. He gripped her long blond hair up in his fist and pulled her face towards him.

'It's been a long time, Elizabeth. Bet you didn't think you'd ever see the inside of this place again.'

'My name's not Elizabeth. What do you want with me? Let me go please.'

Brewster pushed her back in her seat and took a few gulps of whiskey from a bottle he had left behind during his last visit a few nights ago, before reaching inside his jacket and sliding the long sharp blade out of its sheath. He held it up in the light, appreciating the beautiful workmanship, as the light danced off the steel.

'This knife was my best friend in Afghanistan. While you were playing with the tube trains, I was fighting for this country. Keeping people like you safe. It was a shame you didn't show me the same courtesy when I was a young boy, Elizabeth, or whatever your fucking name is now.'

I've told you my name's not Elizabeth.'

'I've heard all this time and time again, over there "my name isn't Abdul or Mukhtar, no, I'm not a murdering bastard terrorist, and you're mistaken".' Brewster stopped and listened, he thought he heard movement but dismissed it when a huge rat scurried along the skirting board, he threw the whiskey bottle at the rodent which disappeared into a gaping hole at the end. 'Stop the snivelling or I'll kill you now.'

Chapter Sixty-Four

They couldn't wait any longer for the uniform to turn up. McNally and Frost put on their stab-proof vests and grabbed their extendible batons.

'Look, Marcia, I know we should be thinking risk assessments and waiting for the cavalry to arrive but I'm going in. I can't stand here if there is any chance of saving this woman. I understand if you want to wait. I will never criticize you for it—it's up to you.'

'I'm with you all the way. How're we going to do this?'

'Neither of us knows the layout, but he won't be expecting us so we've got surprise on our side. I don't think there's any point in trying to talk him down, tell him he has got the wrong woman. I'll go for him; you try and get the woman out. What was her name?'

'Susan.'

'Ready?' Frost nodded.

*

McNally got to the top of the stairs and listened to Brewster ranting about his mother and his ruined life. He could just see, through the gap in the door. Susan Crawford was sat on a chair, her face looking down to her knees, her shoulders moving in time with her deep sobs.

McNally turned and indicated to Frost where Crawford was. He stood back and, with every ounce of energy he could muster, kicked the bedroom door open and screamed 'Police.'

The first reaction came from Crawford, who let out a piercing scream. Brewster turned to face McNally, who was running towards him with his baton above his head, ready to strike. Brewster managed to side step the downward arc of the baton but it caught him on his left arm and he shrieked in pain. McNally's momentum carried him past Brewster, leaving himself unbalanced. Brewster took advantage and kicked the detective's legs away from under him and he landed square on his back. Frost ran to Crawford and tried to untie her.

'Leave her or your friend dies.' Frost looked over. Brewster had pinned McNally to the floor with a foot. She saw a knife in his right hand hovering over her colleague's throat. 'Walk away from her or I *will* kill him.'

McNally pleaded. 'Do as he says Marcia.'

'That's a good girl, Marcia. Throw that baton down, move away and sit on the floor—NOW!' Frost did as she was told.

'You're making a big mistake, Michael.' McNally pleaded his case while, not once, taking his eye off the knife inches from his face. 'That woman over there is *not* your sister. Her name is Susan. You took the wrong woman. Elizabeth, your sister, is safe and well and in our custody. Now why don't you put that knife down and let her go back to where she can be cared for? She's never done you any harm.'

'I'm not stupid, this is just a trick.'

'For God's sake, whoever you are, I'm not your sister. I'm an only child. My mother is from Bulgaria, my father is Irish. Where do you appear in that setup you sick fucker? Let me go, I've got two children at home…just let me go please…' Crawford burst into tears, shouting incoherently.

Frost felt something digging into her leg, without taking her eyes off Brewster she explored with her right hand and clasped a large shard of glass from the broken whiskey bottle.

Brewster crossed the room and put the knife to Susan Crawford's neck.

'You're lying to me. Why are you lying? You're going to die.'

Frost took her chance and thrust the shard of glass into Brewster's thigh. He swung the knife across Frost's face missing by millimetres. McNally got to his feet with baton raised but slipped on the uneven floor and fell. Brewster turned and thrust the knife towards McNally's chest. The knife's deadly point sliced through the air.

'Stop! Put down your weapon.' Brewster, distracted, looked back towards the door and then to his chest, momentarily mesmerised by the red dot dancing around on his black top; he took a step forward.

What sounded like a muffled gunshot lit the room; two probes flew through the air and attached themselves to Brewster's chest. The knifeman shuddered uncontrollably as the high voltage pulse flowed through his body, he lost all voluntary muscle control, and fell to the ground, incapacitated. A uniformed officer, pointing the discharged *Taser*, stood in the doorway. McNally went to secure the knife when a second officer pointed his own weapon at the DI. The red light hovered directly over his heart.

'Don't move—identify yourself.'

'DI McNally and this is DS Frost—BTP.' McNally slowly pulled out his warrant card and showed the officers. Frost untied the hysterical Susan Crawford. It was over.

Chapter Sixty-Five

The team was in for an early morning briefing. An arrest was just the start of a long process, hopefully ending in convictions. McNally spent most of the day being interviewed by the press as the details of the investigation emerged. Frost and Hodge started initial interviews with Brewster, who'd returned from hospital, and Elizabeth Wood, who'd been detained on suspicion of murder. They would remain in police custody until the evidence was passed to the CPS and a decision on charging made by them.

Graves and Wakefield picked up Henry Hayhurst on suspicion of assisting an offender.

By five o'clock, they were all in the World's End pub on Camden High Street, by order of Detective Superintendent Nigel Plummer, who was in the chair. He followed his round of drinks with a stirring speech about their fantastic work and offered them his congratulations.

'Same old management bollocks,' McNally whispered in Frost's ear.

Frost smiled 'Yeah, but it's nice to be praised once in a while. It'll be back to normal tomorrow. Do you think they'll both be charged?'

'Certainly Brewster, but I'm not so sure about Wood. I think the case is so old now, and we have no evidence, apart from the admission in her letter, that she did kill Samantha Kirwin. Even if she were charged, I doubt if she'd be mentally fit to enter a plea and stand trial. Brewster will play on the fact that he was medically discharged for PTSD. All we can do is present the tightest case that we can to the CPS, and then it's out of our hands. The case against him is pretty tight. Jim Wakefield has picked him up on CCTV at both Putney Bridge and London Bridge. How's Susan Crawford?'

'I rang the hospital just before we came in here. She's doing OK. They had to sedate her last night, but I think she's in good hands.'

'Look, I know I asked a lot of you last night but I think we made the right decision. If we'd waited for the uniform, I think we might well have been too late.'

Frost nodded. 'At least, they turned up eventually. I thought we'd both had it.'

'I just want to…you know.'

'Yeah, guv, I know. You owe me one.'

'We got a good team here, Marcia, and I hope you'll stay a while before you're off chasing promotion.'

'I'm not going anywhere for a while, guv. You're right, it's not a bad team, apart from that gob-shite.' They both looked over at Stuart Graves who was deep in conversation with Sara Hallam.

'I think he's met his match there, don't you think?' Frost nodded.

'It looks like it's my round then, sergeant.' McNally looked towards the pub's entrance door. 'Here we go. They say good news travels fast.'

'Who's that?' Frost enquired.

'DCI John Masters—Professional Standards, rubber heelers. You never hear them creeping up behind you. I didn't know he drank in here. No idea who the two with him are.'

'Well, it's either me or you they're after.'

'Probably something I said out of turn at the news conference earlier, or he might just want to buy us a congratulatory drink.'

'He doesn't look happy, guv.'

'No, but their sort never does. Shit, he *is* smiling at me; that's bad news.'

'Ryan, congratulations on the job, just saw your mug all over the *Evening Standard*. Could we have a quiet word, bit of a delicate matter, maybe out in the garden?'

'No. I'm fine here, John. This is my DS—Marcia Frost. You can say anything in front of her; in fact, if this is official, I'd like a witness. You haven't introduced us to your two mates.' Masters turned to his two colleagues.

'This is Detective Inspector Colin Robertson and Detective Sergeant Richard Lewis from the Metropolitan Police, Finchley; they want to have a word with you.'

'How can I help you gents?'

'We were hoping to have a word in a little more private setting but here will do,' answered the DI. 'We are investigating a serious assault at *Da Luca's* Italian restaurant on High Road, North Finchley, last Saturday night. DI McNally, I am arresting you on suspicion of inflicting grievous bodily harm on a Mr Roger Knight.'

The End